The Stones of Bothynus Trilogy

BOOK ONE

Snap To Grid

To: Brian
Thanks for the encouragement!

The Stones of Bothynus Trilogy

BOOK ONE

Snap To Grid

by
D.K. Reed

12/8/16

MCP Books

MCP Books
2301 Lucien Way #415
Maitland, FL 32751
407.339.4217
www.MCPBooks.com

ISBN-13: 978-1-63505-147-6
LCCN: 2016910968

Distributed by Itasca Books

Cover Design by Ryan Qualls
Cover Photo by John Wollwerth
Used with permission of the artist
Typeset by Mandie Brasington

Printed in the United States of America

To my daughters

Acknowledgements

The most important acknowledgements go to my family and friends. The inspiration for many of the characters came from people I know, though no character is based on any particular person. I am especially grateful to my daughters and their friends—truly awesome teenagers that I have been privileged to know and love. A special thanks also goes to my husband, whose support and patience allowed me to have a writing sanctuary. I would be remiss if I did not acknowledge my mother, father, brothers, cousins and friends both old and new. Thanks to my family and childhood friends for sharing with me an idyllic childhood hidden away in a land that time forgot, but magic didn't—the Smoky Mountains. And thanks to my new friends for sharing ideas, gripes and laughter.

Thanks to Rebecca Mahoney and John Jarrold for all their brilliant edits, to Wendie Appel for her great publishing guidance, and to Ryan Qualls for the beautiful cover designs. These books would not have been nearly as enjoyable without their keen insights.

Thanks to the crows of Potomac and Rockville. They have had a difficult time of late with road construction taking so much of their roosting sites and then the West Nile Virus also hit them hard. My wish is for our species to be more aware and respectful of birds and all other species that share the planet with us.

Contents

PART ONE

Red's Viking Ghost

"I thought how fine a scene might be played on a stage like this; if I were a ghost, how bluely I would glimmer at the windows, how whimperingly chatter in the wind.[1]"

The Irish R.M.

CHAPTER 1

The Viking in the Window

September 17

Fifteen-year-old Red ambled up the trail, feeling at home in this wood that ran along the Potomac River near the Maryland portion of Great Falls National Park. She and her sister, Annie, thirteen, had played here for countless hours as children. As always, there was a whisper of cool darkness that drew her in—organic, like the river mud she could smell. Neither girl spoke, but Red could hear Annie's labored breathing below. She thought Annie must be caught up in the river magic, too. Annie was always quiet when they were here, not the usual annoying little sister. More like the Annie at a museum, actually kinda reverent.

Red stopped. She took a couple of deep breaths in an effort to relax. She wanted to enjoy this and avoid thinking of the grim news that had brought them here today. "See anything, Annie?"

A grunt was all she got. She wasn't surprised. Annie was all about teenage indifference.

Red was the one who had suggested looking for wild flowers. She knew it was her hero-compulsion. She wanted to lift Annie's spirits, even if the little ingrate didn't want them lifted. She was determined to find cardinal flowers—their red blossoms would help. They should be in bloom now and she knew they grew in these woods. She and Annie had found them here more than once and a sighting never failed to thrill them both.

She began walking again and felt a drop of sweat trickle down her back from the climb. A glow up ahead told Red they were near the point where the side trail emptied into the backyard of Uncle Alistair's old mansion, slowly being overtaken by English ivy and pokeweed. Red liked the way he had always kept the front grounds tidy, but the backyard wild. Just like him, she thought, cultured enough to sup with crowned heads, but wild enough to sup with fairies. Red had always seen him as someone more mythological than real. When he read to her and Annie or told them stories, she remembered feeling like Arthur being taught by Merlin. It would be just like him to be off doing something intriguing right now. She so hoped that was all that was going on. But she felt uncertainty rear its ugly head in her gut and she knew she had to face the fact that her dad didn't seem to think this was another one of Alistair's jaunts. In fact, he'd called in the police to investigate, since Uncle Alistair hadn't been heard from in over a week. She and Annie were trying to avoid talking about it, but she could tell Annie was shaken, too.

She looked up the trail. It was so pretty, almost hauntingly so. The sunbeam suggested one of those fiery sunsets that only occurred in the fall, when the angle of the sun was just right to make that strange orange glow. She wished Uncle Alistair would be at the mansion when they got back so she could ask him about it; he probably had a name and explanation for that kind of sunset. She heard a crow caw overhead as she neared the break in the trees. She turned and took one last look down the path before leaving the wood and caught sight of a cardinal flower.

"Annie, oh my gosh! There's one." She pointed to a few dark-green fronds peeking out from behind a large sycamore. The fronds were tipped with *blood-red pedals like fingers clawing from flaming spires*; Red loved their description in her field guide. Her long legs, well conditioned from years of tae kwon do, still felt a little sore from a recent tournament as she knelt in front of the clump of flowers.

"Red, don't pick 'em," Annie snapped. "Let's just remember this spot." Red's guilty hand hesitated as she pulled a frond close to her face.

"O-kay," Red knew her voice betrayed a hint of annoyance and she rolled her eyes at Annie rather than respond with her usual passive shrug. Annie needed to tone it down a bit—her nerves were on edge. Nonetheless, she didn't want to make a case of it with Annie today. She let go of the frond and snapped a few pictures of the flowers with her cell phone instead.

She stepped out from the shadows onto the edge of the spongy grass, feeling the warmth of the odd sunbeam.

Momentarily distracted by the orange glow, she caught a flash of movement. Something drew her eyes to one of the third-story windows of the massive structure at the top of the yard.

She stopped dead in her tracks and held her breath. She was looking at a faint apparition gleaming in the window. It looked like a Viking ghost with horned headwear staring down at her. Barely visible, but there—looking straight at her. Dark eyes boring into her very soul. *What the* … Even in its misty form, Red thought she could make out the image of a warrior. The steely-jawed face with the hint of a beard was framed by longish hair. Her eyes were irresistibly drawn to the thick eyebrows—and those piercing dark eyes. Yes, a warrior. Wild, reckless, and … *hot.* Her brain mistrusted what her eyes told her. Her heart pounded.

Annie stopped, too, and stood as silent as a mouse behind her, evidently sensing something amiss. The Viking remained motionless, staring.

Confused and uncertain, Red broke the spell by blinking rapidly and then rubbing her eyes. She looked again.

Now all she saw in the window was a lampshade with antlers protruding from behind it. *What the heck is that? A hat rack? But, no … no, that's not right. That can't be it.* Something was different. The Viking had been more centered in the window. She knew this wasn't what she had seen only seconds earlier. It was wrong. It couldn't have been the lampshade; it was too far to the left. *What the* …

Was someone playing tricks? Was she going insane?

A Year Later
October 20

Red knew her obsession with the Viking ghost she'd seen a year ago wasn't normal. She thought about the sighting now as she dumped an armload of personal bathroom supplies into a box on her bed. She had never dared tell her parents, and especially not Dr. Bennington, her psychiatrist. *Gosh, no.* She didn't know what the good doctor would say about it and she didn't want to take the chance of being labeled any more than she already was. She was having real trouble focusing today on the task at hand. She couldn't keep her mind off her Viking ghost. As he popped into her head yet again, she found herself involuntarily pressing her lips together.

She thought of her initial reaction to the sighting last year. She had been unable to resist telling Annie. She felt pretty close to Annie, despite Annie's annoying habit of trying to be the responsible one even though she was younger. She remembered with anguish that Annie had listened intently, hopeful of some juicy intrigue at first and excited to investigate. This had lasted until Annie had seen the lampshade and hat rack positioned in the window and then totally changed her attitude. She'd made fun of Red for allowing her imagination to run wild. That had stung, but she reasoned that she'd have probably reacted the same way had the shoe been on the other foot. *But I DID see it. It WAS real.* She knew she hadn't seen it in the same way she saw a book or a tree—more like how she saw fog or shadow. Not a definite form, but not a figment of her imagination either. After that, though, Red had decided to avoid further embarrassment by not telling anyone else. Her secrecy, she thought now, probably made her obsession worse.

Red sighed as reached into her underwear drawer; she didn't want the movers to see her boring cotton undies. That was private and embarrassing. She grinned. Nor did she want anyone digging deep into the drawer and finding the leopard print thongs she had bought at the mall, just in case. She sighed, thinking that she hadn't needed them so far, but if that Viking ghost ever came to life ... Then she felt a little creeped-out for thinking that. But what to make of the ghost? She had to forget about the sighting or to make herself believe that Annie was right about it being merely her imagination. Annie was the practical one. Red felt a little annoyed admitting this to herself. Then she changed her mind as she had done a thousand times before: No, Annie was a know-it-all. Red was convinced there had been *something* in the window. What it was, she only wished she knew. She recalled moments of frustration during the past year in not having ready access to investigate the old mansion. Well, that was about to change now that her family was moving in there. She was going to figure out exactly what she'd seen.

Red heard the movers' voices in the hallway just outside her bedroom door and felt annoyed. They had swarmed her family's townhouse all morning and now were obviously upstairs. Oh, she knew she shouldn't feel annoyance toward them; they were just doing their job. But she really wanted to be alone right now to think. She wanted to give in to nostalgia. After all, she was leaving behind the only home she had ever known. She sighed, hearing the voices grow louder.

She unceremoniously shoved the last few personal items into a box, taped it shut, and went downstairs.

Outside, she looked at the orderly stacks of boxes beside the large orange trailer and saw the crate containing Midnight and Roxy waiting in the only shady spot of the tiny yard. *Kitties!* She plopped down onto the grass beside the crate and began cooing to the cats in singsong kitty-speak. Midnight ignored her. She knew it would take a while for him to forgive the humiliation of being crated. Roxy, on the other hand, rubbed against the crate, her multi-colored calico fur poking through the screen. Red poked in two fingers to rub and scratch. She felt the soft fur and could even feel a subtle vibration as Roxy responded with a loud purr. "It's okay, sweetheart, you're going to a new home. And *ders* a kitty door in *da bashment*. Won't that be fun, *kittiesh*?" Red looked around to make sure no one heard her silly voice.

Roxy's purr worked like magic to soothe her frustrated nerves. Red turned her face upward to catch the warm fall sun, still stroking the kitten through the grate, and wondered now why she had felt so annoyed earlier. Was it a feeling of betrayal that her usually frugal and green mom had caved to her dad's plea to hire a moving company? This, despite what Red thought had been a sound argument about the waste of packing materials. *Nah.* Red knew that in all honesty, she really just didn't want to have strangers invade her space. This should be a private day. And it wasn't even so much that she wanted to make this a family-bonding experience. They did lots of that most weekends. In fact, between her nerdy math-whiz-yet-insane-thrill-seeking father and crazy hillbilly-environmentalist mother, Red felt constantly thrown into family outings. In winter they skied, in summer they swam, spring and fall they hiked. She had known how to identify most birds and wildflowers before she could spell their names. And she knew that as out-in-the-ozone as her parents were, they didn't hold a candle to the antics of her dad's uncle, wherever he was. Uncle Alistair felt more like an actual uncle to her and too full of youth and energy to be her dad's uncle.

A part of her wanted to think of him. After all, his disappearance was the reason they were moving today. That was the other creepy thing about the mansion. Red shuddered. She couldn't help thinking of Uncle Alistair and how her family had kept hoping all last year that he would return and all this would just be some silly mix-up. But it just hadn't happened. Her parents at some point had decided that it was time to face the facts and move on. The old mansion couldn't be left abandoned indefinitely or it would succumb to weather, bugs, broken pipes … Red knew her dad felt a huge responsibility to preserve the place. What if his uncle turned up one day? Red knew he couldn't bear to disappoint his uncle by letting the place rot. And the estate was certainly damp, overlooking the Potomac River.

Red knew that Uncle Alistair had willed the house to her dad partly because he was his next of kin, but also because he was the only close family member he had in this country. Uncle Alistair, her Granny Hamilton's brother, had come from Somerset in England some twenty years ago to teach Medieval Religion at Georgetown University. He had bought the old farmhouse mansion, one of a dying breed on the Potomac

River—at one time part of one of the oldest and largest tobacco plantations on the rich Potomac floodplain. Red felt that its grandeur fit his personality to a T since he was the most interesting person she had ever met. Always full of intriguing stories of the crusades, Knights Templar, the Vatican, and even happenings on this continent involving historical inhabitants of the Americas. Oh, how she had loved to visit him in the mansion. She sighed, feeling a pang of regret. It wasn't going to be the same without him there.

As much as Red loved the old place, she had to work to fight the negativity and the long shadow that Uncle Alistair's disappearance cast on the day. It didn't help that Halloween was just over a week away. Red had asked her mom about that—why move into the old mansion near Halloween, of all times? Wasn't this move creepy enough? Red's mom had explained that as sad as they all were about Uncle Alistair, the old place was a magnet for vandals and so the move had to be made as soon as legally possible. Red knew that some evidence of vandalism had been found already. As soon as the police tape had been removed last fall, they discovered that someone had jimmied the lock to the basement door and made a mess of Uncle Alistair's lab, office, bedroom, and library. It had taken a cleaning crew a week to get the place back in order and to box up most of his specimens in the basement and much of his office contents.

Uncle Alistair's disappearance was still a mystery. There had been some evidence that he and one of his graduate student assistants had taken a spill in the Potomac River below the estate and drowned. But the circumstances around his disappearance seemed very fishy to Red, and she still stubbornly held onto a glimmer of hope that he would turn up with another tale of intrigue. It vexed her that they were moving into his house without knowing for certain if he was dead. After all, how could two grown men drown so close to civilization and never have their bodies recovered? On questioning all those who had last seen him, one of his graduate student assistants had reported that Uncle Alistair and another graduate student had planned to look for river stones, something to do with a geological comparison Uncle Alistair was doing with some artifacts. Since park officials found his canoe upturned and caught on some rocks about five hundred yards downstream of his house, many were convinced the two men had drowned. Red had her doubts, though. She knew it was possible their bodies could have been sent miles away into the Chesapeake Bay, but she also knew well the strip of national park land that ran between the mansion and the Potomac River. It seemed impossible that park rangers could scour the river with helicopters, rafts, and dive teams without recovering even so much as an article of clothing. Nothing, except the canoe.

"Hey, Red, can you help me here a minute?" The voice broke into her reverie. Her dad's silver beard and ponytail gleamed in the sunlight as he dragged his scarred-up canoe toward the ancient Volvo wagon.

"Sure." She hopped up to help him hoist the canoe onto the racks atop the wagon. It wasn't heavy to lift, just awkward to maneuver.

"Wait here a minute and I'll get the kayak."

"Dad, you can't put both on the car at the same time. You'll need to make two trips."

Her dad smiled as he walked away. "Just watch and learn."

Red sighed. Her dad had always treated her like a son. She was a big girl, tall and strong for a female. It did come in handy for her dad with all his outdoorsy hobbies, she knew. After helping strap the two boats securely, she began to strap bicycles onto the rack jutting from the back of the already very long wagon. "Dad, are you really going to make your grand entrance into Potomac with two boats on top and four bicycles strapped to the tailgate?"

"No, Red, I'm not," her dad announced. "I'm going to do it with *five* bicycles strapped to the tailgate." She slapped her hand over her eyes as he went to get the fifth.

An hour later, the stack of boxes was gone. "Okay, get in. I think we're ready," her dad shouted as he emerged from the front door.

Red looked down the row of townhouses as they backed out into the street. Each house was pretty much the same. She didn't think her family was at all like the countless "normal" families occupying them. Still feeling pensive, Red mused that her first sixteen years of life had never been typical and she had certainly never been a popular child. Oh, she had friends in Gaithersburg, but no one really special. Her elementary school friends had thinned in middle school, and pretty much vanished in high school as cliques won out over loyalty. Red knew her ADHD had ensured she'd never be part of the popular cliques. Other kids liked her well enough most of the time but she knew she was compulsive and tended to alienate friends by taking jokes too far or blurting out embarrassments without realizing until after the damage was done. She still blushed, remembering how she had taunted Nathaniel in sixth grade after having beaten him at arm wrestling, until he lashed out, calling her *bitch*. She smiled mirthlessly at how taboo that word had been back then. The heartbreaking part was that she'd only teased him because she had a crush on him and it had felt so good to get his attention. But he'd never spoken to her again. She could write a book on how to lose friends and love interests. At least, that had been the case when she was younger. Maybe this move would be a new beginning. She'd like to think she was smarter now.

"Any regrets, Red? In leaving, I mean?" His question caught her by surprise. Her dad wasn't usually this touchy-feely. Perhaps he was feeling nostalgic, too.

"Nah, not really, Dad. I mean, it almost feels like we're leaving mediocrity behind," she said, trying to sound chipper. "I guess I'm ready for an adventure."

"Yep, you know, Red, you've got a point there. Your uncle was … is … a brilliant and special man and I feel like we're going home, moving into his old mansion. I've always felt that our family is kind of unique and fascinating. I've always said that normal families are boring. But nerdy families—" he pointed a thumb at himself "—are creative and unique in their own ways, though admittedly not abounding in social skills." A slight wry smile tugged at one corner of her mouth. As if to prove his quip about lacking social skills, he reached across and poked her ribs, taunting, "Ya gotta admit, kid, that having movers sure made the job easier. Right?" His eye twinkled.

She rolled her eyes, "Okay, I guess … a little."

He wasn't satisfied and started to poke her again, but she caught his hand and giggled. "Hey, you're going to get us killed. Eyes on the road."

He chuckled.

As they rode now in silence, Red had to acknowledge that even with this morning's pensive mood, her emotional state was vastly improved from the time when the decision to move had been made. She sighed, remembering that when her parents first sat her and her sister down one evening a few weeks ago to announce that the family would be moving, their first collective reaction had been to adamantly refuse to leave their friends in Gaithersburg. In truth, that come from an instinct to show solidarity with Annie, Red realized now. For her, the move was more complicated and she had felt torn between reluctance to leave her safe nest and fascination for an adventure. Now, however, she realized she was beginning to feel excited. Maybe it was something about progress and moving forward. She felt a thrill hovering somewhere in the back of her mind as the grand old estate came into view.

The car slowed to turn into the driveway. Buddy barked animatedly from Red's lap, his tail slapping her about the face and causing a long strand of her thick copper hair to fly into her mouth. The two cats began meowing from their crate in the backseat. Red was surprised to see that her mom and Annie had caught up with them in her mom's zippy, bright yellow smart car. Red grinned, remembering how Annie had gone gaga over the color when their mom was looking around for an energy-efficient car. It reminded Red of a bumblebee, with its black top and strange, diagonal black stripe just in front of the rear wheel. She smiled to herself as she opened the door and freed Buddy to explore his new home.

Red stretched and looked up at the mansion with a new eye, trying to come to terms with it now being her home. She tried to focus on the task at hand and began carrying armloads from the car. But her broody nature kept re-emerging and she couldn't stop thinking of poor Uncle Alistair, despite her determination to keep positive. Uncle Alistair, who had obviously met with some kind of foul play here. It seemed unspeakably awful that no one ever *really* found out what happened to him, she admitted to herself. Her family seemed to share a quiet reverence for him and gratitude for this amazing new home. But it felt off to her for them to move in without the mystery being solved. And there was also ... she couldn't ignore it any longer—the Viking to consider. *What's going on here? First a disappearance and then a ghost?*

"Red, you're blocking the movers." Annie's irritable voice seemed to come from nowhere.

Red realized she was standing in the middle of the hallway. She snapped out of her brain-chain, which was what she called it when she lost focus and went into an elaborate daydream. "Oh yeah. Sorry," she said flatly, and moved out of the way of two men carrying a stack of boxes in tandem. Just as they brushed past, she instinctively glided around into a position to catch and rectify the top two boxes that had been about to tumble down as one man began to mount the stairs. Her quick movement kept the boxes from falling. She barely noticed the two men exchange an incredulous glance. Red mentally shrugged off the incident, knowing this was just part of her body's instinctive action from her martial arts training to avert any crisis. She deposited her box and went out for more.

As she carried in the crate-o'-cats, Red lamented that with all its charm and size, the mansion had only two bathrooms apart from the master suite. But at least the one upstairs had a shower. Still, the bathtubs were large and ornate and the lighting was top quality over the massive mirrors. Red smiled, remembering how her uncle had found humor in the American label of "bathroom." Uncle Alistair had also added a teak deck on the river side of the house with a hot tub, of which Red had fond memories. They had a family tradition of having a dip as the culmination of Uncle Alistair's annual Christmas party. She'd had been able to stay awake for those festivities for the last few years. The adults shared a bottle of champagne in the tub, sparkling grape juice for the kids. They would soak up the heat from the bubbling water, scoffing at the cold air temperatures around them, until overheated. Then, the really fun part had been to cool off by rolling in the snow, if it was present, and then repeat the process a few times. There had been such laughter that Red smiled now at the memory, despite the fact that it wouldn't be the same without Uncle Alistair. He had been such a riot.

As she opened the crate door so the cats could come out and explore their new home, Red's thoughts were drawn back to last September and the Viking ghost. She leaned her head against a wall, continuing to recall that day. The daydream took over and she relived that scene as she absentmindedly stroked both cats, each purring and vying for chin-scratching, her hands moving automatically along their soft fur and round heads. She felt a chill run up her spine as she recalled how shocked she had felt the moment she had spotted the Viking ghost in the upstairs window. As time and a busy life had removed her from the event, it had started to feel surreal. Still, she'd been unable to shake the feeling of creepiness she had whenever she allowed herself to believe she had actually seen a ghost. She reasoned that she had never been much afraid of ghosts or angels or anything supernatural. They intrigued her. And it didn't seem at all out of character for the peculiar old house to have a ghost. Or maybe it had been an angel? She remembered that the face had a beauty and glow that seemed angelic. She sighed; she really wasn't sure what she had seen. She just couldn't tell from such a brief sighting and from so far away at the bottom of the yard. And now she feared that time was making it even less real. She needed to figure it out for her own sanity. She wished now that she had given into her earlier urges to investigate, rather than try to convince herself that Annie was right and her mind had played tricks on her—now that she was actually going to be sleeping in the mansion.

CHAPTER 2

Watching!

Erik knew they were moving in. He had mixed feelings about it. It would be easier for him to watch them, but surely it would bring them closer to danger, too. Certainly it would make them known to the cult. The thought made him shudder. As ever, he would do whatever he could to keep them safe, but he wasn't sure that would be good enough.

He remembered last fall. It seemed so much longer ago than one year. It had been just after his transformation. He laughed mirthlessly, remembering how green he had been. He had been here at the mansion, still looking for the key to Professor Hamilton's safe back at the lab—the safe that contained the Stones of Bothynus, the stones that could transform him back to a normal state.

He had heard the front door slam.

In a flash, he had ghosted up the basement stairs and pressed through the door at the top. He didn't notice it anymore, but at the time, pressing through objects felt like slowly walking through gelatin. He had slipped across the room in an effort to move so fluidly that whoever was coming wouldn't detect movement. He was now well practiced in the art of non-detection, but back then he had been nervous about being discovered by the cult. He had melded into the shadow of a bookcase and had stayed perfectly still to listen and observe.

"You two, don't touch anything in case the police aren't done," a man's voice had said as footsteps sounded in the foyer. The tap, tap, tap of nails on the slate floor had told Erik that a dog accompanied the intruders. He smiled now, remembering that Buddy had almost given away his presence.

"Poor Uncle Alistair." The girl's voice had sounded sincere. Erik's prickliness had felt a little smoothed. These were people who cared about Professor Hamilton. They were the good guys, and not the police. He always feared police involvement. The whole thing would be so hard to explain … Even now, Erik still held out hope that he could find Professor Hamilton and the stones before the police—or the cult.

"Look at this, Annie." Erik had heard a slightly lower-pitched voice, perhaps slightly more mature than the first girl.

There had been a low growl, and he'd looked down to see some type of beagle-mix staring directly into his eyes, its sharp black eyes alert, its eyebrows pulled together in a question. He had slowly reached the back of his hand forward to allow the dog to sniff his scent.

"What is it, Buddy?" It had been the younger girl. She had come forward, looking inquiringly at the spot where Erik was hiding, but presumably not seeing anything but shadow and dust motes. Erik was amazed at the beauty of the girl's essence. It was kind of a lemon yellow, but not, and kind of like silver, but not—silvery-blue, he decided. *Ah, the purity of youth*. He had liked the girl instinctively. He had relied mostly on instinct then because that was all he had.

Now, after a year, he knew he still had a lot to learn about reading essences. But he was sure he could see some pretty clear trends. It was one of the few perks of his current and otherwise drab existence. In this state, he could only see the vague outline of a person's physical form. He could just make out the form of his or her clothes and hair, but the most prevalent thing he saw in each human was a fog-like, softly pulsating shape within their physical forms that he thought of as their essence. Some were beautiful, some dull. The hue varied, but not as much as the quality of clarity. He thought of it as clean and pure versus tainted or murky. Was this karma? Or was it more like their spirit or soul? He wished now he had read more about religious beliefs. Was this what was meant by having one's spiritual eyes opened? He recalled a story about a donkey that had stopped in the road because it saw an angel that its master couldn't see. He wondered often whether others had breached the barrier, too, and could provide some insight. If he could just talk to Professor Hamilton ...

"Oh, you silly puppy," the girl had said in a babyish silly voice, ruffling the fur behind the dog's ears playfully. Erik laughed, too, though the girl hadn't heard him. The dog had responded by lobbing his tongue out to one side in a doggy grin and seemed to accept that the girl knew this man and he was one of the pack—or at least was an acceptable intruder. Satisfied, the dog wagged his tail and trotted off.

Erik remembered feeling relief after the close call. He was sure his heart had pounded, though he couldn't really feel that sensation anymore. Since then, he had determined a few kinds of animals could see him—the more intelligent ones, he guessed: dogs, cats, crows, and raccoons, but not deer or squirrels. He thought it must have to do with both intelligence and eyesight.

"Annie, are you going to look at this or not?" the older girl had asked. Erik had looked in her direction. Even now, a year later, he could recall the exact sensation of being frozen to the spot, completely mesmerized. He was sure he had felt his heart stop as his eyes beheld the most beautiful thing he had ever seen—the essence of this girl. Was it even a color? Or was it more of a colored glow, a color's energy? If he were to invent a new color, this would be it. Even now, the memory of that first sighting took his breath away. Like the other girl's, it was kind of lemon yellow, but not, and kind of silver, but not. It also had an aspect of chlorophyll-blue-green, like the earthy energy he had seen in mosses and ferns, but also in emeralds. Primeval, rich, a timeless radiating life force. It glowed with both purity and warmth. How could this impossible color accomplish these very different attributes so clearly, so powerfully? Like he imagined the first woman in the Garden of Eden would have looked, this was radiating, pulsating feminine beauty. There was just something about her essence. Something that spoke to him—something life-changing that he couldn't forget. Like his existence had become somehow better, just knowing she existed.

Erik, who had always considered himself a practical guy, a scientist, had watched spellbound as the two girls explored the room—the silvery-emerald girl's essence had drawn him in a way he had never experienced. He hadn't been able to tear his gaze away. He had watched as she showed something from a book to the younger girl, then re-shelved that one and looked over more titles of Professor Hamilton's books, running her fingers over their spines, an occasional sound escaping the perfect lips. He had memorized their curve. He had been able to do nothing but stand in awe, watching every movement, every breath. He still couldn't explain his overwhelming obsession with the girl.

He watched as she surveyed a group of classics, her graceful fingers removing a volume. *Beautiful and sophisticated—a lover of the classics,* he had thought.

"Oh wow, Annie, remember this? *'Catherine Earnshaw, may you not rest as long as I am living. You said I killed you—haunt me, then. The murdered do haunt their murderers. I believe—I know that ghosts have wandered the earth.'*[2] " She read from *Wuthering Heights* in a curious way, without melodrama, but rather as if she really empathized with Heathcliff. This fascinated him.

"Yeah, Uncle Alistair loved doing Heathcliff. Remember how he did Cathy's voice?" Each girl in turn tried to imitate him and then both tittered in a companionable way.

Erik liked hearing their lighthearted fun at imitating Professor Hamilton reading to them without a hint of fun-poking. He found them to be as pleasant as their essences suggested and saw how much they seemed to love Professor Hamilton. He realized there was a lot about Professor Hamilton he had never known.

The fun seemed to sadden when the younger girl picked out another book and tried reading in what he assumed had been in further imitation of their uncle. "Listen to this—here's one of your favorites. Remember Uncle Alistair doing Reepicheep? *'A dragon has just flown over the tree-tops and lighted on the beach. Yes, I am afraid it is between us and the ship. And arrows are no use against dragons. And they're not at all afraid of fire.' 'With your Majesty's leave—' began Reepicheep. 'No, Reepicheep,' said the King very firmly, 'you are not to attempt a single combat with it.*[3]*"*

Both girls laughed, but their laughter seemed somewhat subdued.

"Hey, Annie, that was a pretty good Uncle-Alistair-Reepicheep. I just wish ..." began the older girl, but didn't finish her sentence.

"Yeah, me too," said the younger girl sadly.

"Don't worry, Annie, they're going to find him." Erik saw her brow furrow and her jaw set with determination.

Erik wondered why that reference had saddened them. Perhaps this had been a favorite childhood memory they thought was now gone from them. Or were they wishing their uncle had been saved by a champion like this Reepicheep?

About that time, the man they had come with had opened the basement door just to Erik's left and called back, "Red, why don't you go on outside with Annie? I really don't want the two of you touching anything yet 'til things are a bit more settled."

"Okay, okay," the girl answered, slipping a book back onto a shelf while the man wasn't looking. *Red. That must be her nickname. Strange, but kinda cute,* Erik thought. He loved everything about her. *She must have red hair to have that nickname.* He had been able to recognize a coppery tint in her waist-length waves. Even in those early days, he had learned that if he stared long enough, he could usually make out physical features, but the essences were more prevalent to him than the visible colors of skin, hair, eyes.

She had turned slowly, still surveying all the room's contents, as if in a museum. As the focus of her eyes moved toward where he stood, he remembered making an involuntary gasp as he saw their brilliant green, so catlike and intelligent. They seemed almost neon with intelligence, echoing the brilliant silvery-emerald quality of her essence. Her features were average, Erik thought, trying to be objective, but now he thought everything about her to be perfect. She had wide cheekbones and a straight nose and the total effect enchanted him. The indescribable color of her essence, the glow of her green eyes, and the energy of her graceful movements mesmerized him.

He felt goose bumps even now as he remembered how Red had started, as though she had heard him gasp. She had looked directly at him. Oh, how that had felt. An electric current had run through him when her eyes met his, though after the initial moment of shock, he realized her eyes seemed to only see the bookcase and adjoining shadowy wall with its faded brick-colored paint. But he had seen into the depths of her eyes. If she'd reached through him to get a book at that moment, Erik was pretty sure he'd have had a heart attack.

But she'd merely shuddered slightly and then drawn away, skipping out the back door that opened onto the deck, following the route of the younger girl.

Erik had breathed a sigh of relief that he hadn't been discovered, yet at the same time, he experienced a sadness that she hadn't been able to see him. Why couldn't he have met her when he'd been normal? He could try to talk to her, but it would only come out as a kind of whispery sound and would likely just frighten her. To be so close and yet so far apart …

He inhaled deeply to see if he could smell her essence. Sweet birch, maybe; woodsy, earthy. Though maybe he had just *imagined* he could detect a scent. Sometimes he imagined his sense of smell worked, but he wasn't totally sure. After all, the molecules would be incompatible with his. Even now he didn't understand it all.

Since that had been a close call, he had stupidly decided to reposition himself while no one was in the room. He had known he was pretty much invisible, but his research with the stones had taught him that in this state, an object could be seen under the right light conditions, like a vapor. He glided into the foyer and up the stairs, pushing himself through the door to the study. It required some effort, but he hadn't wanted the door hinges to squeak. He was now pretty good at pushing his molecules through any solid object, but there was always some slight resistance with certain materials. As a physics major, he understood a lot about his current state, and if his situation weren't so dire, he would thoroughly enjoy this opportunity to learn. He was especially intrigued by the fact that he could stand on a floor, or push himself down *through* the floor. If he grasped objects at just the right speed and pressure, he could move them. Or he could choose to have his hand pass through them. Mastering that ability had taken weeks of concentrated practice and had occupied the first month after his change. On the day he first saw Red and Annie, though, he had still been a novice.

He hadn't been able to resist going to the window to watch the girls. *What a voyeur,* he thought ruefully. He promised himself he wouldn't watch them if they did anything private. He pushed the sheer back so he could see them clearly. They were nowhere in sight at first. He waited for them to come back into the yard, correctly guessing they must've gone down the path to the canal.

The sheer kept slowly sinking into his hand as he held it back until he hooked it over the curtain holdback. After a while, he heard the man come up the basement stairs and open the sliding glass door to the deck.

"Sonia, Anya, time to go," the man shouted toward the trailhead at the bottom of the yard. Hearing no answer, the man called again, this time louder and more authoritative. "Girls. Let's go."

Was this their real names? Sonia, was that the real name for the one they called Red? *Like Red Sonja! No way.* The thought had caused him to laugh slightly, remembering his love for the comic book and movie character, and his fantasy that he'd meet such a warrior woman one day. Could this be the case for the beautiful silvery-emerald girl? In some odd way, that fit with the Reepicheep thing—maybe she had become sad at the mention of a small yet fierce champion, feeling she should have been such a champion for her uncle. But Red Sonja had been tall for a woman and she was somewhat tall, too. Still, he wondered if she and her sister felt some sense of responsibility and sadness that they had not been able to protect their uncle. He hoped not. He longed to tell them there was nothing they could have done—that this bloody mess was a whole new kind of thing.

At that moment, Erik had watched spellbound from the window as the silvery-emerald color appeared at the edge of the forest and moved out into the sunlight. In the sunlight, her essence was even more breathtaking, glowing angelically. Erik wondered if there was a connection, though it wasn't exactly an angel color. A shocking aspect of his transformed state he had needed to process early on was that he could see not only human essences, but other essences as well. He thought of the other beings as angels, though he had never believed in angels before and these beings varied in color and size. The best he had been able to decipher was that each hue designated a type of angel. He witnessed the sunlight-yellow ones hanging around hospitals, tending to the sick. The smaller pink ones were always around children, it seemed.

As he watched the silvery-emerald girl in the sunlight, he had been both mesmerized and shocked by his own reaction, watching in total stillness as if drinking in a Renoir, totally unconscious of himself. He'd been so enraptured that he was been caught off guard as the green eyes rose slowly and obviously saw him. Their eyes met. Electricity sparked. The girl gasped and stopped dead in her tracks.

She remained momentarily frozen in place, as did he. The other girl following her reactively stopped, too, and stood as silent as a mouse behind her. Erik had remained frozen for what seemed like an instant and yet an eternity. Even now, he remembered the feeling of panic that had shot through him. What had he done? His stupid voyeurism may have cost him his secrecy.

As Red rubbed her eyes with her fists in disbelief, he quickly glided out of view of the window and shoved a lamp over to the spot where he had been standing.

He had heard the excited girls' voices outside, though he couldn't hear well enough to understand what they were saying from his position pressed into the corner. Then the voices seemed to change into a few giggles and banter and he could guess the gist. His ruse had worked and they were making light of the sighting.

He remembered being glad the lamp had been nearby and hoping he had covered his tracks adequately. But he also remembered feeling sad, as he had felt earlier when she looked directly at him without seeing him. How he had longed to say something to her, to scream, "I'm here! Please, please see me. I want to talk to you."

How he still wanted to connect with her. He ached, knowing he should leave her alone. He shouldn't get her mixed up with all this. Heck, she'd probably run screaming from the house, back to wherever she came from, if she knew about the whole dreadful mess with the cult looking for the stones. But on the other hand, he had obsessed about her. *What if she never returns?* He didn't want to consider that possibility. His enchantress. He had to think she would return. *But then what?* Would she listen if he could somehow communicate the danger? He was pretty sure it wouldn't work. He had decided it was better to keep quiet and watch. The thought that maybe he could better protect her if he stayed hidden had given him some comfort—he had decided to watch out for those possessed bastards and keep them away from her.

The thought of Roy making any contact with her filled him with rage. He knew the rage he felt was excessive. But this beautiful soul had to be protected from that lowlife. That *traitor.* So he had watched over this lovely family for the past year and knew he would continue to do so. He tried to reassure himself it would just be a little easier to get to them each day, now that they were moving closer to his mom and Ms. Catsworthy; he would be able to watch over them all without so much back and forth. But the thought of Roy still filled him with foreboding.

In an apartment near the Georgetown campus, Roy Oglethorp absentmindedly fingered the thick scar on his right thumb. Even with physical therapy, his hand was still stiff and this affected his handwriting. As he rubbed and stretched it, he was reminded of how he had injured it a year ago. He felt numb, thinking of the awful scuffle with Professor Hamilton and their tug of war over the key ring that had resulted in the deep cut and torn ligament. Even though the thumb had been badly injured, he had held off getting the needed surgery. He had lain low, not wanted anyone to connect the injury with the disappearance. He scoffed. Still, a year later, it was still causing him trouble—partly because he kept re-injuring it. He didn't want to think of the things they made him do to reinjure it. He didn't care if the damn thing fell off, if it would just leave him alone and not throb.

Another part of him longed for a little TLC right now. He had felt that way even back then. But he had waited for the thumb to heal on its own and had kept soaking it in Epsom salts and applying antibiotic ointment to the wound. He had tried to think of ways to feign an injury to get medical attention without causing suspicion, finally resorting to chopping wood for his mom and pretend to injure it then. He cringed at the memory. At the same time, something inside him snickered at the thought of his pain. He felt bile rise in his throat. What had he become?

The doorbell rang and even though he didn't want to answer it, his body didn't obey him. He walked to the door and opened it wide to allow Lorenzo to enter. He watched helplessly as Lorenzo locked the deadbolt before slowly turning to face him.

"So, Roy—did you find it yet?"

"No, Lorenzo … I …" and then he made a huffing sound as Lorenzo punched his gut, forcing air out in a rush. Roy was accustomed to having Lorenzo do this at least once a week in an attempt to force him to find the key.

"That is not the answer I wish to give Signor Pietro. How many days must the masters wait until *il tuo culo pigro* finds the key?" The last word was shouted an inch from Roy's ear.

"I know, I know," Roy pleaded, backing away.

Roy felt Lorenzo's fist hit him square on the lips, followed by a gush of blood. Roy reeled, but didn't fall and didn't fight back, though he wanted to. The things inside him were submissive to the thing or things inside Lorenzo—he knew that much and knew they'd never allow him to fight Lorenzo or Pietro or any of the *Tyrannus-Novum* cult.

"Clean yourself up," he heard Lorenzo spit. He used his shirt to catch the blood streaming from his mouth. He felt some pleasure watching Lorenzo rub his sore knuckles, and then dismay as Lorenzo reached for a bottle of his expensive Shiraz, uncorked it with his pocketknife, and drank straight from the bottle before wiping his mouth on his sleeve.

Roy watched as Lorenzo sank into a chair, facing him. "Signor Pietro sends orders to kidnap one of the family of *il professore*. I think there are two *giovani donne, adolescent,* moving into the old guy's mansion. You should try some moves—use your Casanova moves. You're the best gigolo on the team, so the job is yours. These are his orders." Lorenzo smirked smugly.

"B-But," Roy began but the demon inside him did not allow him to continue. He began to feel a need building in him to toy with these young girls. *Fresh meat.* As he sat staring at Lorenzo, the need built.

CHAPTER 3

Uncle Alistair's Mansion

After the movers left, Red began unpacking and arranging her new room. Her spirits began to lift. This was really cool. She had never before had a room of her own and she was looking forward to space and privacy, though living here was also going to demand more of her time. Her mom had been worried about keeping such a large place clean and they had discussed the pros and cons of hiring a housekeeper. To keep down expenses, they decided they would try to forgo that, at least at first. They had unanimously agreed to close off the un-used portions of the house. But the really exciting part was that Red and Annie had successfully argued that they'd save the family money by doing the housekeeping themselves instead, for cheap, in lieu of finding part-time jobs. Red had been especially keen on this, since she'd be in need of gas money when she got her driver's license.

Red scooted her bed to face the door, then pushed it against the opposite wall, then finally moved it so it was facing the window with the headboard to the left of the doorway. Yes, this was it. She could sit in bed with her shade up and actually see the Potomac River. She had a sudden urge to show someone this cool new room. She didn't have many friends, but maybe one of her tae kwon do buddies might be persuaded to stop by this weekend. Quinn, maybe. *Yes.* This idea felt good, she thought, and decided to call her.

As she walked down the hall, however, she found herself detouring towards the study. She was determined to resist the urge to feel creeped-out here. She wanted to enjoy her new home. She turned the knob and opened the door with a tiny squeak. The office was bare, compared to the perpetual mess it had been when Uncle Alistair was here. After the break-in, a cleaning crew had boxed up much of it; and then after he had been declared dead, her mom spent a weekend boxing up what remained of his stuff. The lamp and hat rack were still positioned in front of the window, Red noted curiously, and felt a chill run up her spine. Okay, maybe she had had enough for one day.

She was just turning to leave when a bulletin board caught her eye. It was hanging on the wall to the left of the large mahogany desk. An old calendar hung there with the leaf still positioned to last September, the month Uncle Alistair disappeared. Red shuddered involuntarily.

Some mish-mash of apparently random notes were still stuck to the bulletin board, but what caught her eye was a picture of Uncle Alistair with two young men—both rather hot, she noted. Must be his graduate students. She hoped neither boy was the one who drowned with Uncle Alistair. She examined the picture carefully, moving close to the board, her fingers uplifted, reaching—reluctant, yet compelled to touch the picture. She felt like an intruder, but then reasoned that was silly. *People pin things to bulletin boards to be looked at.* So, she'd look at it. The picture showed Uncle Alistair standing in front of a table in a classroom setting. The graduate students were facing him, both in jeans, the tall, muscular one wearing a T-shirt with a picture of a crow and a slogan that read, "Save the Rockville Rookeries," and the other wearing a crisp, professionally-laundered linen shirt. *With jeans? Oh well.* She guessed that might work in some cases, but not on him; there was something haughty about the way he looked. Both young men were positioned with their shoulders angled so the observer was directed to look at the table's contents. Rocks. Three glossy, black, egg-shaped rocks were on the table between Uncle Alistair and the boys. Each rock seemed somewhat flattened on the bottom so it rested solidly on the table, and each had a perfectly round opening on each end, but the angle of the shot made it impossible to see what was inside. Each rock was housed inside its own small glass case.

The rocks were probably some museum pieces. Knowing Uncle Alistair, there was undoubtedly some intriguing story about those rocks. Uncle Alistair's expertise was in Medieval Religions, and he often brought relevant relics to the university to show his students. Once, at one of his elaborate Christmas parties when she and Annie were little, he had showed them an authentic gold-leaf icon painting of the Madonna and child he had borrowed from the Vatican. He had it hanging in the living room on the wall opposite the fireplace and everyone at the party had ooh'd and ahh'd over it. She didn't understand why it was so special until he told her about its legendary power to heal the sick and injured. She and Annie had been creeped out by it. Despite his insistence that it was just a story and objects couldn't have power, Annie had cried to go home.

Realizing her thoughts were wandering, Red redirected her attention back to the picture. One of the boys, the one wearing the crow T-shirt, was really cute. He had longish hair and the shadow of a juvenile beard. She stared closer. He looked familiar. She studied his eyes. *Wow*. He had dark cat eyes. His hair was dark brown with some copper-colored streaks from the sun. Had she met him somewhere before? Surely she'd have remembered someone who looked like that. He was *hot*. His pecs, deltoids, and biceps bulged, straining his shirt. And his sharp gaze suggested an inner strength. Yes, she definitely would've remembered him.

As she studied his face, he realized who it was that he reminded her of: the Viking ghost. Her heart started to pound. Yes, she'd seen that face in her dreams! Then she looked closer and wasn't sure. He wasn't close enough in the photo for her to be certain, and it wasn't super sharp. As for the ghost's face, she wondered if her mind had filled in the gaps and imagined a face. After all, the ghost had been too misty to really make out details.

Her gaze scanned the rest of the picture. The other boy looked pale and washed out in comparison, like a bratty cousin of the first boy. He had regular enough features, though, perhaps a weak chin. Now that she looked at his picture, he wasn't at all hot, as she'd thought at first glance. There was something off about him. It was hard to put her finger on the problem with his face and why it just didn't look right. Maybe it was his eyes? The two boys had similar coloration, reddish-brown hair and dark eyes, but the cute boy's eyes were sharp and intelligent, reserved and mysterious, whereas the other boy's were flat and uninspired, even sullen. Maybe it was a lack of warmth. He looked as if a smirk hid just beneath the surface of his pinched lips. Did she see hatred there? Maybe hatred was too strong a word. It was as though he had decided long ago on a course for his life and had given up any excitement or enthusiasm for the unexpected, leaving a surly determination to stick his course. Maybe she was reading too much into one photo.

She unpinned the picture and carried it back to her room, having already forgotten about calling Quinn. She wanted to examine the photo of the cute boy some more, and perhaps sketch him. She loved art. She thought of how she and Quinn had envisioned themselves as artists all through middle school, sitting for hours with heads together, drawing anime figures. They had been so absorbed in art that they seldom socialized with others their own age, living instead in a little anime fantasy world, drawing and talking, drawing and web-surfing, drawing and giggling. Quinn had been the real exception to Red's seeming inability to keep friends. Then again, maybe she just hadn't really needed a lot of friends and her mom had been a worrywart about her not having friends. Or maybe she and Quinn had been friends because their friendship began outside of school where the pressures of the almighty clique were forbidden. She had another friend from tae kwon do, too—Wali, though he and Red weren't as close as she was to Quinn. Wali had never been weird about letting a girl beat him. Master Shah had a different standard at the tae kwon do school, one of honor and earned rank. He would never abide even the remotest hint of a clique, and she respected him for this.

Red realized she had gone down one of her brain-chains and reeled herself back to the moment. She wanted to make this boy from the photo into an anime character—this boy who reminded her of her ghost. She sat down with her sketchpad and began drawing. She sketched half-a-dozen sketches, none satisfactory. She became fiercely absorbed in drawing his handsome and awe-inspiring face. After a while, she sighed with frustration and decided what she really needed was more light and the feeling of the warm sun on her back. She grabbed a quilt from the stack on her bed and snatched up the photo, her drawing tablet, and pencils, priority objects that were among the few things she'd unpacked. She skipped out the back door and found a peaceful sunny spot at the bottom of the yard, near the path.

This was her favorite time of year. Although the peak fall colors were gone, a few colorful leaves still clung tenaciously to the trees. It gave her a warm, harvest feeling, no doubt bred into her through eons of evolution in which humans collectively breathed a sigh of relief to see the harvest, fat and bountiful, except in lean years when they all tried to put on a brave face and celebrate just the same, perhaps with thoughts of enjoying one last feast before the bleak winter.

Once the quilt was spread satisfactorily on the sunny spot, she started to plop down onto its soft warmth, and then, true to her nature, gave herself to the moment. That fall sunbeam was just too warm to resist and she needed to cheer herself up. She raised her face to the sun and felt energized, like a sunflower. No, that wasn't it; she decided what she really felt in this moment was glee, like the young calves during the annual spring release on her grandparents' farm—free to romp in the meadow. Her grandfather would leave all the mother cows in the barnyard that morning and would fling open all the stable doors. Each calf would gingerly tiptoe into first the grand hallway that Papaw called the middle shed and then to the great out-of-doors. The small timid creatures, realizing their freedom, would begin bucking and kicking, running, romping, and eventually butting heads together. Lost in this gleeful memory, Red's free spirit acted upon it. She took a running go and first did one handstand, then another, and then a couple of walk-overs to loosen up, and then began doing flips. After a few of these, she topped it off with two perfect flying side-kicks.

Once her romp was finished, she plopped down onto her back again. She felt the sun's warmth soaked into the quilt and turned her face up to the sun. She slowly filled her lungs with the earthy scent of sunbaked vegetation. With thick forest all around the hidden yard, Red knew the time for sunshine was very short and remembered she had work to do. Her topside warm, she rolled over onto her tummy, luxuriating in the warmth and stretching her legs, arching her back for a trunk stretch and digging her toes into the cool grass just off the edge of the quilt. She had to place her drawing pad in the shadow of her head so she could look at the glowing white paper. She wished she had grabbed her sunglasses. She picked up her favorite graphite pencil and began sketching the boy again. Intrigued by his smooth, slightly convex forehead, and full, thick eyebrows, she tried to lose herself in the moment and allow free flow of her creative energy. Her eyes, however, wouldn't fully cooperate and were repeatedly and irresistibly drawn to the study window. No Viking ghost there any more, just the lampshade she disappointedly saw each time.

Becoming a little frustrated with her lack of focus, she stretched her neck and upper back again by arching upward. She thought about doing a bit of yoga to get the kink out of her neck. Absentmindedly, she sketched a pointy dome shape on the boy's head and made quick strokes along the lower edge, forming a decorative band with geometric shapes with disheveled dark curls lapping upward at irregular intervals. With a wry smile, her pencil moved to the sides of the helmet and within a few smooth strokes, the boy was wearing a Viking helmet with horns. She looked squarely at the drawing. Then she glanced up to the window and back at her drawing. Her heart began to pound and she involuntarily inhaled with a whooshing sound.

The boy and the Viking ghost are definitely the same person. What the heck does that mean?

She shook her head. *Now, wait a minute, no, it was just the lampshade, that's all. I didn't see a ghost.* She tried one final, half-hearted attempt to convince herself there was nothing supernatural going on in Uncle Alistair's mansion.

But there had definitely been something odd about what she'd seen, she had to admit, because even if it had been the lampshade, it had *moved*. And if there had really been no ghost, then how could she recognize this face? Had she seen him somewhere else? *What is it about this boy? Is he really the Viking ghost? This is too weird.* She needed to think—no, she didn't want to think.

"Red, your room is still a mess and I'm going with Mom to CVS in half an hour even if you don't get to," Annie's bossy voice blasted into her consciousness. It had long since stopped bugging her that Annie nagged her to keep her on task. She knew Annie meant well. Her mom had tried to explain their sibling rivalry in one of their many long talks about Red's ADHD. She had explained that whenever a firstborn had difficulty in an area, a younger sibling often tasked him or herself with being the responsible one. Red guessed that Anne felt it was her duty to keep her on task. Understanding this had gone a long way toward encouraging a sound friendship that had grown much stronger in the past couple of years.

Red knew this bossiness from a younger sibling should've grated on her, but it didn't much. Annie was okay. In the good moments, they could talk about anything. She was convinced Annie was only watching out after her best interest. And Annie really was her BFF, even though Quinn competed for the role.

Still, it wasn't cool to answer too quickly, so Red went back to her drawing, trying to force it to feel like a normal drawing and not the image of a ghost. As Red worked, she periodically glanced toward the study window in a faint hope that the spectacle would reappear and confirm her belief that the Viking ghost had been real. A movement up the yard between herself and the house caught her eye and she whipped around. *Only a crow.* She turned her focus back to drawing. Then movements in the crow's direction drew her eyes back to the bird. What the heck was he doing? Was his wing hurt? Was this a mating dance? Being an amateur bird-watcher, Red was always fascinated by birds. As she watched, the crow seemed to be looking at her, extending his wings down to the ground and spreading his tail, strutting and bowing; this was repeated several times. *What the...* To her relief, he flew away.

Red was a bit flustered by the strange antics of the crow. She made a great effort to refocus her energy and attention on finishing the drawing of her Viking. After a few minutes, she had greatly improved the shading and was close to being satisfied when the crow landed on her quilt within a foot of her head. She instinctively pushed herself to a defensive tae kwon do posture and screamed her standard tae kwon do cry, "Aaaaaaaiiieeeght!" She desperately tried to control her breathing, telling herself it was just a crow, but also feeling a little creeped out by the strange behavior. Could crows carry rabies? Could this day get any stranger?

As she began to calm down, she noticed that the crow had something in his beak. He kept one eye on her as he hopped over to her drawing pad and deposited a cardinal flower on her drawing. As Red remained in attention stance, watching this small foe, she noted that he had a crescent-shaped scar

40

or gouge on the left side of his beak. A low, throaty clucking sound came from his breast. Then he turned his head to one side, eyeing her squarely with one black eye, called a decisive, "Caw!" and few away, circling down toward the towpath, into the trees, and out of sight. *Okay, now the day just got stranger. I mean, really weird.*

Red didn't wait for her heart to stop thudding. She snatched up the quilt and bolted for the house. She decided a trip to the drugstore with Annie and her mom would be a welcome change and something normal like buying shampoo would feel good right now. What the heck was she doing, threatening a crow with her tae kwon do stance? She decided to seize this opportunity to confide in Annie about her thoughts on the graduate student and Viking ghost. She definitely needed to get a grip and do some sleuthing work and Annie was actually pretty good at both.

CHAPTER 4

The Crazy Cat-Lady Next Door

On the drive back from the drugstore, Red noticed her mom glancing in the rear-view mirror a couple of times and wondered how much of the whispered conversation between Annie and Red she had overheard. Annie had reacted the same way to the news of the crow's strange behavior as she had last year about the Viking ghost—with complete skepticism. After getting verbally pelted by Annie, Red wondered if her imagination really had simply run away with her. The thought had a calming effect.

So it was a welcome distraction when her mom suggested they pay a neighborly visit to the elderly lady who lived next door. The old lady's house had intrigued Red since she was a child. It appeared to be not quite as old as the original farmhouse; it was probably a caretaker's cottage built on the estate, close to the main house. Both seemed out of place among the cookie-cutter colonials built from one of three floor plans stretching up and down the rest of Chelsea Lane. The cottage sat further back from the road than the other houses, with a thick hedge and an ancient iron fence surrounding the yard. Red glanced toward the wrought-iron gate. To enter through the gate, one had to walk under the lion's head; it seemed to stare at you no matter whether you stepped to one side or the other. Despite this, however, the cottage suggested domesticity and tranquility, with a neatly trimmed hedge, seasonal flowers, and walls painted lavender with pink shutters—totally out of character with the surrounding neighborhood.

It was the old lady's odd ways, however, that made her something of a legend to Red and Annie. Even though she had been Uncle Alistair's lifelong friend, Red and Annie had kept their distance as children, whispering about her oddities under tables and behind hedges, rather than doing what they had really wanted to do—go over and play with her cats. Her house had intrigued Red. And these oddities might've served to make it charming, a fairytale cottage, if Red had known her better. Perhaps she should have accepted one of the occasional invitations to tea. But the old lady had always carried a sadness about her that repelled children. She and Annie had called her Crazy Cat-Lady for so long that Red had forgotten her actual name, Ms. Cat-something.

Red felt a few large drops of rain on her arm as she got out of the car and soon realized a steady rain had set in for the evening. Still a little uneasy from her earlier thoughts of the Viking ghost, and now with the rain pouring, Red thought visiting the creepy old lady wasn't appealing. She was relieved when Annie for once agreed with her and they convinced their mom to delay the visit until tomorrow.

Her dad, perpetually upbeat, further rescued the mood. Red was delighted to note upon entering the library that he had found some firewood and built a roaring fire in the library fireplace. She was further delighted to hear her mom ordering a pizza on her cell. All thoughts of going back outside were blissfully forgotten, and Red felt surprisingly at home, dragging herself drowsily up to bed a couple of hours later, toasty warm from the fire and pleasantly full from the pizza.

The next morning, the rain had stopped and the sun was shining, but Red could tell from the few ice sparkles on the window above the kitchen sink that a frost had bitten during the night. She gingerly placed her hand onto the chilly windowpane for a few seconds before withdrawing it and rubbing the moisture into her fingertips. She could feel the warmth of the sunbeam on her face in contrast to the coolness of the glass.

Her eye caught a movement outside on a tree limb of the old walnut tree. A sparrow, feathers ruffling in the wind, was pounding its tiny beak on a sunflower seed it had evidently taken from the nearby bird feeder. "Mom, did you already fill the bird feeder?" she asked. She noted thankfully that she hadn't seen any crows.

"What, honey?" her mom answered distractedly, shuffling through a box on the counter. She followed Red's gaze. "Hmmm ... who filled the bird feeder?" She shrugged. "We must have nice neighbors."

"Probably Crazy Cat-Lady," Red offered and then immediately felt a pang of guilt.

Red's mom placed a hand on her shoulder and Red enjoyed the quiet moment as they watched several types of birds enjoying the seeds—chickadees, cardinals, tufted titmice, and an occasional sparrow. Red now noticed three crows watching from a large black walnut tree at the bottom of the yard, but not entering the feeding frenzy.

After a moment, Red noted that Roxy, pupils large and black, was crouched at the bottom of the sliding glass door that opened onto the wooden deck overlooking the backyard, also watching the little birds. She smiled.

Her mother picked up the kitten. "No, no, Roxy, birdies aren't to be eaten, but admired for their beauty and song." Red was amused to hear her mother talking in a childish voice. *My mom is such a child,* thought Red. *If Annie were here right now, she'd likely make a gagging gesture.* She grinned at the thought.

The sharp tap, tap of the front door knocker startled them both. Her mom put Roxy down gently and peeped through the keyhole. Red thought she saw her mom brighten as she quickly opened the door with a neighborly, "Good morning."

Red stood behind her mom, who had to look down because the little woman standing in the doorway was a head shorter than she. Wisps of her silver hair had freed themselves from her purple cashmere scarf around a face that suggested aged beauty. Red recognized the face—it seemed somewhat jolly, a Mrs. Santa with rosy cheeks and twinkly blue eyes. *Hmmm, on second thought,* thought Red, *No, that isn't it ... who is it? Oh yeah.* She reminded her of the pretty exotic lady on an

old sitcom she had watched a few times to humor her mom—
Greene Acres, or something like that. Red was loath to admit
that she had actually enjoyed it. The woman on the sitcom
had an unfamiliar accent. Russian? Hungarian? Only this feisty
fairy godmother had a proper British accent and dressed as if
she'd be right at home in a fairytale. Now that Red was more
mature, she found Crazy Cat-Lady's face quite pleasant.

"Mrs. Greene?"

"Yes, Ms. Cats—?"

"Catsworthy, but oh dear, please call me Zsofia." Red
couldn't imagine herself calling an elderly lady, especially one
with such proper manners, by her given name; she decided this
offer was only for her parents. She would try to remember her
real name: Ms. Catsworthy.

"And please call me Kaye." Red's mom seemed very
happy to see the elderly lady and Red wondered if she regretted
letting the rain stop her from calling the night before. "Do you
remember our daughter, Sonia? We call her Red."

Red saw Annie skip down the stairs into the foyer,
curious to see what the commotion was about. "And this is
Annie," her mom said.

"Oh, deary, you're all grown up. Do you remember
me?" She beamed at Red, then, without skipping a beat, tilted
her head and swept her eyes upward to address Red's mom.
"Such a pleasure to have you join the neighborhood. I was
taking my morning stroll and thought to call on you to welcome
you to the neighborhood and bring you and your dear family
some fresh angel cakes for your morning tea."

"Please, do come in," said Red's mom.

47

Zsofia Catsworthy scurried in. "I'd be delighted. Thank you, dear."

Red reaffirmed her earlier thoughts of her mom's childishness as within minutes she observed the two ladies laughing heartily, having a proper British tea using a large box as a table. Red declined to join them, but curiosity and politeness kept her nearby, finding a box to begin unpacking on the large table in the dining room just off the kitchen. She noted that Annie was doing the same.

Red heard her mom say, "Thank you very much for filling the bird feeder—at least, I assumed it must've been you. The birds seem very plump and healthy in the backyard."

Ms. Catsworthy seemed a bit confused for a moment and then responded, "Yes, it has been the strangest thing. I never gave much thought to birds, but since poor Alistair disappeared, I just felt I must feed the birds. It somehow gives me a sense of peace. It's like the thought came to me out of the blue ... and I was compelled to act upon it." She seemed to be in a thoughtful contemplation for another moment.

Red began looking for breakfast cereal and was caught off guard when Ms. Catsworthy turned her focus on her and Annie. "Come, let me look at you. My dear, dear children. Such beautiful children. My, you're all grown up into fine young ladies. It seems like only yesterday the two of you were all dolled up in little flouncy dresses with bouncing curls. Oh my, how time flies." Then, in a barely audible murmur, she added, "And at the same time, drones on forever."

Red felt awkward being admired by Ms. Catsworthy. She was self-conscious about her size because she tended to be the tallest girl in any room and definitely the strongest. She tried not to envy Annie, with her wasp waist and delicate structure. And she felt proud of Annie's graceful physique as Ms. Catsworthy gushed with compliments. In fact, Red began to like this sweet old lady, her warmth growing on her. She felt her childhood opinion that the old lady was creepy begin to melt away. She was certain Annie felt the same way, watching her beam as Ms. Catsworthy praised the fineness of her person.

"Girls, do you remember that Ms. Catsworthy lives in the really pretty house next door?"

"The one with the lion's head gate?" asked Annie. She usually didn't talk much but Red could see she was too bursting with curiosity to pretend to be the shy one right now.

"The very one. I'd dearly love a visit from my favorite new neighbors very soon … in fact, why don't you come round for afternoon tea today?"

"We'd be delighted," Red heard her mom respond and she nodded in agreement. In fact, Red realized she was becoming excited to get to see the inside of the fairy cottage she had admired since childhood but never before had the courage to enter.

"Very good. Three o'clock sharp is when I take tea. Now, don't be tardy," she said with mock severity.

As Red's mom was saying final goodbyes and closing the front door behind Ms. Catsworthy, she heard, "Yeeeeooooooooow!" Red was initially alarmed by the plaintive wail coming from behind a stack of boxes in the dining room, and realized it was just the two cats playing. "Mom, your kitty is getting massacred again," she said, rolling her eyes.

She wasn't surprised to see Midnight lying on his back, his vulnerable throat and black and white, penguin-like underbelly turned up, the completely submissive posture well understood by the carnivore world. Even though he was three times as big as the kitten, Midnight seemed to enjoy pretending Roxy was getting the best of him, a game the two of them had developed and played quite often. Roxy was busy attacking first Midnight's face, then his belly, then his face again, each attack producing a playful meow from the older cat and seemingly encouraging further attacks.

Later that day, Red was escorted by Ms. Catsworthy into her sitting room and was surprised to find the presence of two middle-aged women. Red hoped she was attentive to them enough to avoid the appearance of rudeness. But she had to take a few moments to look around. Annie, she noted, had found her own distraction in the form of an enormous Himalayan cat almost fully occupying an elegant, white, high-backed chair, the style of which Red didn't recognize. Annie had squeezed her hips onto the poufy cushion beside the cat, despite its obvious annoyance, and proceeded to stroke its long silky coat. Red remembered how much, as a child, she had longed to come over and play with the cats and now wished she and Annie hadn't been so fearful. She knew it was because of the sadness she felt here even now, though it was definitely mixed with warmth, too ... oh, this was too much to think of right now. She wanted to explore and her artist's eye was hungry.

If Ms. Catsworthy's house appeared ornate from the outside, it was only a hint of the extravagance of the interior furnishings. They bespoke extensive world travel. The cottage was much smaller than the mansion. But what it lacked in size, it more than made up in splendid furnishings. As in a museum, not a piece of its furnishings was inferior. Not a square inch was left without rich coverings of mahogany, Persian carpets of the highest quality, silk wall hangings, bronze statues, oil paintings—Red was sure one of them must be a Titian. It showed people in different states of undress, lounging in a wood and accompanied by various mythological creatures. The frame itself must be worth a fortune, she thought.

Red was fascinated by art. She was in ecstasy and her ADHD allowed her to wander from the crowd at will without feeling the social constraints that would restrain some people. Red strolled around the room as introductions were made and gave lip-service to the other people as briefly as possible when she heard her name called, but quickly returned to her browsing. Another painting was of a beautiful young girl in a yellow dress, the eyes a dark blue, the hair hanging in golden ringlets, the creamy face with rosy cheeks. The girl must've been seven or eight years old, angelic, with a haze about her as if she weren't entirely of a solid form, but a misty, glowing, ghost-like girl. Red was intrigued and made a mental note to ask Ms. Catsworthy about the painting. Beneath the painting, on a small ornate mahogany stand, sat a framed black-and-white photograph of a young man, somewhat handsome, but with a kind of bent wizard-like nose. His bushy eyebrows were expressive, however, and his warm smile reached his green eyes. *Uncle Alistair?* Red smiled. It had to be him.

"Red, come on over and join us, sweetie," she heard her mom coax. "Did you hear Ms. Catsworthy? She asked if you'd like milk or honey in your tea."

Red blushed and hoped she hadn't appeared rude. "Yes, please, both." She forced herself to break away from her perusal and join her sister on a plump antique carved mahogany sofa with some type of beautiful silver-and-rose-colored tapestry fabric. Red didn't know much about antique furniture, but she could tell this was the real thing. She silently hoped she didn't have any dirt on her jeans as she sat, trying for a graceful motion and hoping the others hadn't noticed the fact that she dropped her weight a little too soon and plopped down with a slight awkwardness. She looked at Anne out of the corner of her eyes.

Her mom was talking with a tall, thin, dark-haired woman seated on very ornate chair with a dark crimson cushion. Did the gold paint mean it was a Louis XIV? Red would have to Google that when she got home. Red noticed the woman had an attractive face with sharp onyx eyes, almond shaped and strangely familiar, and focused her artist's discerning eye on her face.

Her mother asked, "He was Uncle Alistair—um, Professor Hamilton's—graduate student?" Red suddenly zeroed in on the conversation when she heard her mother's question to the dark-eyed woman.

"Yes, his name is Erik Wolfeningen." Could this be one of the graduate students from the photograph?

Red looked at her so intently that the woman seemed to notice the stare and change of atmosphere. The woman,

D.K. Reed

obviously curious about Red's sudden interest, asked Red, "Do … did … you know my son? He's a few years older than you. How old are you?"

"Um, I'm sixteen. And I don't think we ever met … well …. not exactly, but Uncle Alistair left a bulletin board with some pictures of him—that is, I think it was him, in his office. And …" Red was reluctant to talk about Erik, since she was unable to categorize this uncanny interest she had in him. Red hoped his mom couldn't tell she was blushing.

"Ummm." The lady simply nodded, giving nothing away.

"So, it was your son that … drowned … or went missing with Uncle Alistair, I mean, Professor Hamilton?" Red heard her mom ask awkwardly. *Smooth, Mom*, thought Red.

"Yes, but until they find the body, I'll continue to believe that he's alive. I've … well, I just know that it'll all turn out okay," Erik's mom said with a far-away look, gazing skyward through the window, a solitary tear gliding downward.

"Oh, yes, I do hope so. We'll definitely keep him in our prayers." Red's mom placed a hand on her forearm. Red saw the two women exchange a warm glance.

Red wished she hadn't been such an idiot and had listened for the woman's name so she could address her. She'd have to ask Annie or her mom later. The woman was looking away and Red feared she was losing interest in talking to her since her claim to Erik was so slight. How could she tell her she had seen his ghost and believed it to be living in her house? She had to think quickly.

"Yes, Erik and Roy were Alistair's favorite graduate students," Ms. Catsworthy said, in what Red thought must be an effort to steer the conversation onto a somewhat happier theme.

"Your son was also one of Uncle Alistair's graduate students?" Red's mom asked of the other lady. *Hmmm, maybe Roy is the other grad student in the photo*, Red thought. The other woman was seated beside Erik's mom on an identical, also-possibly-Louis XIV chair. She looked nothing like Erik's mom. She had brown curly hair framing a somewhat plump face with a small nose and pouty lips. The term "pleasantly plump" came to mind. *Yes, she could plausibly be his biological mother.*

"Yes, Roy is still in the program, working on his doctorate. His graduate committee is overseeing his studies, though he really misses Professor Hamilton … and Erik, of course." She smiled pleasantly, dropping her eyes, clearly not wanting to call attention to the distinction that one son was alive and the other likely dead. Red liked her tolerably well, though she seemed somewhat lackluster, but certainly harmless. The person who really intrigued her was Erik's mom, with the sharply intelligent eyes. Red decided she had to find a way to spend some time talking with her—she just had to.

CHAPTER 5

Winston Churchill High School

Monday morning came and Red was a little nervous about her first day of school. Although her tae kwon do training had helped develop her self-confidence, it was more of the kind of help that told her she could withstand a physical attack—not much assistance with peer rejection or unaccepting glances.

She sighed. Entering in the middle of the school year was scary for Red, though probably more so for Annie, she thought, since her sister was the shy one. But if she was nervous, Annie didn't let it show. Red raised her own chin slightly at the thought. She had some knowledge of what to expect, having learned something about the school from her mom, who, in the years she had left consulting to spend more time with Annie and Red, had worked part-time as a substitute teacher and had taught at the highly-respected Winston Churchill High School for three months as a substitute for another teacher on maternity leave. She knew something of the differences between this new school and her former school, Gaithersburg High. It was smaller than the mega-high school she had attended up until now, but Red thought it was also probably more snobbish. She wondered why it was named after a British hero, since many of the schools in the D.C. area were named after American politicians. It made her think of Uncle Alistair with his lovely British accent, and she felt a tiny smile play at the corner of her mouth.

Red looked at the clock radio next to her bed and realized she and Annie had best start walking. Just then came a determined knock at her bedroom door. "Red, let's go. I've been ready for ten minutes."

They scurried out the door and began the walk to school. It was a beautiful morning, slightly cool, the leaves just starting to turn. The sky was a deep blue with several whiter-than-white tufts of cumulus clouds scattered about. Red loved looking at the sky. After a moment, she glanced at Annie walking beside her. Annie wore earbuds, listening to her iPod. Red wished she could share her thoughts, but none doing. Red sighed. She drifted back to musing about the school. She knew most of the kids at Churchill were spoiled beyond belief even in these tough economic times. Most parents who didn't work at N.I.H. likely worked at one of the many genetics research institutes or consulting agencies nearby. She didn't have her driver's license yet, only her learner's permit, but even when she got it, she knew good and well that she only might be able to borrow a car once in a while with a really good excuse, and when she went to college, she might get some help in buying a ten-year-old rattletrap. Not these kids. There were Mercedes and BMWs parked in the student lot. In fact, she realized, even if her parents agreed to buy her a car next year, it wouldn't hold its own among most of these.

As she and Annie walked through the parking lot en route to their big first day, she decided the walk really wasn't that bad. She might as well feel that way, since there was no chance of changing it any time soon. It was less than a mile and very level, a good wake-me-up for the mornings and an opportunity to unwind in the afternoons. She was sure her mom would give them a lift when the weather was bad, though it'd make her late for work. And it was only until Red got her driver's license, which she was working on. The state of Maryland required her to log her driving hours over the course of nine months before she could get licensed. She should be good to go in April.

Red took a deep breath of the coolish air, looking up again to the clouds for encouragement and catching sight of at a beautiful solitary whiter-than-white cumulus cloud with some hints of gray in the folds. The beauty struck a chord in her chest and energized Red. Feeling refreshed, she squared her shoulders as she stepped onto the first step leading up to the main doors. Red heard a crow caw from a tree near the main entrance and another caw seemed to answer from behind her.

She prickled slightly and then consciously forced a switch to rational thinking mode as she mounted the steps. Red loved birds and knew crows had a bad reputation. She loved crows because they had such intelligence in their bright eyes and because they reminded her of the cornfields in Tennessee. Her mom had once told her that her grandfather had taught her mom to shoot a shotgun to scare crows out of the cornfield, missing them intentionally. She suspected that her great-grandfather may not have been so compassionate when her mother was absent. Funny, crows seemed a part of such a humble place where subsistence farming was the norm, yet here they were in the trees of Potomac where snobbery likely ran rampant. *Wait a minute. Hadn't the hot guy in the picture had a crow on his T-shirt—something about a Rockville rookery? Hmmm.* She'd have to look at the picture again and see exactly what it said and do some Google research.

Red looked wistfully at the crow in the tree near the entrance and muttered, "Wish me luck." Immediately regretting this, she shifted her eyes to either side to make sure no one except Annie was within earshot. Annie made no sign of hearing. One skinny kid shuffling up the steps a few feet behind, hands in pockets, looking down, didn't seem to hear, either.

Okay, good. Red entered into the grand entryway and turned to the left to the sign that read "Office."

Wow. Red hadn't expected such a modern building. The semi-circular wall housing the office door was made of glass, and a glossy wooden counter just inside the door was also a parallel semi-circle. Further inside the office, three middle-aged women in suits and one bronze-skinned teen with short, glossy hair were busily engrossed with their computers. The closest middle-aged lady had silver, poofy hair, a style that required a weekly visit to the hairdresser. She looked up with a no-nonsense manner, though her voice was soft. "May I help you?"

"Hi, I'm Sonia Greene and this is my sister, Anya. I think Dr. Graham has our schedules." Red tried to present an air of self-confidence.

"Yes, of course, Miss Greene. Miss Greene," she said, nodding toward each girl. "Welcome to Churchill. Dr. Graham should be in her office now. Do you know where it is?" Her voice was friendlier than Red had expected.

"No, but if you could just give us the number, I'm sure we can find it."

She pointed them in the right direction, and soon Red and Annie had their schedules in hand, along with locker assignments. Red looked to see how her day was going to work out. Annie's locker turned out to be nearby. Red wasn't so lucky. Her locker was on the other side of the building. On parting, Annie reminded Red that she'd be staying after school to check out the Being-Green Club and so not to wait for her to walk home.

The halls were getting crowded, but Red found her locker with no problem and hung her Land's End school bag on one of the hooks, wondering if the other kids were carrying Chanel bags or something she had never heard of. She surreptitiously glanced around and was somewhat reassured to see a kid with an angry mop of hair stroll by with rips in his jeans. A short, plump girl smiled at her as she walked by briskly, her long, dark hair swinging around, a faded canvas bag slung over her shoulder. But then two obviously popular girls giggled as they passed without bothering a glance at Red, one with a gorgeous Vera Bradley daypack and the other with some type of red leather bag Red was sure was Italian. She set about comparing the room numbers on her schedule with the locations on a map of the school, awkwardly holding one in each hand, but trying very hard to look like she knew exactly what she was doing. Biology was just after lunch and was furthest from her locker, but she had Digital Art first period. That would be a pleasant way to ease into the day.

Red had removed everything she needed for the morning classes and snapped the combination lock onto the locker when a girl opened the locker to the right of hers.

"Hi. I didn't think anyone had that locker this year," said the sweet-faced girl. She had rich, caramel skin and glossy black hair and was very petite—cute and bouncy was Red's first impression. Red liked her immediately, but her small stature made Red's five-feet-ten-inches seem even larger than usual by comparison. She quickly shrugged off the thought as not worth thinking about. She wouldn't let that stop her from trying to gain a new friend.

"Hi. Well, you were right. No one had it until today. I'm Sonia. New student."

"Nice to meet you, Sonia. And welcome. I'm Uma. Do you need any help finding your classes? The bell will ring in—" she checked her cell phone to see the time. "—four minutes." She tucked her phone into her pocket with a slight flourish. Red was definitely right about the bounciness.

"I don't think so." Red flashed the map she'd picked up at the main office and shrugged.

"What's your first period class? Maybe we can walk together."

"Yeah, great. It's Digital Art. Room 150."

"Great, it's on my way to French."

Red was delighted to find that Uma was in two of her classes. During the course of the day, Uma introduced Red to two of her friends, Tatyana and Gabriella. Tatyana lived on Normandy Drive, the street that T-ed up against Chelsea Lane, Red's street, and the other two girls lived in the same general direction. They decided to walk home together.

That afternoon, the four girls walked together until Red and Tatyana split off, turning left onto Normandy. Uma and Gabriella waved goodbye and continued on to another subdivision a bit further on, past the Shalom Center, the large Jewish community center near Churchill. Gabriella and many of the students at Churchill were Jewish, Red had discovered today, having met several with surnames beginning in Gold- or ending in –stein. This thought-chain triggered an early memory, something about Ms. Catsworthy and Judaism. She'd have to ask Mom about that, Red mused as she walked along, glad for the outdoor open air and new acquaintances.

Red heard a crow caw overhead as she and Tatyana walked. She glanced in its direction and saw a dark blue BMW sports car creeping along toward them. It seemed to be … *following* them. As she tried to shrug off the thought, she realized with embarrassment that Tatyana had been talking to her about one of her classes and she hadn't been listening. She redirected her attention just as they reached Tatyana's house.

"Do you want to come in?" Tatyana asked.

Red accepted with delight, barely able to believe how friendly the kids were here.

She glanced behind her as the girls headed up the walkway to Tatyana's door. The blue BMW was still there. "Do you have a jealous boyfriend?" Red asked.

"I don't think so. Why?" asked Tatyana, starting to punch a code into a keypad next to the garage door.

Red hesitated. "I probably read too much, but I could've sworn that car was following us since we split off from the others."

"Yeah, come to think of it, I think you're right." Tatyana frowned as the blue BMW turned left onto another street and disappeared slowly out of sight. "I don't recognize the car. Hmmm." She thought a moment. "I don't think I know anyone with a blue BMW. Probably a senior checking out the hot new girl."

Red quickly licked her thumb and touched it to her hip, making a sizzling sound. Both girls giggled. "Yeah, that's gotta be it—or maybe he's checking out the hot Ruskie," Red teased back. Tatyana mirrored the sizzle gesture as the garage door began to chatter upward. Tatyana really was a looker, with bronze waves swinging freely to the top of her hips. Red had learned earlier that she was on the cheerleading squad. It showed in her lithe frame and graceful movements. Red wouldn't be surprised if one of the senior boys had a crush on her. The two giggled as the garage door jerked to a halt, allowing them entrance.

An hour later, Red headed home, first-day jitters entirely diminished. She couldn't believe it—three new friends her first day. Maybe this really was a new beginning. Maybe she had learned a thing or two, or maybe life just got better once you survived middle school. And she felt that they sincerely liked her, especially Tatyana and Uma. Gabriella seemed nice, too, but a little more aloof. Maybe just quieter. The best part was that she had already been invited to walk with them to school tomorrow morning, first stopping to pick up Tatyana and hopefully meeting up with Uma and Gabriella again. She hoped Annie had similar good fortune in meeting people.

As Red approached the end of the street, she glanced to the right and was shocked to see the blue BMW parked on the side of the street up about three houses, facing her. A man sat in the driver's seat, the brim of a baseball cap pulled down, covering his eyes and nose. *What the …*

Red stood a moment, undecided about what to do, then felt her inner warrioress awaken. If this creep was really stalking her or any other female, she would have words with him. After all, Annie would be walking this way in an hour or so. And this intersection was the bus stop for the middle school, drawing even younger girls to this spot. If he was stalking young girls, let him get a taste of her tae kwon do kick to the scrotum. That'd teach him. She could break a four-inch board with her kick. Physical danger wasn't scary to her.

She made herself stop and think before she pounced. On the other hand, what if he lived there, or was waiting to pick up his daughter or little sister from the bus stop? That would be embarrassing.

Still, no one else had gathered at the bus stop yet and the bus was probably half an hour away. So she didn't think that could be his excuse. Red decided a friendly introduction was the responsible thing to do.

Red boldly walked over and sharply tapped on his driver's side window. She saw a movement inside the tinted glass—the man started, jerking his head up from something. Was he texting? He fumbled for the window switch and the window slid smoothly down halfway. He sat without speaking, looking at her, his pale face reddening in what Red assumed was embarrassment. He looked older than a high school student, she saw; he was probably a college student, or maybe even older. Red had a sick feeling when she realized this looked a lot like the other graduate student in the photo. In fact, she was pretty sure it was him. If he was Uncle Alistair's student, he must be okay.

"Oh, gosh, sorry," stumbled Red, wondering whether she had overstepped the bounds of civility. "I thought you were someone else."

"No harm done," he said, relaxing. Red relaxed, too, for a moment, until his dark, dull eyes slid over her body in a way she didn't like. She immediately pegged him for a sleazebag, graduate student or not. She backed away from the window.

"Hey, you live around here?" he said.

"Not far." Red said. She certainly didn't want him to know where she lived—or where Annie lived. She could take care of herself, but she felt protective of Annie. She couldn't help but cast a swift glance toward her house. She hoped Buddy wasn't in the yard because he would start barking when he saw her. "Do *you* live around here?" she threw back at him, determined to not leave him to stalking the bus stop—she'd stand her ground. She hoped he caught the challenge in her question. *In other words, creep, if you don't live here, then what the hell are you doing hanging around here?*

"Na, just visiting a buddy of mine up the street." He gestured with his thumb backwards over his shoulder, purposefully vague. "Name's Roy. What's yours?" he said *Roy* in an exaggeratedly smooth way that made Red want to barf. She remembered the woman at Ms. Catsworthy's tea had mentioned her son, Roy. So he *was* the other graduate student.

There was no way she was going to tell him her name. She was busy trying to think of a fictitious name to use, then felt a blast of relief when he started the car engine, apparently out of excuses to stay. *Whew.* An instant later, she was dismayed when he said, "Hey, we should go out sometime." He chewed on something in his cheek as he eyed her, looking more at her hips than her face.

"Yeah, right," Red said, backing away as Roy continued eyeing her. *When Hell freezes over.*

Roy seemed bent on pursuing the matter but was diverted when a huge white-and-green splat of bird guano landed on the windshield. Roy let go with a few expletives as he sprayed the windshield with wiper fluid. Red jumped back too late as the wiper sloshed some of the mess in her direction. "Hey, watch it!" she said, slinging the goop off her hand.

"Damn crows. I'd like to blow up the whole lot," he mumbled, then snickered to himself as if he had remembered something funny, probably something cruel, Red thought. Having apparently either forgotten about Red or deciding not to pursue his advances any further, he pulled out with a squeal of tires, much too fast for a quiet neighborhood.

"Hey, slow down," Red called after him, doubting he heard her. She angrily wiped the wiper-fluid goop on her hand onto her jeans.

What an idiot. Is he on drugs? Red continued her walk home, relieved that Roy didn't know they had been standing just three doors from her house. She hoped to never see him again. She disliked him, and wondered why Uncle Alistair would have such a sleazebag for a student. Maybe it wasn't the same person, she hoped. She'd look carefully at the photo as soon as she got home. She didn't like the idea of him hanging around, and dialed Annie's cell to tell her to wait for her at school. She'd come back to school and walk home with her.

An hour later, a crow cawed from the huge white pine to the left of the driveway as Red stepped back out of the front door to begin her trek back to school, this time a bit lighter without her school bag and with a spring in her step because she dearly loved to feel like she was useful in helping to protect someone she loved. Now that Roy was gone, she regained her upbeat excitement and was anxious to trade first-day-of-school observations with her little sis. She glanced over toward the white pine and decided to find a special treat to give the crows today. What would they like? Perhaps some granola and berries, she decided.

Red didn't see creepy Roy the next day and began to relax a little, wondering if she had overreacted. She had studied the photo and believed it had indeed been Uncle Alistair's graduate student. He'd put on a little weight, but it was definitely him. She wondered about his strange behavior. *What the heck does he want? Why was he hanging around here?* Still, his mother had seemed nice. And Uncle Alistair surely wouldn't have worked so closely with him if he wasn't a good person. Right? *But then, Uncle Alistair had gone missing ...* She shuddered and wondered how she could find out more about him—stalk the stalker. This would be difficult with her busy schedule and lack of drivers' license, but she vowed to keep an eye out.

Over the next few days, her walks to and from school were pleasant and she found she was enjoying the brief time she got to commune with nature. She noticed as the week wore on that the leaves were starting to change—one particularly brilliant maple tree the girls passed each day seemed to flame brighter and brighter. With such a pleasant tree-lined walk, Red noted the whole party looked up more and enjoyed the beauty more and more as the colors ripened into their full autumnal splendor.

Red also noticed the bird-life more and realized how vast the crow population was in the area. Every day she saw crows, and when she couldn't see them, she heard them. She wanted to do some research on the subject. She thought once or twice that she might've caught a glimpse of a crescent-shaped scar on a beak, but she couldn't be certain. Perhaps she'd have to start carrying her compact hiking binoculars on these walks. She was sure that would appear very nerdy to the others, but if they were going to be her friends, they would have to accept her quirks. Maybe she'd be able to teach them to appreciate nature a bit more. That seemed like a good thing to do and would certainly please her mom. This thought-chain led to the decision to ask her mom about the crow population. Even if she didn't know, she would know where to look for information. Red also made a mental note to Google the topic.

Despite the colorful leaves, Red noted that the walks to school were largely spent discussing fashion, boys, teacher unreasonableness, and homework. With two cheerleaders in the group, she was also treated to the politics and gossip of the Churchill football scene, and began to entertain the idea of actually attending one of the games. She had never been much interested in team sports, but the enthusiasm from Tatyana and Uma was contagious.

Being on the cheerleading squad meant Tatyana and Uma were popular. Gabriella seemed popular, too, though much quieter than the other two and maybe a little nerd-like, a trait with which Red could comfortably identify. Red knew she and Annie had never had popular friends at their old school, and they had never really tried for popularity themselves. Maybe this newfound access to the popular clique was due to the new-kid-on-the-block syndrome, or maybe it was just that they were getting older and so the entire cohort was maturing away from cliques and notions of popularity. Red hoped this was the case. She really didn't have time to bother with cliques but her new friends didn't seem clique-y at all. She liked them very much.

"When is the next home game?" Red asked during the walk home on Thursday.

"Tomorrow night. All the rest are away. Hey, you should come. We play Wooton High, our archrival. Should be fun. We'll probably win but it's hard to say this year— we've been kinda on and off. Uma and I have to go over early and stay late, but you should come. In fact, I won't take no for an answer. I'll look for you in the stands and will toilet paper your yard on Halloween if you don't come." Tatyana giggled.

"Yeah, and I'll help!" exclaimed Uma.

"Let's go, Red. I'll walk over with you," Red heard Annie venture.

"I'm going. I'll probably walk over early with Uma, but I'll sit with you if you come," coaxed Gabriella.

"Okay. Sounds like a plan." Red was getting excited. This felt nice—being included. She'd go with the flow, not so much because she was interested in football, but she was interested in the bonding aspect of going to the game together and having something in common to talk about afterward.

The game started at 6:30 and Red and Annie arrived half an hour early to look for Gabriella. No one from the football team or cheerleading squad was out on the field yet. The band was assembling in one area of the bleachers. Annie spotted a new friend among the band members; Red saw her wave until she caught a girl's attention and the girl waved back. Red scanned the bleachers in a pattern designed not to miss a bench and after half a minute spotted Gabriella, who evidently had been watching for them, too, because she was waving and laughing good-naturedly. Red punched Annie lightly and pointed to the spot where Gabriella sat—the noise was already too loud to easily talk. Annie nodded and followed

Snap To Grid

her to the spot Gabriella had claimed for them. Red was starting to feel that this was grand fun. Annie pointed out a couple of students she now knew, stating their names and her impressions of them. Gabriella, though more reserved, did the same and Red was able to point out a few whom she recognized and get information about them, mostly things like who their boyfriends or girlfriends were, their club memberships, and whether Gabriella had previously known them from middle or elementary school. Red hoped she could remember at least some of what she learned, though a lot of information was exchanged by the time the game started.

Red knew by the hoopla around her that it was an exciting game, though she was more focused on the feeling of new friendships and people watching. Eventually, the game was over and Churchill had won, though Red wasn't sure what had been going on half the time. Still, it was fun to feel the enthusiasm and Annie seemed to enjoy it, too. The bleachers were filled with activity as the crowd began to collect their things and climb down in a mass exodus. She and Annie were saying goodbye to Gabriella, who was going down to the locker room to await Uma and Tatyana, when someone tapped her shoulder from behind. Expecting one of her new acquaintances, she was shocked to turn into the face of Roy, who was leaning toward her from the bleacher just behind them. Had he been there the whole time, watching them?

"Remember me?" he said in a greasy voice intended to sound smooth. He reeked; Red was sure he had been drinking and smoking. She drew back from his breath involuntarily.

"Uh … yeah," she responded flatly, trying not to encourage further conversation.

"Hey, what about that date we talked about?" he crooned.

"No, thanks, I'm kinda busy." She grasped Annie's arm to pull her attention away from the girl she was chatting. "We better get going," Red said, infusing her voice with a sense of alarm, a tone she hoped Annie would recognize.

Red saw Annie look at her and then up at Roy, who was still leaning forward, a silly grin on his face. She started to speak to him but Red pulled her up off her seat and practically dragged her down the bleachers. "Don't talk to that creep," she snapped.

"Calm down, Red. Why are you so paranoid?" Annie protested. "He seemed nice enough, just kinda old."

"Didn't you smell the alcohol on his breath?"

"So what? Dad smells like that sometimes."

"Just keep walking."

The crowd was thick and progress slow. Red kept casting glances backward and saw that Roy was following them. He seemed to be laughing about it, apparently unashamed. If fact, he seemed to enjoy upsetting her. His eyes were always on her each time she looked back and he didn't try to look away.

"What's going on, Red?" Annie was obviously starting to get that this really was upsetting to Red and not a joke.

"I think we can get through there under that sign," Red said determinedly, spotting a small gate in the chain-link fence, under a huge metallic sign advertising an upcoming musical at the high school. The gate wasn't locked, but a sign stated that it was an emergency exit only. *Well*, though Red, *this is an emergency*. She pulled Annie through the crowd and broke away toward the gate. She heard someone behind say aloud, "Hey. That's an emergency exit!" But she ignored them. She was used to thinking on her feet from her years under Master Shah. She knew she didn't want her little sister having a conversation with that creep, but wasn't going to show her panic any more than was warranted. If it were just he and she, she was pretty sure she wouldn't be running away.

She and Annie bolted through the gate and crossed Goldsborough Lane. Red pulled her off in a different direction than their house, since she knew Roy knew the general direction where they lived.

"Hey, Red, what the heck are you doing? This is the wrong direction!" Annie protested.

"Shhh. Don't let him see you. Let's see what he does," she said, and pulled Annie into the darkness behind a tree.

She looked back just in time to see Roy approach the gate to follow them through. He grasped the handle and just as he started to pull it open, the huge metal sign fell down on him, sliding downward with a sickening metallic scrape against the metal fence and onto his outstretched wrist. They heard a scream from him and then a few screams from onlookers.

The girls turned and ran. They took a long way around their neighborhood and constantly glanced behind them, but to Red's relief, they did not see Roy again.

As they reached the safety of their house, Red stopped Annie. "Annie, I need to explain what that was about before we go inside." Red quickly tried to explain her previous encounters with Roy and her fear that he was a stalker and definitely up to no good. "And, Annie, I don't know how to say this other than to just spit it out ... I'm pretty sure he was one of Uncle Alistair's grad students— not the dead one, of course. We met his mom at the Crazy Cat—I mean, Ms. Catsworthy's house."

Even in the dim light, Red saw Annie roll her eyes, "You don't say."

"No time for sarcasm. What if he's a murderer? What if he had something to do with Uncle Alistair's disappearance? I mean, Annie, I've been thinking about this whole thing for a while and I don't trust that creep. I don't want to scare you, but I don't think you should walk home alone from school for a while."

"Do you think he got his hand cut off?" asked Annie with a shudder.

"I don't know. Could be. Guess we'll hear on Monday. It was amazing timing that the sign fell just as he was about to come after us."

"Creepy, that's for sure. He'll probably sue the school."

"Yeah, but he probably deserved it."

"I hope we don't get in trouble for taking the emergency exit," Annie sounded worried.

"Oh, don't worry about that. No one who saw us knew who we were. Besides, if I have to, I'll tell about his stalking and I'm sure no one will say a word to us." Red tried to sound reassuring.

There was a flash of white movement in the nearby trees and both girls jumped. "What's that?" Annie said. They listened hard, but there was no sound.

"An owl?" asked Red. "Boy, aren't we jumpy."

"Red, let's go inside." Annie shivered.

"Okay, but one more thing. Don't say anything to Mom or Dad about Roy until we can figure out what's going on or they won't let us go anywhere by ourselves. You know how Mom can be when she gets an anxiety attack. As long as you're with me, I'll watch out for you."

As she followed her sister into the house, Red couldn't shake the feeling that this Roy character was a real threat. Not just a voyeur or some comical stalker. There was something really creepy about him. He wasn't right. And he meant business.

There had been a lot of strange things happening since Uncle Alistair's disappearance—the Viking ghost, the odd behavior of the bird, and now this. She couldn't help but feel it was all connected. Red didn't know how the Viking ghost thing or the bird thing fit in, but she didn't feel threatened by them as much as this real flesh-and-blood man. She knew she needed to get to the bottom of this.

CHAPTER 6

All Hallow's E'en

Red approached the dining room, stepping gracefully, first one timid foot and then the other, as if she were in a ballet, her hair and long sleeves blowing back behind her, even though she felt no wind in her face. A piano played something that sounded like Wagner. Though her steps were hesitant, she felt graceful like never before, and beautiful—beauty itself to present to him whom her heart adored. She saw his erect form, his back massive and strong, his shoulders broad and square. His glistening black hair playing in the same non-breeze that assailed her. Step, glide, step, glide. As she approached him from behind his shoulder, giving a graceful wide birth, keeping in time with the music, her steps became faster and more exaggerated, building to a climax— when their eyes would meet. She swung lithely around, as though skating on ice, to the back of the tall ladder-backed chair pulled up to his right. She knew her place at this table was at the other head—not head and foot, but two equal heads at this table. But she wanted to be close today. She needed to be close right *now, this instant. As the motion of her body halted behind the chair, her hands grasping the chair back for support, she brought her eyes up to see that beautiful face ... aaaaaaahhhheeeeeeeeeee! She heard a blood-curdling scream somewhere. From her. She jerked back, still clutching the chair. She saw his eyes squeeze shut in pain, and his enormous black beak slightly turn away, shrinking from her eyes. She stood frozen, staring. Her heart ached for him, his beautiful raven hair still blowing in the wind, his hideous crows-face rendered expressionless by the stiff beak, except for the eyes, still squeezed shut against the pain of having her see him this way. Time stopped as she gazed in horror, not knowing how to react. She watched as one enormous tear formed in the corner of the eye, slowly grew until it pooled, then slowly glided down the black gleaming pinfeathers until it fell. Red felt tears pool in her own eyes as she watched. She gazed through her tears as the scene blurred and the crow's face gave way to the handsome face she sought. Like a mist, it curled into one form and then the other until she wasn't sure if the crow-face was the imagined form and the handsome Erik-face the real one, or if it was the crow-face that was real. She watched, spellbound, wanting to hold him, but repulsed by the hideous face of the crow. Finally, the handsome Erik-face began to take dominance and her heart swelled in anticipation. Then the massive black eye jerked open and the sharp crow-eye glared at her. She felt herself recoil, flying backward into abysmal nothingness, falling, falling, hearing her own screams growing faint ...*

After a fitful night of dark dreams, Red awoke at nine a.m. With a sigh of relief, she remembered it was Saturday and drifted back into another fifteen-minute nap. Her dad was probably off on his bicycle exploring his new surroundings—no moss growing on him. Red grinned and shook her head slightly as she thought of the child-like energy of her dad and was glad he let her sleep in this morning.

With the first week at the new school behind her, Red began preparing for Halloween. She only had one weekend to put a costume together. Tatyana was coming over this morning to help her and to have some bonding time. Red was really looking forward to it. She couldn't wait to tell her about last night and Roy's behavior. Annie would be spending the day with her old Gaithersburg friends. Both Annie and her mom were early risers and had likely already left. Red was glad that Annie would be trick-or-treating in Gaithersburg this year, rather than their new neighborhood—away from Roy.

Red needed to organize her thoughts. Tatyana would be arriving in an hour. She had decided to forgo her usual martial-arts costume for a change. This year she'd go all out and be Red Sonja, the Marvel Comic female barbarian for whom she'd been jokingly nicknamed by her dad back when she'd started taking tae kwon do classes. This felt right this year—she could use a strong female role model right now. She thought she still had a grey plastic helmet, sword, breastplate, and shield left over from when she was eight—that should work. It was actually a Viking costume, but it would work for Red Sonja. Tatyana would have definite opinions about whether this was too childish. But Red had to find it first. No doubt it would be somewhere in the boxes stacked in the back room of the basement, not yet organized in any way. The area Uncle Alistair had used as storage was now a mish-mash of their stuff and his. Red guessed it was all theirs now and felt a twinge of sadness. The Forest of Darkness; that's what she and Annie had called the back storage area when they were little; this area also housed the doorway to the Pit, the dug-out part of the basement that Uncle Alistair had used for wine storage, but which Annie and Red pretended held unspeakable horrors. Actually, she didn't think she had ever actually entered the Pit. It had held as much mystique then as the Mines of Moria did later on when her dad read *The Lord of the Rings* to them every night for months until it was finished. Red sighed dreamily, remembering those wonderful close family times.

Realizing the hour was quickly slipping away, she ate a piece of bread, not wanting to take the time to let it toast, drank a glass of orange juice, and headed down the stairs to the Forest of Darkness.

Red was initially relieved to be reminded that her mom's organizational skills—well, her OCD—knew no bounds. She easily found a large orange plastic box with a black lid: of course, the Halloween box. Red carried it upstairs so she and Annie could go through it later to find the yard decorations. There would be a battery-powered, sound-activated ghost inside they'd hang from the crabapple tree in the front yard. It made eerie ghostly sounds when anyone clapped hands near it, though it was getting harder to activate each year. She hoped it still worked; it was a really fun prop and part of their annual traditions. And there was a giant spider web, too. She'd show it to Tatyana; maybe they could even do something with that for costumes. *This is going to be fun.*

After a few minutes of rummaging around in the box, though, it was clear the plastic Viking costume wasn't there. *Hmmm, that's funny.* She was sure they hadn't given it away. A Viking helmet was just too classic, and it was one-size-fits-all so would never be outgrown. But it wasn't among the Halloween decorations.

She glanced at the clock on the microwave. She still had half an hour, time enough for a more thorough search in the Forest of Darkness.

She decided what she really needed was a flashlight for her search. *Where did Mom unpack the flashlights?* They were always in the cabinet under the microwave in their old townhouse, so she checked the same location here. *Yep, good ol' reliable Mom.* She selected one that reminded her of a long, black metal policeman's combination flashlight and nightstick.

Just in case Tatyana came while she was out of earshot of the door, she decided to text her to let her know she'd leave the door unlocked and to come on in and call to her in the basement. *There. Done.*

Flashlight in hand, Red headed down to the basement. Buddy came along, presumably to see what all the fuss was about. At the bottom of the stairs, he made a beeline for the small Dora the Explorer cushiony children's chair where Midnight lounged, filling the entire space. Red was glad the cats had ready access to the basement via a cat door her dad had installed so the litter box wouldn't have to be upstairs. "Found your favorite chair, huh, Midnight?" She couldn't help but smile.

Midnight opened one eye and then hissed at Buddy, who'd thrust his nose too close. Buddy looked hurt and backed away. *Those two.*

Turning to the task at hand, she flipped on the overhead bulb in the Forest of Darkness, but her mom had already replaced all the light bulbs in the house with compact fluorescents, and this particular one was an older one that didn't give off satisfactory light. It only illuminated the front part of the basement. Red switched on her flashlight and shined it back into the distant part of the room. She noticed an odd-looking lamp sharing a small table with some other objects that all looked like they belonged in a lab—a microscope and some types of little boxes with knobs. She tried the lamp and was glad to find it actually produced light, though the light it gave off had a strange orange glow, almost like a sunset. Funny how it reminded her of the day she saw her Viking ghost. She wondered if it was something from Uncle Alistair's lab that only emitted some peculiar set of wavelengths. Whatever it was, it didn't help illuminate the room very much and so she mostly had to rely on her flashlight as she began to search each box.

After about twenty minutes, Red had made a mess, moving the boxes around, stacking and restacking. She hoped Mom didn't have them in any particular order. She cringed slightly at the thought of her orderly mother's reaction to Red's mess. But all she found were boxes of old tax forms and her parents' graduate research notes and old green-and-white computer printouts with the little holes in each side. Why did they need to keep that? *Where would I be if I were a Viking costume?* Her mind went to their old dress-up box from when they were little. *Of course.* Red was both annoyed and grateful that Mom had kept their dress-up box, a large, plastic, pink pig with a hinged lid that held their old costumes. She really needed to talk to Mom about getting rid of some of this—give it to some poor kid who could enjoy it. She thought she could see something pink behind a short stack of clear plastic file boxes and was pretty sure that was the pink pig. She pocketed her flashlight to free her hands and had to rely on the orange light from the lamp.

Just as she turned toward the boxes, she caught sight of a movement against the wall behind them. She stared hard and got the fleeting impression of a human shadow behind the boxes. "Here," a voice whispered. At that instant, Buddy turned from what he'd been sniffing and looked directly at the same spot and wagged his tail. Okay, this was weird.

She stood still for a few seconds and breathed deeply, trying to allow her heartbeat to slow down. Then she switched back on the flashlight and swept it all around the room. Nothing. Not even a cat. Had she imagined the whole thing? Buddy certainly seemed to think something had been there a minute ago. But now he'd lost interest and was rummaging elsewhere.

She felt a little disappointed; part of her had been hoping it was the Viking ghost again. She sighed. The movement must've been her own shadow cast by the orange lamp, the almost-sound just some natural house creak. She climbed over the boxes to the pink plastic pig and lifted the lid. As she looked around for a place to put it, the flashlight beam swept the wall and lit up the spot where she had thought she'd seen the shadow. She noticed there was a trail of what looked like sawdust clinging to the cinder block wall. Curious, she moved her flashlight around and spotted a pile of sawdust on the floor beneath the wall.

Termites? Carpenter ants? Or something else? She scooted a couple of the boxes over so she could climb up and see if there was anything amiss in the wooden rafters. Shakily raising herself up first on one box, then two stacked boxes, she peered just over the top of the cinderblocks and into the overhead rafters. She saw mostly spider webs. The web over the sawdusty area had sawdust clinging to each silken fiber, exaggerating the shape of the web.

She shone her light all around over the area and didn't see any sign of ant tunnels. She pointed the beam at the top of the cinder block wall and used her fingers to feel for grit on top. It felt like one of the cinder blocks was hollow, with something sticking up ever so slightly. Red gingerly reached her fingers to the opening, thinking warily of spiders. Her fingers touched something that felt like a spring. Red recoiled her fingers instantly in case it was an electrical wire, then lifted up onto her tiptoes and looked closer. *Oh.* It looked like the spiral wire on a notebook. Excited, Red pulled it up and over to reveal a yellow spiral-bound notebook. It had been partially rolled to fit into the opening. *Was this Uncle Alistair's, or maybe a previous owner?* This place was so old it wouldn't surprise her if it came from Colonial times. *Did they have spiral notebooks then?*

She heard the floor creak overhead and stilled to listen. Buddy's head rose suddenly, obviously hearing the same sound. He barked questioningly and then raced up the stairs.

Maybe her dad was home after all, she thought, then realized: *Oh, no. Tatyana. What time is it?* Red pulled out her cell to check the time—five past ten. *So it must be her upstairs,* Red thought, then saw she had a text message from Tatyana: "Running a bit late. Be there about 10:30."

So who was upstairs? Red could hear Buddy barking, but wasn't too worried. Her calmness was from more than just her tae kwon do training. She just didn't worry. It was like some worry gene had been left out. It drove her mom crazy. Red liked to think of herself as being peaceful. The noise was probably just her dad, anyway. But given that this was a creepy old mansion where a mysterious death had recently occurred, and sleazy Roy was now in the picture, she should investigate.

She snapped off the flashlight and silently crept down off the boxes, squirreling the notebook away under the stairs as she tiptoed to the landing. She slowly mounted the stairs, trying very hard to move smoothly without making the stairs creak. One creaked a bit anyway. *Oh, shoot.* She froze for a moment but didn't hear anything from upstairs and crept onward.

Reaching the top step, she was glad she had left the basement door ajar. She slowly pushed the door open wide enough to get through.

Once through the door, she tried to muster all her senses to determine if someone was in the house without revealing her position. But as she peered around the corner, she saw Buddy was barking at the front door. Whoever had been here had left. Maybe she shouldn't have left the door unlocked with Roy in the picture. She shrugged, walked over to the door, and was just about to turn the deadbolt lock when she heard the sound of a key scraping into the lock from the outside.

The door pushed open and relief flooded her when she saw her dad enter; Buddy rushed past him into the yard. She had to admit to herself that she was glad to see her dad, despite her thoughts of bravado.

"Hey, Red, did I scare you? You look like you've seen a ghost."

"No, just down in the basement and thought I heard something up here. Did you just go out and back in again?"

"No, I did a bike ride down into Potomac Village to get … this. Tada." He lifted his left hand to reveal a bag from their favorite French bakery, cocking one eyebrow and pressing his lips together to look prim, like the cat that ate the canary. Both Red and her dad had a real sweet tooth and their favorite breakfast was French pastries.

"Yum," Red responded, hopefully showing her usual enthusiasm. She didn't want to worry her dad.

She casually stepped over to a window opening to the front of the house and looked up the street in time to catch the sight of a blue BMW disappearing up the street. Buddy stood just inside the fence, barking at the receding car, his whole body bouncing with each bark. A shiver ran up her spine. *What the heck is going on?* Red thought of Annie and felt a chill. Red could take care of herself, but Annie didn't know the first thing about self-defense. She had dropped out of tae kwon do after only achieving the first level. She didn't share Red's aggression.

Let this creep come after her—she wasn't worried. And just let him try to lay a finger on any member of her family. He'd have to get past her. Still, she couldn't help but feel increased pressure to solve the mystery.

She heard Buddy's familiar toenail tap at the front door and let him in. He immediately took on his bloodhound persona, nose to the ground, following some invisible trail. The trail went from the front door, through the foyer, and started up the stairs, then back to the sliding glass doors leading to the deck. He scratched on that door and Red let him out, following him. His trail went down the deck stairs and around to the front of the house, where Buddy once again barked in the spot where he had barked at the BMW. Obviously Roy had come in through the front door and started up the stairs. *Did he think someone would be asleep up there?* Red's skin crawled at the thought. *No, he probably thought everyone was gone.* She'd certainly make sure not to leave the door unlocked again, and it was chained at night. Of course, the ever-faithful Buddy was always here at night, but then, hadn't he been here this morning? Some watchdog he'd turned out to be. Red sighed and re-joined her dad.

Red politely accepted a pastry, though she wasn't particularly hungry. She didn't want to disappoint her dad. What she really wanted to do was squirrel away in her room and read the spiral notebook. She leaned against the kitchen island as she pinched off pieces of the pastry.

"What're you doing for Halloween?"

"My new friend, Tatyana, will be here in about fifteen minutes. We're going to put together costumes for tonight and then I'm going trick-or-treating with her and some of her buddies."

"Haven't you had enough of trick-or-treating yet? I think I stopped in seventh grade." Her father smiled. "But whatever floats your boat, I guess."

"Yeah, I don't really care about the candy—just about spending some time with my new friends. They seem pretty cool. And I'm wearing a cool costume."

"That's great, Red." Red knew her parents worried about her socialization, given her tendency to drive friends away by her compulsive behavior. Only Quinn and Wali had withstood all her embarrassing hyperactivity. Oh, there were a couple of girls at her old school that she was still kind of friends with, but not on the level of Quinn and Wali. These new friends were a nice surprise for Red as well as for her parents, she thought; she was pretty sure her mom was thrilled with all her recent attention from other teens.

"Well, I need to pop upstairs for a few minutes before Tatyana gets here," she said.

"I think I'm going to try and set up that entertainment center now." Red thought of her dad as quite a wizard, capable of fixing pretty much anything, though his quirky habits didn't always give that impression to others. But that only applied to those who didn't know him well.

As he started to open a box, Red took the opportunity to slip downstairs to retrieve the notebook and make her escape back upstairs. She tried to look nonchalant lest her dad notice; after all, it was totally out of character for her to be studying on a Saturday morning.

Once in her room, Red locked the door and dove onto her bed. She quickly gave the book a once-over and decided it must be a lab data book. It had columns of numbers and lots of notes written very small in the margins. Her heart gave a leap when she saw the name *Erik Wolfeningen* written in a neat and matter-of-fact script. There was something in the way the pen's contact with the paper was so direct and solid. Red thought she sensed masculinity leaking from the script, then laughed at herself. *Oh, stop that.* Why was she so connected to this boy? And what was he trying to tell her? After all, he was probably dead … but she couldn't think of that. Even if he was a ghost, it didn't seem creepy to her. She signed as she ran her hand over the notes. They had been written with his hand.

Erik watched Red. The keenness of his interest in this girl continued to surprise him. He saw Red's fingers caress the words he had penned and one corner of his mouth tugged upward slightly. He wondered at his strange connection with this beautiful, glowing girl. He had always admired beautiful women and he'd had his share of flings, but his studies had always occupied the chief part of his attention, especially given his obsession with the Stones of Bothynus. *Those damned stones.* He had been far too preoccupied to devote himself to a relationship. Now, watching this girl study his notes, totally absorbed in something that was connected to him, he was filled with a curious warmth. Maybe he was mistaken about her interest in him. But why else would she be caressing his notebook? Was he just being silly? He tried to reel in this strange hopefulness, then sighed and continued watching her.

He wanted so desperately to communicate with her, to

tell her he wasn't dead. He could try using Moon again. He had to think hard. He didn't want to scare her away. Sending Moon over with the cardinal flower had worked a little, but the gesture had also backfired. He laughed softly, remembering Red's hasty departure. But something was better than nothing. Moon's guano-bomb on Roy's windshield had certainly worked. He felt a bleak inaudible snort. He longed to be himself again. But it seemed so hopeless sometimes. He had looked so hard for the key, but turned up nothing. There were times when he just wanted to give up. But to what? He couldn't even starve himself to death. Apparently the little bit of food he had eaten before his change had stored enough energy for more than a whole year. He wasn't even hungry yet. He reasoned that his low mass did not require even a fraction of the energy for either internal functions or movement as what would be required in a normal state. Good thing, since there wasn't anything to eat as far as he could tell—no food existed in this state. He sighed. Yet as he looked at the girl, he felt a tiny thread of hope. He didn't know why she was so compelling to him. Her strength? The clarity of her essence? The way she romped in the backyard like a meadow nymph? He had never before seen anyone give themselves to the moment so completely. Maybe it was the strong connection he felt to her. Somehow, he felt that she, of all people, could help him.

"Red," he heard her dad call from downstairs. "I think your guest is here."

The girl quickly stuck the notebook under her mattress and ran downstairs, and Erik was left alone once more.

***

Tatyana left mid-afternoon. Red's dad had finished

organizing the entertainment center in the den. Back from Gaithersburg for now, Annie was stretched out on the floor, propped up on her elbows with a Wii control in one hand. Red plopped onto the couch with one of Uncle Alistair's old file boxes. She began rummaging through the box, examining each object she came across.

"What are you doing?" Annie seemed mildly curious.

"None of your business. But if you must know, I'm examining the contents of Uncle Alistair's desk drawers, like any good sleuth." Red felt a little annoyed at that interruption.

"Give it up, Red. The police already did that and they're way smarter than you," Annie said. Red heard a mocking singsong tone in Annie's remark, meant to annoy.

Red stuck out her tongue, feeling sassy. Now, distracted from her work, she noticed the cats were playing under the dining room table.

"Roxy, you silly, what are you up to?" Red said, using her customized kitty-speak voice. Red saw that Roxy was now lying on her back with her nose and front legs invisibly tucked upside-down under the fancy wooden scrollwork adorning the bottom of a built-in hutch, like an auto mechanic.

"Oh, my gosh, kitties at battle—waaay too cute," cooed Annie.

Annie suddenly jumped up and waved the Wii controller, saying energetically, "I challenge you to a melee." Red couldn't resist. Within a few minutes she was totally absorbed in the Wii game, jerking the controls around in swift movements. Sometimes it was fun being a kid again with her sister, Red thought. She knew their bond made even video games seem like a warm-and-fuzzy celebration of togetherness, though neither would ever admit that.

Behind them, a *Yeeeooollll* distracted Red as the cats romped. "Quiet, kitties," said Red.

Their yowls continued at a higher pitch and frequency, as though the cats were determined to be heard.

"I said *quiet*, you naughty kitties." Red paused the game and stomped into the dining room with mock severity. "We can't focus on our game, you silly things." She heard a curious scrapping noise as Midnight slid something across the floor. Red bent down to look. Roxy leapt forward and batted the shiny object like a hockey puck across the polished wooden floor.

"What's that, kitties?" Annie asked, apparently noticing it, too.

"Looks like a key," Red said. It was an unusual key, short, yet very thick. She had never seen one quite like it. It was too big for a jewelry box or diary. "Wonder what it goes to?" She shrugged and stuck the key into her cell phone case, then sat back down to resume their game.

CHAPTER 7

Red Sonja Begins to Emerge

Feeling stalked by Roy caused Red to rethink the break from tae kwon do she had planned on taking for the move and new-school adjustment. It was time to resume her classes. On Sunday afternoon, in catching up on her email and text messages, she had announced this decision to her two best tae kwon do friends, Quinn and Wali. The move had actually brought her closer geographically to them, though not close enough to go to the same high school—which was a shame because both would have been in her class. Both lived a little to the west, just north of Potomac Village, and attended Wooton High School, the archrival from the game last Friday. She had mildly teased both about this fact in their email exchanges, but it went right over their heads. Like her, they weren't great football fans.

Red was delighted when Wali asked to come by soon to practice sparring for next weekend's tournament. It was so cool that she was now close enough for him to ride his bike to her house. Red hadn't yet decided if she would enter the tournament, but Wali always entered them and it had become their tradition to practice together before a tournament.

She decided, too, that the fall sunshine looked inviting and she wanted to spend as much time as possible sketching in the sun before he arrived. So down she went with her quilt and sketchpad to the sunny spot at the bottom of the yard. She sketched the crows for about half an hour and then gazed at the photo from Uncle Alistair's bulletin board. *Erik.* His eyes were amazing. They looked right at her from the photo and made her heart pound. She sketched him looking into the wind, his hair blowing back and his hand holding a sword as if he were really a Viking. He wore a tunic belted with leather and leather sandals that laced up his muscular legs.

She sketched herself beside him, her hair also blowing dreamily, entwining with his and swirling in the air around them. She sighed and immediately realized how school-girlish she was acting. But her embarrassment didn't last long. She allowed herself to be drawn back into the romance of the drawing, becoming so absorbed that the sound of steps coming down the yard made her jump. Before she could react, she felt a form pounce on her, straddling her back and pinning her neck to the ground, her face pressed into her writing tablet.

"GET … OFF," she spat.

"*Joon Bi.*" Wali laughed impishly as he belatedly called the tae kwon do command for combatants to ready themselves for battle.

"A little late for *Joon Bi*, you barbarian," Red spat teasingly and looked up as Wali leaned to one side and began to remove his leg from across her back. At that instant, the crack of a tree limb sent a shockwave through the air. Before he could move, the branch crashed downward toward him. Red's training kicked in and she rolled away from the falling limb, while Wali rolled away in the opposite direction. Red felt a soft pressure pushing her away from the quilt. Somehow, miraculously, the limb totally missed her, but hit Wali.

"Wali, are you okay?" she shrieked, almost afraid to look for fear that he had been impaled. She lay still for an instant, trying to decide whether to help Wali or run to the house and call 9-1-1.

"I'm fine," coughed out Wali. "What was that? I mean, it's not like it's windy or anything."

Red tried to collect her thoughts and figure out what just happened. What *was* that pressure she'd felt propelling her away? And why did the branch fall away from her? She could've sworn it had been about to snag her leg. "Don't know," she panted. She could see a thin stream of blood trickling down Wali's right arm and a nasty scratch under his eye. "Better get those scratches disinfected."

Carefully, she pulled the branch away from Wali. "It's a miracle this thing didn't do more damage." She caught Wali's hand and pulled him to his feet. He brushed off his shorts and stiffly followed her up the yard and into the kitchen to find the hydrogen peroxide.

After doctoring Wali's scratches, she put on her pads and helmet and they sparred for an hour with no further mysterious occurrences.

"Want to see a movie tonight?" he asked hopefully.

"No, thanks. I have to finish a report," she answered regretfully. "I think Quinn said she was caught up with schoolwork, though. She might want to go." She slightly tilted one brow, hoping Wali wouldn't notice her matchmaking push.

"Yeah, maybe I'll give her a ring," said Wali, almost absentmindedly. Red sometimes wondered if perhaps Wali liked her just a little bit more than she liked him. He had been one of her best pals since second grade, but now that their bodies had matured, there was some obvious awkwardness when they sparred and grappled. Still, it was fun and she valued his friendship. Overall, they had an easy comfort that came from years of practicing tae kwon do together. Whenever the air became awkward between them, one or the other would come up with a wisecrack to set them both at ease again.

As Wali walked up the yard, Red called after him, "Later, dude."

"Later," was his easy reply. He didn't bother to look back—he just gave a quick wave with his chest pad and headed toward his bike. She was glad they could have practice sessions now without having to bum rides from their parents.

After Wali disappeared around the side of the house, Red took off her pads and settled back on the quilt. She picked up her sketchpad to survey the damage. The last sketch she had been working on was slightly wrinkled and she tried to smooth it out. She collected her sketching pencils and continued to work on the picture. She began to daydream of her Viking ghost. Thinking of the story of Red Sonja and her proclamation that she would only fall in love with a man who could beat her in battle, she couldn't resist drawing herself, dressed in a skin tunic off one shoulder like a stereotypical cave-woman. She wore leather thongs on her legs and battled with her Viking, who was similarly dressed. His face was only inches from hers, their swords pressed together. Her full pouty lips wore an expression of determination, but there was an ever-so-subtle amused question in her eyes.

Realizing she had goose pimples, and caught up in the moment, Red turned the page and started sketching her Red Sonja character with submissively lowered eyelids, the Viking with passion burning in his eyes, their lips only centimeters apart, her lips slightly parted …

Just as she was putting the finishing touches on his lips, she heard an audible sigh near her left ear, a deep voice confined to a whisper, like air flowing through a primitive horn. Electricity sparked her spine and she heard an ear-piercing scream, a split second before realizing it came from her own lungs. She rolled automatically into a crouch, ready to defend herself. She stayed deathly still, allowing her heart rate to slow and adrenaline to dissolve back into her tissues. She listened intently, hearing no sound other than Buddy barking to be let out of the house—her ever-ready hero desperate to come to her rescue.

"Re-ed," called Annie, emerging from the sliding glass door onto the deck. Red heard Buddy's tap-tap-tap on the deck as he rapidly scaled the steps and bounded toward her. "What's wrong?"

"Nu-uh-thing." She tried to sound normal. Buddy arrived with a "Brf, brf" and a panting waggle. He came over to allow Red to celebrate his arrival by scratching between his ears, and then he went to a spot a few feet away and looked up expectantly again, as if someone were standing to her left. "Bud-ster, what is that all about? You trying to freak me out?" She noogied Buddy on his head, calmed a bit by his infectious playfulness. After all, if there *had* been a ghost or some random evil thing nearby, Buddy would've doubtlessly been irate. Red laughed at her own stupidity.

With the interruption, she decided to change activities, collect her things, and bite the bullet to finish her history project. She gingerly approached her quilt and gasped. There was a cardinal flower lying on her writing pad.

An hour later, the history project and Red were at an impasse. She had intended to do a report on the Cherokee, since her Mom had recently discovered they had a Cherokee ancestor, something a cousin of hers had speculated from the results of one of those send-away genetics test kits. But Red just couldn't reel in her thoughts and she knew very well why—she couldn't stop thinking of her Viking.

Had she really seen a ghost? Were all these mysterious things—the flowers, the shadow in the basement—related to the ghost? The possibility that ghosts could be real had some serious implications for things like religion and afterlife. Red wasn't sure how she felt about that. She wondered if she should be scared moving into this old place. She remembered Annie's teasing justifications for all she had told her about the ghost. Despite trying to use this to reassure herself that nothing was there, Red felt jumpy. She had probably been imagining things. But what about the two cardinal flowers? Did they both just happen to be blown by the wind onto her quilt?

Another thing bugging her was that somehow she couldn't allow herself to think of the Viking as dead. She had already formed a strange and powerful attachment to him. She needed to find out more about him. How could she access Uncle Alistair's records? She was sure if she mentioned it to Mom and Dad they would think she was being really weird and might ground her or worse. If she could get another chance to talk to his mom, she'd figure out a way to bring up the subject.

She was moping for who knows how long when she heard a few familiar musical notes and then Quinn's ringtone on her cell.

" 'S'up?"

"Hey, Red." Why did Quinn sound funny? "I have a question for you," Quinn said, sounding nervous. "Are you sure you don't like Wali? I mean, he's pretty hot. And so nice."

Red made a face. "Quinn, you know how I feel. Wali is one of my best friends, but anything more would be like kissing my own brother—yuck. And I'm sure he's a really hot guy to some, but I just don't see him that way. You like him and I think that's awesome. Go for it, girl." *I'm perfectly content with my Viking ghost.*

"Well, he asked me to a movie." Quinn could barely say the words without squealing. "It might be just as friends, though, 'cause he said he asked you and you had to work on something."

"Doesn't matter. Just go and have fun. Be yourself and let nature take its course," Red said. "You underestimate yourself. You're smart and pretty and beautiful inside and out. What's not to love? The more you two hang out together, the more likely a spark will ignite and then, who knooo-ows."

"Oooh, I hope so. We're going to see *Vampires Suck*. I can't wait to see it. It's going to be so awesome. Will tell you how it goes."

After they hung up, Red reveled a few minutes in Quinn's glow. She loved to play matchmaker, and what could be better than her two best friends getting together? The unexpected joy distracted her from her ghostly contemplation long enough to boot up her computer and begin searching for some interesting angles to write about on the Cherokee. She didn't want to do the obvious Trail of Tears report and so decided to do something more uplifting, like their spiritual beliefs. Soon she was fascinated with the project and deeply immersed in her research, especially the legends of the *Yunwi Tsunsdi*, or Little People. They sounded so much like elves that she wondered if there must be some basis to the legend. How else could two such similar legends parallel each other with an ocean between them?

Since the Little People had so completely captured her attention and imagination, her report was quickly written and put to bed. She glanced at the clock and saw it was almost eleven.

She decided to take a relaxing bath and carefully drew water of the perfect temperature, which for her, was almost too hot but still bearable when she slowly immersed herself. She looked in her bath travel kit for a razor and some soap since she hadn't unpacked those essentials yet. She noticed a very slim bottle of bath salts that Annie had given her for Christmas last year. She sprinkled a few of those in as well.

She undressed and gingerly stepped first one foot and then the other into the heavenly water and slowly sank the rest of the way in to relax, lingering until the water was cool enough to lose her interest. She toweled off and realized how tired she was from sparring—she needed to get back into a good exercise routine to regain her stamina. And there was the emotional strain of constantly thinking of her Viking.

She opened the window even though there was no screen upstairs, hoping no wax beetles or moths would venture in, and turned off her light so as not to encourage them. She slipped on her favorite oversized Life is Good T-shirt and slid beneath the cool sheets. She lay awake for a while, staring through the open window at the stars and thinking of her Viking until she finally lost the battle with tiredness and drifted off, only to see her Viking again in her dreams.

Chapter 8

Moon-y

"Prophet," said I, "thing of evil—prophet
still, if bird or devil.
By that heaven that bends above us—by that
God we both adore—
Tell this soul with sorrow laden, if, within
the distant Aidenn,
It shall clasp a sainted maiden, whom the
angels name Lenore—
Clasp a rare and radiant maiden, whom the
angels name Lenore?
Quoth the raven, "Nevermore."[4]

Halloween fell on Wednesday night, so Red didn't have much time to savor the experience. She did her homework and then quickly dressed in her Red Sonja outfit, barely in time for the rendezvous with Tatyana and her friends.

The night was a whirlwind of laughter, candy, and gossip, and before Red knew it, she and Annie were both back home, comparing loot and exchanging stories, as they had done every year since she could remember. Both girls had a huge haul of chocolate bars, tiny lollipops, gum, Twizzlers, and other assorted dental anathema.

Thankfully, they hadn't run into Roy, a concern that had been in the back of Red's mind. But the only unusual event Red had to share was a puzzling sight. "Someone dressed like Darth Vader was running down the street being attacked by crows," she told Annie.

"Crows?" Annie sounded like she suspected Red of embellishing.

"Yeah. It actually happened. There were two or three swooping down and seemed to be clawing at the guy. I mean, it was dark and hard to tell, but you could hear more of them in a nearby tree cawing and squawking. It was pretty loud. And of course the Darth Vader guy was screaming and cursing."

"Huh," Annie snorted. Red wasn't sure whether she was ambivalent about the truth of Red's story, or amused that something so weird had really happened.

"I'm serious," Red insisted.

"Yeah, Red, no offense, but I haven't forgotten that you thought you saw a ghost last year. How's that going for ya? Seen any little green men lately?"

"Whatever," Red was annoyed and a little hurt by Annie's disbelief.

Annie seemed to realize it and softened. "It's just that,

crows at night? I'm not as much of a birder as you and Mom, but I do know they roost at night. Maybe it was some other bird. And where was it you said it happened?"

"One of those lanes off Normandy Drive," Red said. "But I do know a crow when I see and hear one. I just hope the crow population doesn't catch flack over it. If people complain, the county might use one of those chemicals they use to kill birds. Poor things. I'd bet the guy they were attacking deserved it. He probably littered or something." She couldn't help but smile at the silliness of the thought. Annie giggled, too; they were both on a sugar high from the candy. Red felt a pang. How she would love to confide in Annie about all the other creepy crow antics and Erik's save-the-crows T-shirt, but she felt a little too emotionally vulnerable and let it drop. She pictured Erik in his crow T-shirt. *Yes, crows are awesome.*

The remainder of the week was uneventful, with the exception that Friday was the end of the first marking period and Red had arranged an appointment with her guidance counselor after school that day. Even though Red had been able to get all the same classes she had at her previous school, she'd missed some work during the transition. She knew Annie had done everything perfectly, as always. She didn't really resent her for it, but it did make Red more aware of her own grades— mostly A's with a smattering of B's, but a few dips into the E-zone that discomfited her. Red knew she could make good grades when she did the work, but was so easily distracted that she tended to miss whole sections or assignments. Realizing she wouldn't be walking with the group today, she suppressed a shudder as she thought briefly of Roy, and was glad to know Annie was going home with a new friend after school and so wouldn't be walking alone.

She said goodbye to Tatyana, Gabriella, and Uma at the lockers as they packed up to go home and walked slowly toward the counselor's office. She had a half-hour to kill, and thought about pulling out the novel she was reading, but put that off to lazily scan a large bulletin board. It was awash with notices for tutoring services, an advertisement for a trip to Greece for forty-five hundred dollars. *Hmm, that would be nice,* she thought, until she realized it would take ninety weeks of doing housework to earn that much. She could join the French Club, Chess Club, Gay-Straight Alliance, Environmental Club, Manga Club, Hiking Club. *Wonder if there is anything about bird protection? Like the Audubon Society?* She saw a Biology Club and a Save the Bay Club advertised but nothing specific to birds. She made a mental note to ask her mom about a birding club.

That night, she stayed home to enjoy her family's standing movie-and-pizza Friday night. She would make a point of inviting her friends over for next Friday night. "Hey, Mom, do you know of any birding clubs?"

Her mom, always ready to help a budding young environmentalist, went directly to the computer in the library. "There's the Potomac chapter of the Audubon Society," she said after a quick search. "It looks like they're having a hawk migration watch tomorrow at Snicker's Gap. It's about an hour away."

This would mean they would need to leave the house at

seven-thirty. Red almost wished she hadn't asked—there went her plans for a relaxing Saturday morning. She'd need to work doubly hard Saturday evening and maybe even part of Sunday afternoon to finish all she had to do. Still, she was compelled to go. Her mom seemed to think this was the only group in the area dedicated to bird protection and enjoyment. Red was determined to get involved and try to learn something of the world of this mysterious, intriguing man, who had so obsessed all her waking, and sleeping, thoughts. And anything she could learn about him might shed light on the mystery.

As she mounted the stairs, a brilliant thought occurred to her—she would wear a crow T-shirt tomorrow. A few minutes later, she was in her room, her artistic fingers fast at work, making a drawing on an old T-shirt using a tube of neon fabric paint. "Ta-da," she exclaimed out loud, viewing the finished product. From a graceful minimalist sketch, a perching crow's beady eye stared sharply out. The crow had a crescent-shaped scar on his beak. Red smiled at that. And the caption read "Save the Rockville Rousting Sites." *There, that should draw them out.* She hoped to attract the attention of anybody who might have known Erik and could tell her more about him.

Red's greatest challenge the next morning as she and her mom emerged from the yellow bee-car was to distance herself enough from her mom to do some sleuthing, hopefully without hurting her feelings. Her mom had been excited to see that Red was championing a cause when she first noticed the shirt. Red wore the T-shirt over a white turtleneck, hoping to stay warm enough in the mountain-pass winds without needing to cover up the shirt with her jacket. Red had tried to avoid in-depth explanation for her sudden interest in crows by telling her mom that some kids at school were into the crow thing. She knew it was a lie, but reasoned that she didn't say which school, and so it wasn't a barefaced lie, more a half-truth. And who knew, maybe she would start a crow club. This didn't salve her conscience much, though—she really hated lying to her mom.

Once at the bird site, Red focused on her mission. She was dismayed there was such a short hike to the bird-viewing spot—in fact, it pretty much adjoined the parking lot. As they walked toward the overlook, Red worked on getting her mom engaged in conversation with someone other than herself. Her mom was pointing and whipping off bird names right and left—here a robin, there a thrush. "Look, Red, a slate-colored junco! We must be pretty high in elevation to see one of those this early in the fall."

Red caught sight of a promising larger bird sitting in a dead tree in a small grassy field just below the lot. The field contained tall tufts of wild grasses of a soft golden color, waving in the pleasant mountain breeze. "Mom, what's that bird?"

Her mom whipped her binoculars into position as fast as a trained assassin, and proclaimed it to be a sharp-shinned hawk. Red, with her binoculars likewise poised, said loud enough for other nearby birders to hear, "Are you sure, Mom? I was thinking Cooper's hawk." She so hoped that made sense—she just pulled the name out of the air.

"Hmmm … maybe." Her mom took the bait. "Granted,

it's a bit on the large side for a sharp-shin, but ..." Because they had stopped, a couple walking directly behind them also stopped on the side of the trail beside her mom, binoculars raised, anxious to see the object of interest. The woman sided with her mom, totally convinced it was a sharp-shin. However, the man wasn't so sure. Red's artist's eye yearned to take time to enjoy the attractive outdoorsy pair. But she had work to do, so she took the opportunity to ease quickly away while her mom chatted with the young couple. She pretended to look into the trees, but in reality, focused on distancing herself. *Sorry, Mom,* she thought. A quick glance backward brought a smile to her face as she watched her mom gesticulating, apparently in some description of wing movement, while both the woman and man watched and listened, and then responded with some gesticulations of their own. Red breathed a sigh of relief and estimated that her mom would be engaged for at least an hour, and possibly until lunch.

She spotted a group of college-aged people and moved closer, zeroing in on a young couple. "Hi, I'm Red," she said. They greeted her warmly. Their names were Rachel and Daniel, and were both in pre-med at Georgetown. *Promising.* Red learned they had attended Churchill. *Even better.* Now she was getting somewhere. Red didn't have long to wait. Rachel glanced sideways at her T-shirt and asked, somewhat excitedly, "Does Churchill have a bird-club now? Or a wildlife group dedicated to protecting the crow roosting sites?" *Bingo.*

"Well, not yet, but I'm trying to get one started," Red said. Okay, she was tired of lying—she would, in fact, start such a club, she pledged to herself. "My uncle's graduate student got me interested in crows, actually." She glanced at both significantly, hoping that Daniel, too, had heard the remark.

"What is his name? I probably know him if he's local. We crow-lovers are a tight bunch," said Rachel.

"Erik Wolfeningen." Red watched as excitement gripped both Rachel and Daniel. Their heads fully turned toward each other, their mouths dropping open.

"Erik?" they said in unison. Then Rachel's face darkened. "Poor Erik. Did they ever find for sure what happened to him?"

"Are you talking about Professor Hamilton?" Daniel said at the same moment.

Both looked to Red expectantly, wide-eyed with curiosity and obviously intrigued by the coincidence of meeting someone who seemed to be part of their small group of crow-enthusiasts and yet who was previously unbeknownst to them.

Red filled Rachel and Daniel in on the details of the police investigation and mentioned shyly about her great-uncle being declared dead and her dad's inheritance of the house. She had to admit she didn't know the particulars of whether Erik had been declared dead, but said she guessed he had since he disappeared with her uncle. *But I can't think of that. Not him. Not dead.*

"I love that old place," Daniel said, a spark of recognition in his eyes. "Erik talked Professor Hamilton into allowing us to use the mansion for our Save-the-Crows summer cookout a few years back. Remember that, Rach?" Daniel winked.

"How could I forget it?" Rachel blushed. "That

was when Daniel and I'd first started dating. We had a very romantic stroll on the towpath that evening." She smiled, then added, "It really is a great place to view herons, and some folks have seen bald eagles up-river, though I've never been lucky enough to catch one there. I saw a pair up-river from the Great Falls platform, though, once. You know, on Olmsted Island overlook?"

Red nodded and tried to steer the conversation back toward crows and Erik. In the midst of this thought process, she had an amazing idea. "Hey, perhaps you can have more Save-the-Crows meetings at the mansion. Maybe my Churchill group could tie into your group in some way. After all, I'm a novice on the subject and have a lot to learn." Red was delighted that this turned out to be exactly the right thing to say, reasoning that enthusiasts of all types love to teach a novice.

Red learned more than she would have thought possible about the historical number of crows in the area, about the formerly extensive wetland environment of the whole Washington, D.C. area, and a lot about crow life history. Red felt she got an outstanding overview and was sincerely becoming interested in crows.

Red was about to bring the conversation back to Erik when Rachel exclaimed, "Look, Dan, there's Xenia." She waved toward a petite, very cute girl with a cascade of long, dark, wavy hair flowing in the breeze as she advanced toward them. She waved back at Rachel, obviously intent on joining their group. To Red, she said innocently, "Here's Erik's former girlfriend now. She'll probably be able to tell you more than we can."

Red's heart sank. She didn't know why this announcement

affected her so much. After all, Erik was dead, or at least might be. But Red recognized a pang of jealousy for anyone who had been fortunate enough to be close to her Viking.

The young woman dropped her daypack onto a nearby stone, took out a hairband, and proceeded to restrict the wildness of her long hair into a ponytail as she greeted Rachel and Daniel, with whom she was obviously very close friends. "Xenia, this is Red. She's Professor Hamilton's niece and lives in his old mansion," Rachel said. "Can you believe that? And she wants to start a Save-the-Crows club at Churchill."

Her enthusiasm was infectious and Xenia took Red's hand in both of hers and gave her an unexpectedly warm welcome. Red blushed and felt ashamed of her jealousy. She seemed like a truly nice person and she was glad Erik had had the pleasure of her company—well, at least in theory, though some prickles of jealousy still remained.

But how could he fail to fall in love with those eyes? Xenia's hair and skin were dark, but her eyes were white-blue, something Red had never before encountered in real life, only in magazines, and she had assumed those had been photoshopped. What was more, she seemed unaware of her appeal, totally immersed in the easy exchange with her friends. Red had a compulsion to draw her. *Maybe later.*

Red's artist's eye for beauty had, for a couple of years, been so obsessed by the beauty of the female form that she wondered if she was gay. But now her fantastic crush on Erik had made her realize she wasn't. If she had him, she was certain he would be all she could ever want.

As the three friends chatted, mostly about birds

each had seen that morning— comparing notes with just a smidgeon of one-upmanship, Red began to feel she might be getting close to overstaying her welcome, and began to look around with her binoculars and ease away from them. Then she was jolted into instant attention when she heard Xenia say, "I haven't seen Roy in over a month."

Red glanced toward Xenia—something had definitely darkened in the beautiful face. *Did Xenia seem sad? Hurt?* Red listened intently, pretending to survey the trees for more hawks.

Red listened as Xenia excused herself and left the group to speak with another nearby birder. While Xenia was tied up in that conversation, Daniel, obviously unaware that Red was still listening, ventured privately to Rachel, "Why did you say Xenia was Erik's girlfriend?"

"Oh, that." Red saw Rachel shrug out of the corner of her eye. "It's just that I wish it were true, I guess. You have to admit they seemed to be on that track for a while—they definitely had a flirtation. I mean ... promise you won't tell Xenia I told?"

"Told me what?"

"Roy hit her." She lifted a hand as if taking an oath. "I swear. Xenia told me. I mean, Roy has changed. I—I don't trust him anymore. I told Xenia she can do better. I wish she'd been with Erik. I know she flirted with him. He's a better guy than Roy."

Daniel shook his head, concern lining his face. "Wow. I guess I can't say I'm surprised, though. You're right, Rach, he certainly has changed."

Xenia returned and said something to Rachel that Red

couldn't really make out. After a few minutes, Red realized the subject of Roy was finished for now, and, feeling that she didn't want to ruin her good fortune in meeting them by seeming like a cling-on, decided to move away. She made a show of lowering her binoculars and as she passed by the three now-clustered friends, and addressed Rachel. "It was so nice to meet you. Let's do keep in touch about the crow club." Rachel heartily agreed and they exchanged email addresses.

Red puzzled over the new information as she moseyed over to where her mom was still chatting with the couple from earlier. Thankfully, upon seeing her approach, her mom excused herself from her newfound friends and said in a chipper tone, "You hungry for lunch?"

Red realized she was famished. She and her mom found an unoccupied rock and Red tried to position herself in a lounging position on the hard rock in the way customary to hikers, trying to appear to luxuriate in nature's beauty and the golden warmth of the sun. It felt good to have a mother-daughter lunch of peanut-butter-and-banana sandwiches and crisp, juicy apples. Her mom was ecstatic to learn of Red's intent to start a Save-the-Crows club at Churchill and gladly granted the use of the mansion and grounds any time, even going so far as to offer her services in the provision of refreshments. Red was cautiously pleased with this all-too-expected response from her mother, but hoped it wouldn't lead to her mom's disappointment. Red was honestly becoming interested in crows, but knew something else was the true driver—learning more about Erik and Roy.

The next morning, Red awoke to a dreary, rainy Sunday.

Her mother and Annie were at a worship service, and the house was quiet. Red made herself a cup of tea in the kitchen and sat in one of the ladder-backed chairs, Buddy at her feet and her hands cozied around her teacup for warmth. She breathed deeply, thoroughly enjoying the muddy smell of the river, and closed her eyes, enjoying the broody moment. A few minutes later, she opened her eyes and gasped. Perched firmly on the other side of the window screen and eyeing her with his sharp, intelligent eye, was a crow—*the* crow. The one with the crescent-shaped scar. Then she realized a screen was between them and felt a little better. After a few calming breaths, she began to think rationally and wondered why Buddy wasn't barking. She looked around and found him around the corner at the end of the bay window, away from the open-window breeze but with his head up, watching her with an occasional glance at the crow. Likewise, both cats were sitting on the other side of the bay window, away from the draft, watching both her and the crow. *Strange.* She felt goose bumps again. She spoke first to Buddy, who wagged his tail and regarded her warmly, and then to the cats, who ignored her. Midnight began preening Roxy. The seeming state of contentment among the pets made her feel a little less creeped out. *Okay, so they're not afraid of the crow. They seem to accept him as one of them. That's odd, but we'll have to go with it.*

The crow began to make a low clucking sound. He lowered one wing and started to dance. *The mating dance again?* "Okay, you. Enough is enough." She looked squarely at the crow. Buddy seemed to hear the tension in her voice and rose from his tranquil pose and pranced toward the window, his toenails tapping on the wooden floor. The crow eyed him and voiced a caw that sounded somewhat irritated and flew away.

Red closed the window. She wanted to enjoy the deep gloomy mood of the day rather than be overly creeped out by it—she thought it was good to see aching beauty in gloom as well as sunshine. She smiled to herself, wondering if anyone else had a crow suitor. Was there a support group for this? Perhaps he just wanted food. She filled a lid with a few clumps of granola and half a dozen raspberries she found in the fridge and carried it up to her room.

Back in her room, she popped the screen out at one bottom corner, placed the lid on the ledge, and put the screen back in place. *There.*

CHAPTER 9

It's Complicated

Red felt excitement as her parents began their holiday preparations. Thanksgiving Day had always been the biggest annual event on the Greene family calendar, with Uncle Alistair hosting the Christmas festivities in former years. But this year it fell on them to host both events and Thanksgiving was fast approaching, less than a week away.

Red knew her mom had tried, as she did every year, to talk her own mother into coming up from Tennessee to spend the holiday with them, but as usual, to no avail. Red was intrigued by her Mamaw Jefferson, who lived alone on the family farm in the Smoky Mountains, even though she was over eighty years old, a hold-out from an earlier time, keeping the farm running by hiring help to get the work done and by sharecropping. She had long since stopped making any significant profit from the few cattle and little bit of corn, but it had always been part of her world to check the farm every day, rain or shine. She always seemed to feel too tied to the farm to travel up to see them; after all, it was a ten-hour drive. She had visited them only twice during Red's lifetime.

The real pressing issue right now was the Thanksgiving invitations. Red's mom and dad always liked to have a full table for this event, which in prior years had always included Uncle Alistair. Red felt a pang of sadness as she remembered. This year, the family didn't take long to decide whom to invite: Ms. Catsworthy. Red wondered why they hadn't asked Uncle Alistair to bring her to their house in the past. After all, she lived so close to him and seemed close in a personal way as well, but then, that could just be Red's imagination. Ms. Catsworthy had typically attended Uncle Alistair's Christmas parties with the family, but never stayed long and had tended to be very quiet on those occasions. "Maybe we should also invite Ms. Wolfeningen," Red suggested, fervently hoping she didn't color as she made the suggestion. But it was a legitimate request, Red reasoned; Erik's mother would be alone this holiday season and her fate was very connected to theirs, given that they'd lost a loved one in the same event—whatever it was that happened that fateful day. Annie eyed her furtively, obviously wondering at Red's gumption.

"That's a lovely idea," her mother said. Red flushed with warmth, gratified by her mom's acceptance. Then she was caught off-guard by something she hadn't considered. "Let's also invite the other woman we met at Ms. Catsworthy's tea," her mother suggested.

Roy's mom, Red thought, her stomach plunging. *Stupid. Stupid. Stupid!* That meant they'd be inviting him too. Then he'd know where she and Annie lived. What had she done? She wanted to investigate him from afar—not invite him to dinner.

After a momentary shocked silence, Red regained her composure just enough to stammer something about there not being enough room. "And hadn't that lady said they had family locally?"

"Nonsense," Red's dad chimed in. "We now have enough space for a dozen families. We have a ballroom, for crying out loud. We have all those folding chairs in the basement and, what the heck, we could rent equipment if needed."

Red knew her dad loved to entertain, but this didn't mean he loved to prepare for the guests. In fact, he had a much lower standard for such preparation than her mom. She watched her mom stiffen, clearly worried, no doubt thinking of all the boxes still unpacked in every room. Her mom, evidently seeing trouble in their future and wanting to nip it in the bud, quickly interjected, "Honey, we might have enough room, but I, for one, don't have enough energy to entertain more than two or three couples in addition to ourselves, unless, of course, you want to hire people to get the whole thing done—cleaners, caterers, and so on. And you'd have to manage the whole thing because I've got too much else to do." Red's father seemed to entertain a mental vision of lots of time away from bicycling to do all this work and so docilely went along with the idea of keeping things reasonably small. "Of course, honey, I just meant we could accommodate several families, not that we wanted to have a huge event." He snorted as if she were silly for thinking it. Red's mother smiled, seemingly satisfied that the crisis was over.

But the crisis wasn't over for Red. *Roy might be coming.* All she could do was drag her feet up to her room and cast herself facedown onto her bed. She lay like that for a half an hour, but two thoughts emerged that made her feel like she could possibly cope with this situation. First, because of the move, they were really late in planning for Thanksgiving dinner, and so, chances were anyone they invited would already have plans. And second, in less than a week it would be over—at least, the meal would be. Of course, there was always the possibility that shortly thereafter, Roy might have Annie and herself chained in some dungeon, making them rub lotion on themselves so that after he killed them, he could make a suit out of their skin, like in *Silence of the Lambs.*

By Sunday evening, however, things started to look up again when Red's mom told her she'd called Roy's mom but his family already had plans for Thanksgiving. Red tried to avoid an audible sigh of relief. And more good news—both Ms. Catsworthy and Erik's mom had graciously accepted the invitation and both ladies had offered their services in bringing a dish. Ms. Catsworthy would bring homemade rolls and a dessert. Red fondly remembered her fairy cakes. And Ms. Wolfeningen said she'd bring a Thanksgiving favorite—sweet potato tempura. Red had never been crazy about the sweet potato part of the meal, but had to admit this sounded delicious. She and Annie would make pumpkin pie and cranberry sauce. What a difference one day made. Now she was really looking forward to the occasion and the three days of school she had to endure first seemed much too long.

***

Red awoke on Thursday to a very pleasant aroma. Her mom must be sautéing onions and celery to add to the stuffing before baking the turkey. She'd undoubtedly bake the turkey for many hours—always way too many for her dad. This was an annual argument; he was much more of a carnivore than her mom. She usually started an argument for tofurkey instead of real meat, then reluctantly agreed to real meat as long as it was free-range; but he liked his meat practically raw, even his poultry. *Eeeesshh.* Perhaps *argument* wasn't the correct term because they really didn't argue about this—it was understood that her dad would do whatever was needed to please her mom. Even if he decided to smoke the turkey, he'd keep the smoker going until her mom was satisfied. Their dynamic always fascinated Red. Her dad was such an independent, strong-willed, healthy man, yet was totally subservient to a much smaller, quieter, socially awkward woman. Red was only now beginning to explore the effect love could have on a person—totally conquering a person's priorities. She smiled, threw on some sweats, and went downstairs to help.

Red reveled in the mouthwatering aromas filling the old mansion: cinnamon, onion, cloves, and toasty pie crusts. By three o'clock, their guests began to arrive as fires blazed in both grand fireplaces—the one in the library for the guests' enjoyment while the final meal preparations were completed, and the one in the dining room for the dining ambience. This had been mildly contested by her mom, citing global warming and wasted resources, so her dad had lowered the thermostat so the heat from the fires wouldn't be wasted. Red wasn't sure about the logic in that, since with the fires the heat pump wouldn't engage, anyway, *but whatever* ... Red knew the fires were a must for any gathering her dad hosted; he was well on his way to becoming a pyromaniac. She was pretty sure not many families had quite the enormous fires they had on camping trips, even during the summer. He seemed to love the elements—rain, wind, fire. Now, Red watched as he shuffled between tending both fires and arranging the wine glasses while her mom finished the cooking in the huge kitchen.

Zsofia Catsworthy arrived first, carrying heavenly-scented bread in a basket covered by a cotton towel. Red thought she must be very hungry to notice this so keenly. The stack of covered dishes she carried also contained a plum pudding and a gingerbread-stacked cake—wow, this would indeed be a feast. With these newly added aromas, Red wasn't surprised to note that Annie had left her computer to join the gathering.

Minah Wolfeningen arrived next with her sweet potato tempura, but before Red could do more than greet her, Tatyana and her parents arrived. Red was surprised and delighted to see her. Her dad mentioned that he'd called them at the last minute, realizing that there would be way too much food for so few guests. Since Thanksgiving wasn't a holiday Tatyana's family customarily celebrated, they had gratefully accepted the invitation and had many questions for Red's parents about the preparations. This, of course, was a big hit with Red's mom and dad, she noted, who competed in sharing stories about past Thanksgiving successes and failures. She heard her dad enthusiastically retell the first year he tried to smoke the turkey, when he couldn't manage to get the charcoal to stay lit and resorted to using a gasoline-powered leaf blower to fan the coals and ended up with a turkey with a uniform black crust.

Red was a little embarrassed at her parents' exuberance in telling tale after tale, which seemed to grow in humor as more wine was consumed by the adults. A part of Red wanted to excuse herself and Tatyana from the meal and escape to her room to have some private time. But she also wanted to try and get Erik's mom to herself so she could find out more about Erik. She so hoped she wouldn't say anything really stupid. She knew it would be seen as abnormal to be so obsessed with a dead guy. She couldn't even talk to Tatyana or Quinn about it. Annie knew a hint of the truth, but even with her, Red had treated it as a joke and they teased each other about the hot Viking ghost. Red's heart went out to this woman who had lost such a beautiful young son. *And what about Erik's father?* Red hadn't heard anyone say whether he was still alive. He obviously didn't live with Erik's mom or he'd be with her this evening. Red frowned at the sadness of that family. But Minah didn't appear sad. She seemed very serene and almost joyful. How could she be?

Red's chance to speak with her came as the main part of the meal drew to a close and Red's mom suggested that everyone withdraw to the library, which functioned this evening as a cozy sitting room. Her dad's efforts at fire building had created a fire so hot Red was a little concerned the old chimney might melt. Red noticed the guests choosing the seats farthest away from the fireplace. Even though this room was massive by Colonial standards, it was still relatively small and cozy. It reminded Red of a hobbit hole, with its short doors but floor–to–ceiling, dark bookcases. These were replete with grand volumes of every sort. Red was sure this had been Uncle Alistair's favorite room—the old wizard certainly would have felt right at home here. As they all sat down, Red maneuvered herself near Minah and motioned for Tatyana to join her in a nearby seat.

Eventually, Red caught a moment when the other guests were involved in lively conversations all around and Tatyana was attentively listening to one of her dad's tall tales from a backpacking trip. She pulled the photo of Eric and Roy from her pocket, where it had been protected by a leather photo wallet. She held it in her upturned palm and, reaching it toward Minah, awkwardly stammered, "Ms. Wolfeningen, I found this on Uncle Alistair's bulletin board upstairs. Is this your son, the one with the crow T-shirt?"

Minah reached for the photo appreciatively and held it delicately. She brought it close to her eyes and smiled. "Yes, that's Erik. With his friend Roy. They studied together, both your uncle's graduate students." She smiled warmly. "That crow T-shirt. How like Erik." She clutched her hand to her bosom poignantly.

"Was he really into birding, then?" Red felt like she was walking a tightrope. Minah seemed to be enjoying the conversation, reminiscing pleasantly, and Red wanted to keep it that way. Any hint she was probing would likely put the woman off.

"Well, yes and no. He was a member of the Audubon Society and he and some friends organized an effort to save the crows. Erik and his friends worked with the city Planning Commission to salvage as much of their roosting areas as possible."

"That is so cool," Red said. "Mom and I were just at an Audubon Society meeting last weekend and heard something about that. Tatyana and I were thinking of starting a Save-the-Crows club at Churchill." She glanced sideways at Tatyana to make sure she was in agreement, but Tatyana was still listening to her dad's story.

"I don't know much about the project first hand, but it certainly seems like a worthwhile effort. Crows are such intelligent creatures. I could probably find some names and email addresses of contacts involved in this effort if you like," Erik's mom offered helpfully.

"Was Roy also involved in the crow project?" Red hoped this was still an okay question. It seemed reasonable, since he was pictured on the photo Minah still held in her hand.

Minah's face darkened perceptibly. "How do you know Roy?" she asked with some alarm, apparently forgetting that she had just identified him in the photo.

"We talked about him at Ms. Catsworthy's tea," Red responded timidly, trying to remember if he had been mentioned.

Minah relaxed. "Oh, that's right."

Red made a sudden decision to confide in Minah, afraid that otherwise the subject would be dropped. She glanced to each side to see if anyone else was listening. Thankfully, Annie had pulled up a chair beside Tatyana and the two were doing something with an iPod, sharing a set of earbuds, each with one in an ear. "Roy, well ... he kind of hangs around."

Minah's sharp, dark eyes immediately bore into Red's face, searchingly. "Red, this is important," she said with urgency. "What exactly has he been doing?"

"Nothing really threatening," she said quickly, swallowing hard, her mouth suddenly dry as she realized maybe she hadn't been imagining his rudeness. Minah certainly appeared concerned. "It's just that I see him around every time there's anything going on. Like, I saw him at the bus stop one day and I asked him what he was doing and he said he was visiting someone up the street, but that didn't seem to be true. And he drives by sometimes when we're walking home from school, and, oh yeah, he showed up at the football game and tried to talk to me. He—he said something about going out on a date." Red made a face of disgust.

Minah gasped. "Red, I want you to listen to me. You need to stay away from that boy. He's not right. I mean ... can we go somewhere more private to talk?"

"Of course." Red glanced around. Tatyana still occupied, check; no one else was looking in their direction. She said loud enough for anyone within earshot to hear, not that it mattered in the din of multiple conversations, "Come and I'll show you."

Minah stood to follow. Red led the way across the room. Just as they were almost safely away from the others, Ms. Catsworthy, seated in one of Uncle Alistair's leather wingback chairs near the door, looked up hopefully from a discussion with Tatyana's dad on football. Not wanting to appear rude but not wanting to invite her along, Red racked her brain for an excuse as to why the two were taking a stroll. Minah saved the day by placing her hand on Ms. Catsworthy's forearm as they walked by her chair and whispering something to her. The only word she could make out sounded like "mole." Ms. Catsworthy immediately nodded her approval and turned back to bravely rejoin the sports discussion.

"What did you tell Ms. Catsworthy?" Red asked as soon as they were out of earshot.

Minah tittered lightly. Red felt warmed by her good nature, especially in light of the immediacy of the subject they were to discuss. "I told her you had a mole you wanted me to see. I hope you don't mind. I'm a pediatrician." She had a mischievous sparkle in her eye.

Red reddened with embarrassment, then quickly saw the humor in the situation and laughed. "Actually, that's pretty brilliant. So I guess we should take our stroll upstairs to my room rather than outside."

"Yes, that would make more sense. It's a bit nippy outside." Minah took Red's arm and the two quickly slipped upstairs to Red's room.

Not wanting to waste any precious time alone, Red immediately turned to Minah. "So Roy is mentally ill?" Red felt sick remembering the morning she had thought he was in her house.

"Yes, Red, or ... worse. I know this sounds strange in today's world, and especially coming from a medical doctor, but—how to say this ... Erik thought he was, well ... *possessed.* You know ... demonic possession."

Red gasped. "What?"

"Red, you have to be very careful with whom you discuss this. And more importantly, you need to stay clear of Roy. I love his mom. We've been friends for years. My Erik played with Roy throughout his childhood—well, when we were in town. We lived abroad some years. My husband was with the State Department and worked overseas during some tours of duty. Roy was a good kid, a couple of years older than Erik, but they knew each other through Scouts and living in the same neighborhood."

She sat down on the chair as Red sat opposite her on the bed, both women leaning toward each other in urgent attentiveness.

Minah continued, "When Erik was finishing his bachelor's degree at Georgetown, he was applying to graduate programs and ran into Roy on campus. The two re-kindled their friendship. Roy introduced Erik to your uncle and the rest was history. Erik was so excited about a project Professor Hamilton had underway, something about some ancient relics from the Vatican—Erik didn't tell me much in the way of particulars. I guess it was top secret. I used to laugh about his attitude toward the project, but then after he disappeared …" Erik's mom stopped momentarily to collect herself and stifle a tear. "Well, I probably should've taken that aspect more seriously."

Minah inhaled deeply and then continued, "So, getting back to Roy. Just about a month before their disappearance, Roy returned from a summer program in Italy. I don't know all the details—I only saw Erik once between Roy's return and Erik's disappearance. But Erik came for dinner one Sunday, August 26, the last time I saw him." She paused a moment, looking upward dreamily before collecting herself again and continuing. "He told me he had made a breakthrough on the relics, though he didn't give any details. He was very excited."

She smiled with the memory of parental pride, but her face darkened once more. "He also confided that he was worried about Roy. Roy had returned from Italy changed. His good-natured personality had been replaced by a sharp, business-like one, and he had become … well, cruel, I guess is one way to describe it, though I don't think those were Erik's words." She thought a moment and then shook her head. "Kind of … evil. Cold. Erik said Roy had become 'cold and vacant.' He said he was convinced Roy had become demon-possessed during his time away. This was amazing coming from Erik, because I'd begun to think he was slipping into atheism before that. Demon possession was definitely not something I'd have expected him to suggest."

"Possessed?" Red was trying to grasp the concept. She had seen the Hollywood version of demon possession and read a miniscule amount about it, but really didn't know if she believed it ever really happened, at least not in the modern world.

"I'm so sorry to have to tell this to you. And I should talk to your parents about Roy—it sounds almost like he's stalking you." She placed her hand comfortingly onto Red's. Red felt warmed by this woman who had lost her son, and apparently her husband, but at the same time, was a little alarmed at the thought of bringing her parents into it.

"Dr. Wolfeningen, please don't worry. It doesn't frighten me." *Well, it's only a tiny lie.* "I'm very strong. I have a black belt—well, a junior black belt—in tae kwon do. I like to think that I'm a strong woman. And, really, please don't tell my parents. He hasn't done anything and I don't want to worry them."

Minah smiled with her eyes at Red. "I'm sure you're a very strong young woman. Tell you what—I'll see what I can learn from Roy's mom about his current state. In the meantime, you have to promise me you'll use extreme caution and tell me or another adult if anything happens. Promise?"

"Promise."

Red was relieved when Minah continued, "Where do you study tae kwon do?"

"In Potomac Village, with Master Shah."

"Ah, yes, Master Shah. He's wonderful. My Erik also studied under him during the years we lived here."

"Oh, wow." Red's fantasy world just got a major perk. She'd find a way to bring up the name to Master Shah and see if she'd learn anything about Erik. She refused to think he was dead, and if not, she would find him. She made this vow to herself. She'd help this kind lady find her son even if he was dead. One way or the other, she'd get to the bottom of this mystery.

"Re-ed." It was Annie calling to her and it sounded like she was coming up the stairs.

"Oh, shoot, it's Annie," Red said urgently. Knowing they were about to lose their privacy, she quickly asked. "Do you think Roy had something to do with the … disappearances?"

Minah's face was deadly urgent. "Yes. I do. I can't prove it and I don't know what happened, but that boy knows something."

A knock sounded at Red's bedroom door and the conversation was over.

"Call me." Minah pulled a business card from her purse and placed it into Red's hand, squeezing it urgently.

***

The next morning, Red slept in until ten o'clock. She yawned and stretched, having passed the night in dreamless sleep for a change. Somehow, even with the bittersweet discussion with Erik's mom and her warnings about Roy, it had felt very good to be able to share some of her inordinate love for this missing beautiful young man—her Viking. The result was that she felt peaceful, as though simply sharing the burden had eased the solitude and loneliness she felt. *It must be that way for his mom, too,* she thought. She felt a sudden urge to talk to her again. She would go downstairs and make sure she'd have time for an extended conversation before calling—she didn't want her mom walking into her room while she was talking with her—and she knew this was a very real possibility because the Greene women were very casual with each other, walking in on each other without a thought during even the most private moments.

She wasn't worried about Annie walking in on this anticipated conversation. Last night when Annie and Tatyana had barged in to see what was up, Red had come clean with them after Minah rejoined the adults downstairs—about Roy, and about her love for Erik. Both girls had told her in no uncertain terms that she was insane for loving a dead guy and that they would taunt her unmercifully if she kept it up. But they also agreed to stick by her and support her right to love whomever she chose, and to cover for her as needed. Red felt lucky to have loyal friends. They had also been on board with thinking Roy was a danger they needed to watch. Especially Annie, after the football game stalking, but Tatyana, too, revealed she'd noticed more of his drive-bys, a thought that made Red's blood run cold.

Red, still barefoot, slipped on a pair of comfortable grey sweats along with her oversized T-shirt. She headed downstairs to the kitchen to check the occupancy of the house. Annie was watching television and didn't look up when Red entered, but still answered her questions grudgingly. Their dad had gone to work as usual, but their mom had taken the day off and gone over to Ms. Catsworthy's—Annie didn't know why or when she'd return. Red decided to lock herself in the upstairs bathroom to make the call.

She managed to sit comfortably on the cool, tiled floor, leaning her back against the cabinet, and used her cell phone to dial the number. She was delighted when Minah answered right away and seemed very pleased that she had called. Red learned that Roy's mom was at her wit's end from worrying about her son. Minah was keeping Ms. Oglethorp's little dog for a while, because she had, on multiple occasions, witnessed Roy being cruel to the little thing, jabbing it with sharp objects and slapping its face to elicit a snarling response. She had been afraid Roy would ruin its training and disposition if this continued and it did no good to take him to task on the matter. He just laughed and claimed the dog was lazy and need to be razzed a bit. "He was such an animal lover as a boy, but now seems like such a cruel, cold-hearted person," Minah said. Other animals seemed to sense this, she said, and avoided him. He had been a bird lover but now only said derogatory things about birds to the effect that he wished they were all dead. He had stormed at his mom that birds were pathetic things, so cheerful despite being perpetually on the brink of starvation that it vexed him to see them enjoy life. "Even his own mother is afraid of him," Minah confessed.

This made Red's heart race. After having met Roy's kindly mother, she had questioned her own prejudice against him and felt she must have exaggerated his ill manners. But this confirmed her worst fears. When she said goodbye a half-hour later, she felt the need to do something. She dared not go to the police—they had investigated the disappearances already. What more could she tell them except that Roy was acting very strange and was possibly possessed? *That'd go over well.* She snorted sardonically to herself.

There was only one course of action. She'd need to solve this mystery herself and put to rest one way or the other what actually had happened to Erik and Uncle Alistair. And somehow, she'd need to figure out what to do about Roy and how to protect his mom and others from his insanity, or worse—his possession.

An opportunity to learn more about Erik and Roy presented itself when Red checked her email that afternoon. She had a note from Rachel, the girl whom she'd met while bird watching, saying she'd love to take Red up on her offer of allowing the Save-the-Crows group to meet at the mansion. Their regular meetings were held the last Friday of each month from six to eight, and they usually ordered pizza, she said. They'd love to meet at the mansion the following Friday if it happened to work out, but could accommodate pretty much any time that was convenient for the family.

Red realized she had mixed feelings about this. She was thrilled to associate with college-aged kids, especially very likeable ones like Rachel and Daniel. On the other hand, the shock of hearing the term "girlfriend" associated with Erik hadn't fully worn off and she'd probably have conveniently forgotten about the agreement to have the crow meeting at the mansion had Rachel let it drop. But, since that wasn't the case, she was sure her mom would be thrilled about the environmental aspect and her dad about the socialization aspect—he seemed to think his daughters should have friends around at all times. She worked herself up into quite an excited state with the opportunity to learn more about Erik and to be around people who knew him. It'd be nice to hear of Uncle Alistair in his professor role, as well, she thought. She cleared it with her mom and emailed back that the next Friday would work well. She'd make sure to help with the set up, but also tried to calm her nervousness by reminding herself that she wouldn't be in charge of the meeting but a mere bystander. She longed to find out more about Erik and felt she needed to learn more about Roy so she could help protect those she loved from the creep.

On Sunday evening, Red received the official email invitation and agenda for the upcoming meeting from Rachel, who identified herself as the club president—okay, that made sense. In bold green letters, the change in location was announced and Red saw her address printed along with a small map showing the location. Red noted that the club would be discussing plans for an upcoming joint meeting with members of the Maryland Ornithological Society and the

National Wildlife Federation about the possibility of a drive to encourage Rockville and Potomac residents to turn their backyards into wildlife habitats, with special emphasis on the needs of crows. She noted that someone named Jennifer was scheduled to bring the snacks, so Red wouldn't have to worry about doing that.

She scanned the recipient list in an attempt to see how many chairs would be needed and let out a gasp. Among the addresses as plain as day was royoglethorp@gmail.com. *Oh, my gosh. I should have known—why didn't I think of that? Stupid, stupid, stupid.*

Of course he'd be on the club email list. Hadn't she even heard the three discussing the fact that they hadn't seen him in a month or so? Now he'd know she lived here, if he didn't already.

Red thought about cancelling, but there was no graceful way to bow out. Maybe there would be a huge snowstorm and the meeting would have to be postponed, she thought hopefully.

She thought about the situation. Roy probably didn't know she and Annie were sisters, so she'd at least warn Annie not to be around the night of the meeting. Maybe he wouldn't come. Maybe he wouldn't notice the address was his old professor's house. *Yeah, right.*

She shuddered upon realizing the biggest creep she had ever encountered would be in her house in less than a week. She tried to reassure herself that if he came, it might actually be good to confront Roy while there were others around. She could watch him interact with others on her own turf.

She found Annie in her room, finishing some last-minute homework, and told her about the new development. Annie chastised her for worrying too much and said she'd go home with a friend that night or stay in her room or something. She admitted he was creepy but thought he probably wouldn't come. "People sign up for all kinds of clubs and just delete the emails," she suggested. Red wasn't quite so nonchalant about it and suspected Annie was more worried than she admitted.

Red slept fitfully that night. She dreamed that Roy suddenly appeared at the foot of her bed. *She couldn't see his eyes in the darkness but he seemed to be creeping toward her silently, his hands outstretched like claws. She screamed and leapt out of bed, assuming a defensive stance. All of a sudden Roy was tackled from the side by another man. Two men in her room? She screamed a bloodcurdling scream again. A brief scuffle ensued, but Roy disappeared out the door and the other figure stood up slowly from the spot where the scuffle had occurred. As the figure turned to face her, blazing black eyes looked at her with concern. "Sonia, it's me. It's me. Shhhhhh," he whispered, slowly moving toward her with his arms outstretched as if to comfort her, but her brain was muddled—she couldn't tell whether he was good or evil. She knew she wanted to trust him, to run into his arms. "It's okay, baby. Shhhhhh. It's me ..."*

"Red, it's me. It's me." Red heard a familiar voice and realized her mom was standing beside her bed, shaking her shoulder. "Sweetie, it was just a dream. Shhhhhhh ... you okay?"

"What—" Red shook herself awake. "Thanks, Mom. I'm okay now. Just a ... dream." Red tried to smile to assure her mom she was fine now.

Red looked at the neon numbers on her clock-radio. Five a.m. She lay on her back for a few minutes, trying to make sense of her dream, still feeling the adrenaline surge. He had called her *baby*. Oh, what was she doing? Falling in love with a ghost? A longing in her ached to know that he was real and not evil. In a rare moment, she prayed, begging, with tears spilling now from the sides of both eyes onto her pillow behind her head. *Please, please let him be okay ...*

The whole week was rainy and bleak. Red's sense of foreboding about Friday night grew, but she knew if she cancelled the event, she'd probably never have occasion to talk to Rachel, Daniel, or Xenia again. Some door would close and her Viking ghost would dissolve into the ether. She might never know what happened to him and Uncle Alistair. She had to try.

Her warrior instincts came to her rescue, building a fierce determination by Friday to stick with the plan and to find out all she could about Erik, his friends, and, yes, even his girlfriend and creepy Roy.

Jennifer, the girl in charge of the snacks, emailed her on Thursday, asking if it was okay to bring alcohol. She related that the group usually had beer and snacks at their meetings, but since this was happening at Red's family home, rather than a college-student apartment, she thought she should clear it. Red responded that she was sure it would be okay. After all, her dad had wine with his dinner every night. They had never had anything like a keg party but there were drinks served at most social events at her house. Her parents even allowed Annie and herself to have a glass of champagne on New Year's Eve and other such occasions. Still, she quickly asked her dad, who responded just as she had guessed—no problem. In her email exchanges with Jennifer, she learned that in prior years, when Uncle Alistair was here, the group had also been allowed to use the hot tub for some after-meeting relaxation. *This must be a fun group,* thought Red. She had also asked about that and her parents said they saw no problem as long as nothing lewd occurred. Red assured them this wasn't a wild group. The group would have their meeting in the dining room. Red would make sure a nice fire blazed, or, better yet, hint to her dad that one would be needed and allow his inner pyromaniac to play. They'd bring their own refreshments and would be very happy if any or all of the family members joined the meeting, enjoyed the snacks, and joined them in the hot tub afterward. Red was sure she and her mom would be involved; as planned, Annie would stay away, but her dad could go either way.

The next day, as Red walked home from school, she waved goodbye to her friends and continued on alone. She had invited Tatyana, Uma, and Gabriella but all three had previous commitments, and Annie had gone home with a new friend from school.

She sighed and looked to the sky for comfort as she walked alone. The rain had ended yesterday and only a few puffy clouds remained, though some still held grey undersides. *Guess it doesn't matter if it rains tonight since the meeting will be indoors. And the hot tub will feel great with cold drops of rain stinging the shoulders*, she thought. She was glad her dad had already serviced the hot tub in preparation for the traditional hot-tub-snow-roll that had always occurred at Uncle Alistair's at the first snow and at Christmas, with or without snow. Red suddenly felt nostalgic and smiled at the likeness between Uncle Alistair and her father. They were both very creative and fun-loving individuals. Engrossed in her musings, it almost startled her to hear a crow caw from a tree nearby and as she came to her house, she noted that the trees in front of the house were full of crows. She looked up at the sky and said a silent *thank you*. She didn't think this was a coincidence—the crows felt like guardians. Her life had taken on a surreal quality since moving here—actually, since she saw the Viking ghost.

The first to arrive were Rachel and Daniel, and then a young woman who turned out to be Jennifer, who had carpooled with Xenia. These four arrived a few minutes before six to help with any last-minute set up and seemed very appreciative that Red had all in order. They arranged snacks on the table, placed two six-packs of bottled beer in the refrigerator, and set a pot of mulled cider on the stove in the kitchen. The aroma rapidly filled the downstairs rooms and made the gathering seem holiday-ish. Jennifer also carried in a hefty platter of homemade gingerbread cookies, which added to this ambiance. Red regretted briefly that she hadn't thought to decorate the room with pine ropes and holly. Her family would likely put up their Christmas tree and decorations very soon—probably next weekend, or even later this weekend. They hadn't yet talked about it. It would have been nice to have thought of it, but the group seemed very appreciative of the efforts that had been made and made rumblings of wanting to get the meeting done so they could enjoy the hot tub.

Ten people showed up, but no Roy; Red realized she'd built up her battle-readiness to the point that she almost felt disappointed. Her mom and dad joined the group, her mom serving as the greeter and ushering people into the dining room. Her dad began to futz with the fire again. Red helped take coats and couldn't help but smile as she heard a couple of comments about the crows in the trees. "I knew we were at the right address by all the crow-greeters," Daniel joked. Red agreed; that aspect truly was surreal.

Red had previously brought up a few wooden folding chairs from the basement to supplement the dozen nice chairs around Uncle Alistair's dining room table, but decided to go down and bring up a few more just in case. She carried two folded chairs in each hand up the stairs, showing off how strong she was. She silently chastised herself, realizing it might not be cool to be tomboyish to a college-aged crowd. As she entered the dining room, she almost dropped the chairs. There was Roy.

Their eyes met and he winked. *The nerve.* Red flushed hotly as Roy regarded her smugly. He was seated next to Xenia and she had her hand on his arm, talking to him and laughing, but he was ignoring her and watching Red.

Red positioned the chairs around the periphery of the room, behind those at the table, taking care to place one behind Roy, where she quickly sat down. This would give him a taste of his own medicine. She'd watch him for a change. She noted that Xenia jumped up from the table and fetched a beer for him. *Figures he'd want to be served. I'd make him get his own damn beer.* Red was surprised at the warmth with which he was treated by Xenia. It made her a bit sick. *Had she fallen into his clutches as a rebound when Erik disappeared? Had Roy taken advantage of her vulnerability?* Red was a little bit hurt for Erik *in abstentia*—shouldn't his maybe girlfriend have been more faithful than that? She had liked Xenia, despite her jealousy the day of the hawk watch, but now, she wasn't sure. She knew if she had an awesome boyfriend like Erik and he disappeared, it would take longer than a year for her to forget him. Like a lifetime. She sighed.

As Xenia returned with a beer for each of them, Roy pushed back her chair without rising. *Forget standing and doing it properly,* Red thought wryly. As if he read her thoughts, he glanced back to Red with a smirk and a snicker and then his eyes fell unashamedly onto Xenia's backside as she positioned herself to be seated. Then he looked back to Red with another wink and chuckle. *What is that creep trying to convey, that this is his woman? That he can get one woman and therefore I should be interested?* Was this a slam on Erik? The whole thing made her sick. She tried to ignore him and listen to the meeting.

Rachel was leading a lively discussion. There seemed to be a lot of interest in this project. Evidently, the National Wildlife Federation had a program already in place for declaring backyards as wildlife habitat. The homeowner got a little sign to display out front and the hope was that when others saw it, the popularity would catch on. It didn't require a great deal, but it did require drastic limits on the use of pesticides. The homeowner needed to provide food of fruits, nuts, or even flowers for pollinators, as water. The water requirement was what limited most ple, a young man was saying; she recognized him from the hawk watch. Unlike this place, which backed up to the canal, most people needed to actually build a lily pond or keep a birdbath filled with water. If a container such as a birdbath was used, there was an added complication of needing to do something to keep mosquitoes from breeding in it. This could be accomplished by emptying and refilling twice a week or so, depending on the species of mosquito. He said he'd do some research and get back to the group during the next meeting. Rachel jotted this down.

Red felt her head might spin with all this lively exchange but also had to admit she'd learned a thing or two from the meeting and was sure her mom was fired up to get their yard inspected right away to see if they could qualify. And this yard thing did seem like a win-win situation. Why would anyone doggedly keep using pesticides in their backyard? The front yard she could understand a little better, since it was visible from the road.

Red's mom took over the hostess duty now that the meeting was breaking up and announced where people might change into their swimsuits. Red thought she detected a special emphasis on this—her mom's way of saying that *yes, there must be swimsuits worn.* Red was relieved at this—she had no desire to see any rowdy play from Xenia and Roy. About half the people said their goodbyes at this point and thanked either Rachel or her mom or both. Red's dad, already in his swim trunks, his hairy chest proudly displayed, was busy stoking the fire, which was now an inferno for guests to use for a quick warm-up before and after the tub.

Red mentally weighed the pros and cons of joining the group in the tub. If Roy went in, it would be a little too close for comfort to join them. Still, she'd play it by ear and do what was needed to watch him. Her chief objective had been, and still was, to learn about Erik, but she might be able to do some of both if she were clever. Two of the spare bedrooms upstairs were in service as changing rooms, as well as the downstairs powder room. She tried to blend into the woodwork and watch, feigning busyness by picking up empty bottles for the recycle bin. She noted that Roy and Daniel went upstairs together, as well as Xenia and Rachel, along with a handful of other people. Good, he was with Daniel. She instinctively trusted Daniel—he and Rachel had seemed very kind and normal the day of the hawk watch. She followed them up the stairs, keeping her distance, and went into her own room. She quickly slipped on a one-piece suit and puffy bathrobe. She opened her door slightly and watched until everyone had gone downstairs. Then, she decided she could best spy from her window since it overlooked the deck. She turned all lights off in her room in hopes that no one would see her. She eased up her window just an inch to hear. A cold blast of air felt refreshing and she could clearly hear the group teasing and giggling on the deck. Several *ooh*'s and *ahh*'s expressed satisfaction with the water temperature. Overall, this seemed like a very nice group of people—considerate, fun-loving, and dedicated to a better world. She liked them very much—all except Roy.

Red remained still at one side of the window, the curtain slightly pushed aside and her eye positioned in a way that she was sure no one could see her, and watched. Xenia and Roy emerged from the house together. They seemed to be catching up, as if they hadn't seen each other in a while. Though Red couldn't hear every word, she got the impression that Roy was being cold and aloof and Xenia encouraging, but obviously a bit hurt by his distant behavior. He was complaining about his workload, perhaps as an explanation for neglecting her.

Then, as Xenia and Roy approached the tub, Red was shocked to watch an owl silently breeze in and attack Roy's head, its great white wings beating in the dim light.

Several gasped from the hot tub and one girl screamed. "Get off, you bloody mother—" Roy shouted. The bird was gone before his upswept arm could contact it.

Xenia quickly helped Roy stand under the light fixture and surveyed his face and head, looking for damage, and proclaimed that his eyes were unscathed, to the general relief of the group. Then she and Roy went back inside.

Red quickly went downstairs and entered the kitchen, where her mom was dabbing some antiseptic on a cut on the back of Roy's head and apologizing profusely. Roy was obviously angry and she heard him mutter something under his breath. Xenia stood by, anxiously wringing her hands.

Then Roy barked at Xenia, "You coming with me?"

Xenia obviously didn't know how to reply, and stammered that no, she'd brought her own car.

Roy stomped up the stairs to retrieve his clothes.

Red followed to make sure he wasn't left unwatched while in their house. His anger riled, he didn't look back, but went directly into the spare room where he had dressed and slammed the door.

Not more than a minute later, he emerged fully dressed, probably having just pulled his jeans and shirt over his trunks. He left in a huff without a thank you, goodbye, or even a glance toward Xenia, who stood dumbfounded, her eyes tearing up momentarily before she composed herself and re-joined her friends in the tub.

Red heard a car fire up and screech away. Buddy began to bark from her parents' bedroom, where he had been contained during the gathering so that his poor manners and persistent barking wouldn't annoy the guests.

Red decided to join the remaining group in the hot tub to see if she could glean any new information. She heard voices in the dining room, and upon entering, was disappointed to see the party was breaking up. Everyone was out of the hot tub and most had gone upstairs to change. Rachel, Daniel, and a woman she didn't know were still discussing the likely species of owl that had attacked Roy. As Red approached, Rachel turned to her and thanked her profusely for the use of the mansion and hot tub.

"You're more than welcome. I just feel really bad about that owl attack. I don't know what to make of it." Red hoped for some insight.

Rachel was profuse in her reassurance that the owl incident was actually a boon for birders and would be the talk of the club for some time to come, definitely making their newsletter. Red was disappointed that Rachel hadn't offered any useful information or made the obvious connection that birds didn't like Roy.

Rachel expressed regret that she had to be getting on and asked Red to please let her know anytime they wanted to have the meeting here and that they'd love to come again. Red expressed an enthusiastic hope that they'd come again very soon, but didn't commit to a date. She needed to think about the fact that Roy was part of the group, and should probably clear it with her folks, though she didn't say all that.

Before Red went to bed that night, she slipped outside and placed some bits of meat on the deck railing—a reward for the owl for attacking Roy—along with a few cranberries just in case the crows had anything to do with urging the owl onward.

As she lay in bed, she decided she learned at least two things tonight. First, Xenia seemed to have displaced her affection for Erik onto Roy, who was undeserving and evidently only interested inasmuch as he could play a cruel game with her. If Erik were around, he'd probably be heartbroken over this. And, second, birds didn't like Roy. The windshield droppings, the crow attack on Halloween … Red was sure now that Roy had been the one in the Darth Vadar costume, the one the birds had attacked. For that matter, Buddy didn't like him, either. What was that all about? She suspected Erik's mom was right about the demonic possession. But why was he interested in birding, with all that bad karma? *Is it a cover? Is he trying to get in with the group for some sinister purpose? And how can a woman like Xenia fall for a creep like that?*

PART TWO

Altered State

Quote from <u>Perelandra</u>: The distinction between natural and supernatural, in fact, broke down; and when it had done so, one realised how great a comfort it had been— how it had eased the burden of intolerable strangeness which this universe imposes on us by dividing it into two halves and encouraging the mind never to think of both in the same context. What price we may have paid for this comfort in the way of false security and accepted confusion of the thought is another matter.[5]

CHAPTER 10

An Unexpected Ally

The next morning, Red thought of calling Minah to tell her about Roy coming to the meeting, but decided the woman had enough to worry about without adding to her burdens. Wali and Quinn were competing in a tae kwon do tournament that morning and she realized she'd waited too late to get a ride to go see it. She and Quinn competed occasionally, but not nearly as much as Wali—he was a real competitor and loved for her to come and cheer him on. But Quinn and Wali could cheer each other on. *That's probably better, anyway*, she thought. That brought a smile, and she thought about how excited Quinn had been when he'd asked her to the movie. Maybe Red's absence would help fan the spark.

As she descended the stairs, she heard Christmas music coming from the ballroom. Now she had a better idea of how her day would go. It had totally slipped her mind that this was the second Saturday after Thanksgiving. Mom would no doubt be itching to drive out to one of the orchards and cut a Christmas tree. This was one of Red's favorite things to do, and they usually took Buddy with them, but she didn't think the house should be left alone without Buddy there to bark in case Roy came again.

She decided to stay back under the guise of offering to dig out the decorations from the basement and maybe even start putting up some outdoor lights. Her mom and dad seemed pleased at her maturity and independence. Annie was definitely annoyed that she wouldn't be coming along. Red decided she'd tell her the real reason behind her offer at the next opportunity. But in the end, the others left in her dad's Volvo wagon and Red was left alone.

Red immediately put the chain on the front door and then decided to call Tatyana, Uma, and Gabriella to see if anyone wanted to join her in the decorating. Tatyana didn't pick up her cell, so she left a message. Gabriella was going shopping with her mom for Hanukkah, which started next weekend, and Uma had to babysit her little brother but could come over later in the afternoon. *I'll have to hold down the fort alone this morning.*

Without even planning to do it, she did a few warm-up exercises and started rehearsing her forms in the huge ballroom. She felt like a warrior readying for battle. She had an adequate view of the driveway through the floor-to-ceiling windows and she kept an eye on it as she practiced her forms, blocking, thrusting, and kicking in various graceful ways— abduction, adduction, front-kicks, back-kicks, flying side-kicks.

She felt magnificent, feeling a fierce determination she had never before possessed.

About half an hour into her practice, with sweat spots under her arms and on the back of her T-shirt, her foe arrived. Red wasn't surprised. She had to give him some credit this time—he didn't sneak in. She saw the glint of a car in the driveway and then heard a knock at the front door. She could've left the chain on the door and spoken to him through it but she didn't want to cower. Her inner-warrior had been awakened.

She went to the door and calmly opened it. No mincing words. "What do you want, Roy?" she said coldly and without any softening.

"Well, Miss Greene, it appears that I'm interrupting something." He eyed her sweat-stained T-shirt and boldly looked at her breasts, which were still heaving up and down from the exercise. He rudely pushed himself past Red into the house. "Nonetheless, I seem to have left a favorite windbreaker here last night after your watch-bird attacked me. By the way, I've alerted Animal Control and demanded they get rid of the rabid beast."

Red wheeled around but left the door partially ajar. She was a warrior but she wasn't stupid. He could have a weapon, or for all she knew, the demon-possessed might have supernatural strength. She braced in a preparatory stance. "Get out. I'll mail your stupid windbreaker."

"No, I need it tonight. I'm taking Xenia out to get a little action for myself. One must dress nicely to impress the babes." He snickered. "Stupid bitch thinks she loves me. Well, no matter. A man has his needs and she'll do in a pinch. Not like fresh meat, though. What I really like are virgins." He slowly walked toward Red. "Ah, come on, I know you want it."

"Yeah, well, come and get it, creep."

Roy tried to snatch her wrist, which she easily deflected, though she noted that bone-to-bone combat smarted. She had never before sparred without padding.

Roy rubbed his forearm. "You little—" He lunged for her with all his weight.

No problem, Red had this. She easily twisted away from his grasp and captured him from behind in a chokehold.

Roy began yelling profanity. Behind him, Red saw two movements from different directions. To the right, both Midnight and Roxy sprang to positions in front of Roy's feet, growling menacing, guttural growls Red had never heard before. He tried kicking them but they sprang back out of his reach, keeping their positions in front of him, ready to pounce. From the opposite direction, Red saw the door fling wide open and a figure appear in the doorway. For an instant, with sunlight streaming in, she couldn't identify the newcomer. But the voice was unmistakable.

"Roy Oglethorp, you leave this house immediately or I shall call your mother," Ms. Catsworthy demanded with unexpected command and clarity.

Roy went slack in Red's grasp. He almost seemed to become a different person for an instant. His voice was softer, almost pleasant. "Yes, Ms. Catsworthy," he said dutifully. "I'm sorry. We—there was just a … misunderstanding." He flicked a desperate look back toward Red to see if she'd play along.

In response, she dropped her grip, pushing him away from her emphatically. He awkwardly reeled, almost falling.

"No, Roy, I understood quite well what you wanted. Please leave and don't come back to this house. I'll search for your windbreaker and mail it to you if I find it," Red said. "I'm sure Ms. Catsworthy has your mailing address."

"Yes, Roy. I'll assist Miss Greene. Now, don't you have work to do at the university? A paper to write or something?"

Roy stood, brushing himself off, and looked from one to the other. His face had lost the docility of a few moments before and now exuded hatred. He muttered something under his breath, but left. The cats sauntered away as well.

Ms. Catsworthy came quietly forward, closing the door behind her and locking it. "Now, dear, did that rascal harm you?" She approached Red with concern. Red realized she was still positioned in a defensive stance. She took a deep breath and forced her body to relax.

"No, I'm good. I'm glad you came over, though. I think you saved Roy from a serious shredding by my cats." They both glanced in the direction the cats had gone and simultaneously let out a guffaw.

"Very curious," mused Ms. Catsworthy, nodding her head. "Now, I think you need a nice, relaxing bath. I'll stay here to make sure Mr. Oglethorp doesn't return. I'm sure he'll not return today, but just to be on the safe side. You go on upstairs and do something to relax and I'll stay until your family returns. Okay?"

"Oh, thank you so much, Ms. Catsworthy." Red suddenly realized how sweaty she was from the adrenaline. She really could use a bath.

Half an hour later, Red returned with wet hair, clean jeans and T-shirt, to find Ms. Catsworthy seated in one of the comfy wing chairs in the library, reading one of her mother's bird-watching books. Her feet were propped up on an ottoman. She looked like she belonged there. Red guessed this wasn't the first time she'd sat in that chair.

"You look very comfy, Ms. Catsworthy. Thank you very much for staying. I confess I was a bit shaken. Can I get you something? Some tea?"

"Oh, that would be lovely, dear. But I'll come with you to the kitchen. I think we need to have a little talk before the rest of your family returns."

Red nodded, wondering if she was going to get scolded for allowing Roy in the house.

Red put the kettle on and turned to Ms. Catsworthy, who looked at her seriously. "Red, I don't wish to alarm you, but I need to know exactly what Roy said to you and whether he hurt you. His mother is a dear friend of mine and he was poor dear Alistair's student. He was a fine boy at one time, but he has changed. I don't know what happened, but his mother and I are worried sick about him. And I'm not totally convinced that he had nothing to do with the disappearance of Alistair and the other young man," she said.

Red nodded. So while she made the tea, she recounted each incident with Roy.

They carried their tea back into the library, where Red built a fire. She found that she really did like Ms. Catsworthy. The lady was calm, sincere, non-judgmental, and quite knowledgeable. She found herself pouring out all the secrets she had been keeping inside, from seeing the Viking ghost to finding the lab notes.

Ms. Catsworthy took it all in without seeming the least surprised, which puzzled Red. "May I see those lab notes?"

Red retrieved the notebook. Ms. Catsworthy flipped through the pages, nodding. "You know, it might be safer if I keep them. I know Roy has been looking for something here during the past year. Before your family moved in. I'd seen lights flickering in the house late at night on several occasions."

Red instinctively trusted Ms. Catsworthy, but was reluctant to part with the notes. They made her feel connected to Erik, and parting with them made her a little sad. Apparently sensing something close to the truth of this, Ms. Catsworthy said, "The notes will be perfectly safe at my house. I will make sure to give them back to you when this business with Roy blows over."

"Oh, of course." Red saw the logic of this and had to admit to herself that it felt good to have someone else involved. Ms. Catsworthy slipped them into the pocket of her very smart, green tweed jacket. Red couldn't shake the feeling that there was more she should tell Ms. Catsworthy, but for the life of her, she couldn't remember what. "Are you going to tell my parents?"

Surprisingly, Ms. Catsworthy left this up to Red. Red thought about it. The whole situation was a little off-the-beaten-track and parents tended to worry. They might decide that Red had mental problems if she told them she'd seen a Viking ghost. Red decided to table telling them unless a real need-to-know situation occurred. She could handle Roy, and now she had an ally to watch the place lest he break in again. Ms. Catsworthy agreed to suggest to her parents that they change the locks, citing that Alistair had given keys to several students so they could work in the basement and retrieve life vests and oars when they wanted to use the canoes.

Red felt so close to Ms. Catsworthy at this moment that she couldn't resist finally asking why she and Uncle Alistair never got married. Usually so impulsive in her conversations, it felt somehow new to push a question out that hesitated behind her teeth. She sensed there would be a depth to the answer and didn't want to offend her new friend. Softly, she said, "I always knew you and Uncle Alistair had a very high regard for each other, and hope you don't think I'm being nosy in asking this, but why didn't the two of you ever get married? I mean, you just seem so perfect for each other. But, please, you don't have to tell me anything you don't want to. And I'm sorry if I'm being impertinent."

Ms. Catsworthy patted Red's hand in a grandmotherly way, pressed her lips together, and nodded for a moment, seemingly rehearsing her answer in her mind. She finally said simply, "Red, dear, would you like the short answer or the long answer? Oh, never mind. I'll tell you a bit of both. The short answer is that he never asked me. A longer answer is that we met during a time when the whole world had gone crazy and things, well, just didn't get off on the right foot for romance. But you know what? We were always better than lovers. We were friends."

The rest of the family arrived before Red could learn anything more detailed. Red's dad called to Red from the door, asking her to come and help get the Christmas tree off the canoe rack on top of the Volvo.

"Okay, Dad, coming." She turned to Ms. Catsworthy, who sat tranquilly by the fire. "Please won't you stay for a while? We're going to be decorating and it'll be fun."

Red's mom entered at that moment and implored her as well. Ms. Catsworthy seemed unable to find it in herself to decline. Red was glad and went to help fetch the tree, looking forward to a festive afternoon with Christmas music and the aromas of cider, baking cinnamon, and fresh-cut greenery.

For the next two weeks Red couldn't help but bask in the joy of the season. The decorations made the house smell of evergreen boughs. Whatever Ms. Catsworthy had told Roy's mother seemed to work. There was no sign of him in the street or knocking at the door. Red knew she would have to figure out ways to find out more about him, but it was nice to have him at a distance; it felt more like she was in control of the situation. Relaxing from that stress allowed the energy of the season to invigorate Red into action on a couple of fronts. First, there was Christmas shopping to do. But during the time she spent with Ms. Catsworthy, she had learned that the dear lady was, in fact, Jewish. So she suggested to her mom and Annie that they do something to make Hanukkah special for her. They had wholeheartedly agreed and spent a day baking dreidel-shaped cookies decorated with icing and blue sprinkles, then shopped for perfumed soaps and bath oils at the mall in Rockville. For the whole week of Hanukkah, they took a small gift or baked-good to her each evening.

In turn, Ms. Catsworthy had invited them to a small party on the last night of Hanukkah. Red loved the fragrant latkes and applesauce and warm atmosphere. She also noted that the guest list included Minah Wolfeningen and Sally Oglethorp, but no Roy. At one point in the evening, Minah asked Ms. Catsworthy to tell her story of the Holocaust.

Everyone became silent. Red noticed that Ms. Catsworthy assumed a far-away gaze, looking upward, as if trying to connect to a world of yesterday. "I was a baby at the time," Ms. Catsworthy said. "So parts of my story come from what I was told later."

Ms. Catsworthy had lived in an enormous, ornate house, with all the finery life could afford, surrounded by artwork, a grand piano, and lush rugs and tapestries. She had an older sister, Victoria, who had been as beautiful as the doll her parents had given her, with long, golden ringlets and blue, blue eyes. Ms. Catsworthy fetched the doll and passed it around the room. Red felt honored to hold such a well-loved, yet delicate treasure. She felt her eyes swelling with tears and quickly passed it on to Annie. A glance told her that Annie was in the same emotional state.

"Your Uncle Alistair was there," she said. Red felt a shock, and a glance around the table showed her family felt the same surprise. He had been Victoria's playmate, Ms. Catsworthy said. They were the same age. Alistair's father had business dealings with her own father and the children were often together while the fathers worked; both mothers, too, were often present, helping out with record-keeping. Several times a year Alistair usually accompanied his parents to Budapest, where Ms. Catsworty's family lived. "And it was their presence there that saved my life," Ms. Catsworthy said, her voice thick with emotion. Red drank in every syllable.

Red learned that Ms. Catsworthy's family hadn't been classified as Jewish early in the war and had been largely left alone by the Nazis. Her father's original surname was Katz—a very well-respected Jewish name, but since her grandfather had died and her grandmother remarried, her father had taken the surname of his step-father. Then one day, a band of Nazi soldiers burst in and took her family away. Her beautiful sister, too. Ms. Catsworthy, the baby, had been asleep at the time and they didn't know at first that she was there. She had been born at home and was never registered as a citizen. Her sister was six years old and had attended school, so the soldiers knew about her, and had been looking for her sister and parents. Ms. Catsworthy had started to cry while the soldiers were there, but Alistair's mother went to her cradle and retrieved her, pretending she was her own child. She was able to escape with Alistair and his parents to England. There, she was adopted by a nice family, who changed her name to Catsworthy to honor the name Katz while still being different enough that if the Nazis overtook England, she wouldn't be recognized as Jewish.

The family had two other little girls, and she had a normal upbringing with her adoptive sisters, but both were deceased now. She had been raised with the best of everything: servants, tutors, beautiful clothes. Best of all, the family lived near the Hamiltons in London, so she was never far from Alistair. Red could tell as she listened that Ms. Catsworthy was purposefully espousing the bright side of a truly gruesome situation. "Your uncle and I remained the best of friends our whole lives. I felt I owed my life to his mother and father." She remained dry-eyed despite the overwhelming emotion in the room. *Such a gracious lady,* Red thought.

Red wanted to ask the unspoken question, the elephant in the room. *Do you know what happened to your parents and sister?* But she couldn't. She was afraid she knew and didn't want to circumvent the obvious attempt to put a positive spin on the story.

Neither did Red bring up anything further to Minah about Erik that evening. It felt like an evening of bonding, not a night to speak of death. It was about survivors loving each other and loving the ones who hadn't survived. Of connecting. Red could feel love for the beautiful Victoria, who had likely perished in the gas chambers of Auschwitz, and for Uncle Alistair, who might be at the bottom of the river, but whose personality still lingered in the old mansion. And, of course, for Erik, whose vivacity for life called to her from a photo, and from the ether.

CHAPTER 11

Christmas Eve

Christmas Eve came like an unstoppable train. Red wanted to get Annie the perfect gift and feared she had waited too late to order online for delivery through the regular mail—she'd have to pay the extra rush charges. Nonetheless, she was looking forward to the freedom of using her new debit card to order online. Never before had she been able to order without having to ask her mom to type in her credit card number and then repay her by counting up her saved dollar bills and quarters. Without any censorship, she was able to surf the web and find the perfect T-shirt. She laughed aloud at several options—it was great fun picking out the perfect one. Annie was into horror movies, supernatural romances—anything shocking. She chuckled with glee as she clicked on "Purchase Now" for a T-shirt showing Abraham Lincoln as a werewolf. Her parents wouldn't get it but Annie would. She heard Annie chuckle while doing something on her own computer. Red thought she'd likely receive a similar gift.

On Christmas Eve afternoon, Red ambled into the kitchen to find that her dad had put out an array of cheeses, chips, dips, breads, and veggies. She peeked into the oven and found miniature quiches and stuffed mushrooms warming. *Wow.* Her dad had been busy. Then she spied a full trashcan topped by boxes that had contained pre-prepared hors d'oeuvres. Red grinned.

Only a handful of people had been invited, unlike Uncle Alistair's much larger affairs of yesteryear. Red mused that this must be why she had never really gotten to know Ms. Catsworthy. The quiet lady seemed shy around crowds and pretty much had disappeared into the woodwork during the events her uncle hosted. But she'd be joining them tonight, along with one other family, Red's friend Gabriella and her parents, Dr. and Mrs. Epstein. Red's mom and dad had encouraged their daughters to invite their new friends and their families, but all others were already tied up or out of town for the winter break. Dr. Epstein was a researching physician at the National Institute of Health and his wife was a "professional volunteer," as she described herself. They were both originally New Yorkers and were very sociable. Her dad really hit it off with Dr. Epstein and the two agreed to play racquetball together on Wednesday nights after winter break.

Red felt the evening had been mostly pleasant. She, Gabriella, and Annie spent a large portion of it upstairs in Red's room. She'd been a little worried Annie wouldn't have a buddy, but as it turned out, Gabriella and Annie seemed to enjoy each other's company more than Red's. Red felt just a little left out, which was often the case in a group. Her parents had allowed them to have champagne on this special occasion and Red had greedily downed two glasses, obtaining one from each parent separately early in the evening. As they climbed the stairs, she had been loud and exuberant and some of the impulsivity of her ADHD had reared its ugly head—she had slapped Gabriella on the back and received a reprimanding glare. *Whoops.*

The embarrassment affected her and now she felt withdrawn. Now, watching the two giggling over something silly on the computer screen, she sat on the edge of her bed and pulled out the picture of Erik. This always made her feel better. Feeling just a tad sorry for herself, Red let a tear escape. It just missed landing on the photo. She pledged to make copies at the first opportunity. This close call made her realize how fragile the tiny thread was that connected her to her Viking. She only had one photo and a few drawings—well, that and her memory of seeing his ghost and the dreams she often had of him.

Red didn't get to spend much time mulling over Erik, however. "It's hot tub time!" Annie exclaimed. Red suspected Annie had done this on purpose, having sensed Red's dejection. Red would've preferred to stay in her room, but decided to humor Annie.

In the hot tub, it didn't take long for Red to note that Gabriella had apparently also felt the champagne and had become boisterous, making Red realize perhaps she had been too hard on herself. Her mood became light and playful. The adults shortly joined them and Red heard her dad tell Dr. Epstein it was too bad there was no snow because the family tradition was to get overheated and then roll in the snow. As if on cue, humongous flakes began falling, quickly producing a white blanket over the deck, handrails, and hot tub cover. The snow clung beautifully to the tree limbs at the bottom of the yard, so pure and white it seemed to glow.

Red wasn't surprised her dad was the first to do the snow roll, followed by Dr. Epstein, not to be outdone. Then she and Annie and Gabriella, with reckless abandon and steamy skin, made snow angels and frolicked about barefoot in the snow for a few brief minutes before scampering quickly back into the embracing warmth of the bubbling water. Red was delighted to see that even Ms. Catsworthy took a turn. Then Annie did a slide into the snow and they laughed some more.

Just like polar bear cubs. Erik thought, chuckling. He was totally smitten with Red and her family. He had never seen such a free-spirited, fun-loving family as this. He knew Professor Hamilton was fun loving, but a whole family like that? How zany it would be to belong to such a family. He had been such a serious student that he now wondered when he stopped being playful. Erik felt like a poor kid looking in the window of the candy store. All he could do was sigh and watch. Oh, if he could just communicate with her. He might have to take the risk and try to talk to her soon, maybe in a place where he could be sure she'd hear him. Moon wasn't cutting it. He thought of his mom and knew she'd be home now from the party she had attended, all alone. He needed to go see her and try to make her feel better with his positive energy, but he had to admit he was having a difficult time tearing himself away from this happy scene.

Christmas Day was relaxing and low key. Annie seemed to like her T-shirt, but obviously liked the Wii game her parents had given her even more. Red had reluctantly agreed to join Annie in her gaming, at least for part of the day. But Red had her own gift of new art supplies to enjoy. Their parents had also splurged and gotten both girls iPhones. Red needed to spend some time figuring out all the features. But most importantly, everyone seemed happy and content. Even Buddy and the cats got a special treat of giblets from the pasture-raised organic goose her mom prepared.

A new movie version of *Les Misérables* that Red really wanted to see had opened in theaters on Christmas Day, so the day after, Red and Annie called their friends and arranged for their mom to drive them to an afternoon showing. Only Tatyana and a new friend of Annie's named Nyah were available.

It was fun to be on an outing with friends and Red felt like part of a giggling gaggle of girls as she approached the theater. But as Red watched the movie, she realized she couldn't eat her popcorn. There was something about the gut-wrenching hopelessness of the film that got to Red; when Fantine sang "I Dreamed a Dream," her words rang too true to Red, reminding her of her own hopeless dream of Erik. When she listened to the lines, *I dreamed that love would never die,*

I dreamed that God would be forgiving, she began to sob as though her heart would break. Great tears began to stream down her cheeks as she sobbed silently. Tatyana handed her a tissue and used another to blot her own eyes. Many people in the theater were crying, too, apparently touched by the song, but no one as much as Red. As the song ended, she reached into the pocket of her hoodie and touched Erik's picture—her only concrete connection to him. She held it to her bosom and wept anew.

Erik saw her clutch the picture of him to her heart and weep. He was sure it was the picture she had removed from Hamilton's message board. He was distraught as never before. He had scarcely allowed himself to hope that this exquisite girl could love him. But here he was, watching her heart break for him. Him, the total nerd who had never been particularly smooth with women—not like Roy. Roy had tried to teach him how to be more sociable and popular. Erik had been frustrated then, but nothing like now. He had dated, but had always been more interested in his intellectual pursuits. He had never really deeply desired a woman before. He had been attracted to them but had never really connected with a particular woman on such an emotional level. But Red—he loved this woman, this girl so pure and strong. So kind to old Ms. Catsworthy, as well as his own dear mother.

From watching her these many months, he had learned she lacked self-confidence. If she only knew how beautiful she was, inside and out. If she only knew how much he loved her. And to see her so heartbroken over him … "No, my pretty one. No, baby. No." He tried to whisper to her, but he knew his voice could be heard only faintly to those in the normal state, and certainly not over the loud movie. He could only watch her heart-wrenching sobs. If he could only tell her how much he loved her, she would surely feel better.

There *was* one way, he thought. He could mind-meld with her and try to communicate his love. He had never allowed himself to do this with her because he felt like it would be intrusive. And he wasn't completely sure until now that his presence would be welcome. What if he mind-melded with her and discovered she was pining away over someone else? Over that tae kwon do kid, or someone at school? If he ever got back into his normal state, would she forgive him for invading her mind? For possessing her very thoughts? He knew it was inexcusable to meld minds without her consent, but he felt her act of clutching his picture to her heart was a kind of signal that she loved him. He allowed himself a moment to savor the thought. Then, he made his decision—he couldn't bear to see her so heartbroken.

He concentrated hard, preparing his own mind for the meld, then moved silently into position, into the same space she occupied, not even noticing the feel of the back of her seat as he passed through it. He positioned his brain inside her brain while she sat in the theater. He focused on allowing her to feel his love for her through his thoughts of her, her inner-beauty and his wish to hold and comfort her. He savored the picture of himself in her mind and the love she felt for her Viking ghost. *Cute.* He had never thought of himself as a Viking before, though he supposed his dad did have some Viking ancestors. He spent the most blissful half-hour he had ever spent, enjoying her love and communicating his love to her.

As Red emerged from the movie theatre, she felt as though she was walking in a cloud. The other three girls talked excitedly about the movie, but Red was too enraptured to join in. How could she tell anyone about what had happened? She had been totally distraught one minute and enveloped in love the next. She couldn't really explain it, but she seemed to have a confidence that love would find her. Mechanically, she got into her mom's car and tried to make small talk on the way home, but Tatyana nudged her and asked why she was grinning from ear to ear. "I'm just happy," Red said.

At home, Red really wanted to be left alone with her thoughts and was very pleased to find that her dad wasn't home and Annie and her mom were heading out to take Buddy to a boarding kennel, where he'd stay while they went to Colorado for their annual winter-break ski trip.

Once alone, she went onto her computer and began watching videos from the *Tess of the D'Urbervilles* movies. She found several made by fans, set to haunting love songs. One in particular matched her mood, set to a modern song with a waltz beat. She watched it a couple of times and then went to the computer in the library, found the song, and set it on repeat play through the speakers in the ballroom. She thought of the scene where Angel sees Tess and the maidens, all dressed in white, flowers in their hair, dancing in a spring meadow. With tears trickling occasionally from her closed eyes, she danced in that same meadow. Time was non-existent to her. She was totally immersed in the haunting sweetness of young love that could never be. She whirled with the imaginary maidens and with Angel, who had the face of Erik.

Erik stayed with Red on the drive back from the movie to make sure she was okay. He watched as Red whirled in the ballroom. He had to know what she was thinking, and so once again, he mind-melded with her, moving fluidly until he got the picture she was seeing of Tess and Angel in the meadow. Then, he left the mind-meld to take the place of Angel and danced with her, trying to imagine the same meadow he had seen in her mind. He felt they were lovers separated by invisible walls, yet together somehow, tasting the sweetness of love in the spring air when the world was blooming in an ancient cycle of death and renewal. He knew he had to find a way to bridge the gap. He had to find the key to the safe and retrieve the stones. He had to find a way back to her world.

CHAPTER 12

Ski Vacation

Red hurriedly stepped into the gondola. She had both her white fleece hood and black ski coat hood over her head. All that was exposed of her face was a horizontal oval with her sunglasses and nose. She felt like a blind person, feeling for the doors on either side and trying to get out of the way before Annie, who was beside her, got left behind. She felt a light pressure on the small of her back directing her into the seat.

Annie sat facing Red. Red sat beside her mother. The other side was empty, but Red could've sworn she felt the pressure of a thigh pressing against hers. *What the ...* With the tunnel vision of her ski mask, she couldn't see what might be beside her and surreptitiously reached her hand down to check. Nothing.

Red's dad handed her a soft glasses cloth so she could wipe her glasses and see more clearly. After she cleaned her glasses, her dad handed her his pocket camera and asked her to take a photo of him and her mom. She snapped a few quick pictures. While leaning forward, she almost stumbled, and definitely felt a hand steady her. This was just too weird but she guessed she was pretty good with weird. She decided she was going to confront whatever this was.

"Oh, no," Red began. "I forgot my iPod."

"Red, we're up here to enjoy nature's glory and get some exercise. You don't need an iPod," her dad said authoritatively.

"Then what'll I do while waiting for you slowpokes at the bottom of the run? Guess I'll have to strike up a conversation with some random boy. Maybe the one in that gondola up ahead with the skull tattoo and all those facial piercings. He looked pretty hot."

"Red, that's not funny." Her mom glared at her with one eyebrow raised.

Dad sighed, having clearly fallen for her bluff. "Do you have your room key?"

"Of course."

Annie gave her a secret, questioning look, but Red kept a stony face and nonchalantly watched out the window, trying to hide her nervousness. As her family piled out at the top, leaving Red alone in the gondola car to ride back down the mountain, she took a breath to steady her nerves.

"Okay, who or what are you? I know you're here," she said aloud once she was alone. She could hear the tremor in her voice as she made the sign of the cross. Her hair bristled and her heart felt like a frog was leaping in her chest.

"I am not evil," came a whisper. Her heart skipped a beat and a shock raced through her. "It's a very long story," the voice said with a sigh.

"Okay, then please begin," she said. She tried to identify the exact location of the source of the voice. It was coming from the bench directly facing her.

"My name is Erik Wolfeningen."

She gasped. *Erik?* Shakily, she said, "Uncle Alistair's assistant."

"Yes."

"Did you kill him?" She gripped the seat so hard she felt her fingernails making permanent cuts in the plastic. She wondered if she'd survive the fall if she jumped from the gondola right now.

"No, no, no. Please, hear me out. Listen to my whole story before you bolt." They were halfway down now.

"Are you a ghost?"

"No. Well, something like that. Professor Hamilton, your Uncle Alistair, is in a similar boat. He isn't dead, either. At least, I don't think so," he said. "I'll tell you what happened to us, at least some of it, but you have to keep it secret. Our lives, and now yours, may depend on it. Deal?"

"Okay, I guess." Did she have a choice? She *had* to know the truth. And Uncle Alistair wasn't dead! But where was he? She was flooded with emotion and confusion.

As the gondola glided over the platform at the bottom of the run, Red stepped off and others entered. She tried to look nonchalant as she retrieved her skis and poles and found a rack nearby to place her equipment so she didn't have to carry

171

them. "You still here?" she whispered, making sure nobody else was in earshot.

"Yes."

They didn't speak again until Red had entered a secluded wooded area nearby and was definitely out of earshot, though still visible to people walking from the parking lot to the lodge. She fished in her fanny pack and was glad to find she had her iPhone. She took it out and pretended to take pictures of something on one of the trees.

"Erik?" she spoke louder than a whisper this time, but still softly, trying to keep her lips still in case a bystander walked by. Wait, she thought, she'd just pretend she was talking on her iPhone. *That'll work.* She raised it to her ear.

"Okay, Sonia, I need to stress the utmost secrecy. There are forces involved that are not trustworthy and certainly not after your best interest, nor that of your family. I don't want you to know more than is absolutely necessary, but I do need to tell you that both your Uncle Alistair and I are alive, though in a different state of existence. We're trapped in an alternate reality. I know that this sounds like science fiction, and in a way it's exactly like that. But it's also real, and we need your help."

Red liked the idea of helping her Viking ghost; this certainly was a twist, though, him being something other than a ghost. "Okay, I'm game. What do you need?"

"There is a key that is essential to our transformation back to our normal states. I think it may be somewhere in Professor Hamilton's—your—house. It's a very distinct-looking key—about three inches long and heavy. It's brass and has a crown emblem on the oval head."

Oh my gosh! She reached into the small pocket on her cell phone case and drew out the small key Roxy had found. "Like this?" She was thankful she hadn't yet gone shopping for a new case that better fit her new iPhone. For that matter, wasn't sure why she'd continued to keep the key in the case; there was just something curious about it.

She heard an audible gasp. "I think that's it! Where did you get that?" Even given the whispery nature of his voice, Red heard extreme emotion behind his words.

"My cat found it under the built-in hutch in the dining room. I guess it had gotten kicked under there. You know how it has a curlicue design carved into the wood at the bottom?"

"Of course. Why didn't I think of that a year ago? I've been looking for this for months. I thought I'd overturned every single hiding place in that house. I can't believe it was there all the time. What if Roy had found it?" He seemed to be getting agitated at the thought.

"I'm glad to be of service," Red said. She wanted to ask him more about Roy, but that would have to wait. "What do we do now?"

"Sonia, please listen carefully. The lives of your Uncle Alistair, as well as my own, may depend on that key. It's difficult for me to carry an object with a normal molecular structure for more than a few seconds and so I'll ask you to hold onto that key until we can get back to Maryland. I guess there is no more that can be done this week. Just enjoy your ski vacation and know you're a real lifesaver for finding that key. I could hug you right now—well, I would if we had the same molecular structure." Erik sighed. "But, most importantly: Do. Not. Lose. That. Key."

"I'll guard it with my life," she said. She felt like she was glowing from the feeling of making him happy and that he'd like to hug her.

"Thank you, Sonia."

A thought struck her. "Should I tell Dad and see if we can go back home early? I mean, he'd want to help Uncle Alistair as soon as possible."

"That is a noble gesture, but I think it would be better not to risk it. First, what if he didn't believe you? I don't want to put you though that. We've waited a year to get back. What's a few more days? Second, and more importantly, it might alert Roy that something's happening if you change your plans. I take it you know he's involved. I know he's stayed away lately, but I don't think we should chance it."

"Okay. Do you ski?" she asked, feeling timid about asking him a personal question.

"I used to. Tell you what, just enjoy the week. Ski your heart out and know that I'll be nearby, enjoying it with you. And when we return to Maryland, I'll take the key over to Georgetown University somehow and rescue your uncle and myself."

"I can take it for you," she offered.

"Oh, Sonia, I really don't want to involve you any more than you already are. This is a dangerous game."

Red felt a mixture of weak-kneed giddiness at his concern and disappointment in his intent to leave her out. Then she felt her inner warrior become slightly miffed. "Oh, don't be silly. I'll be okay. Just try to stop me."

She heard Erik sigh, and smiled.

CHAPTER 13

Sleuthing at Georgetown

Red's heart was pounding as she sat on the R15 bus heading toward Georgetown University, wondering where Erik was. It felt strange having a friend she couldn't see. "Erik," she said, trying to whisper loudly without moving her lips, while hoping the perfumed lady in the business suit sitting across the aisle didn't hear her.

"I'm here," came the strangely familiar wind-whisper voice from the empty seat to her left.

"Say something when it's time to get off, okay? I'm not exactly sure where to go." The lady to the right shifted and seemed to stealthily eye Red, obviously thinking Red to be deranged. A well-dressed couple directly in front of Red continued a conversation in low tones, totally oblivious to the ghost sitting behind them. Red fought to suppress a grin.

"What's the grin for?"

"Tell ya later."

"I like seeing you smile."

Red's heart skipped a beat but there was no time to think of flirting now. She had to make sure she got off at the right stop.

"Now," Erik said a few minutes later, and Red rose from her seat. As Red stepped from the bus in front of a massive old library, she felt an unexpected soft support on her elbow and blushed as she realized Erik was steadying her, showing an almost forgotten type of chivalry from a bygone era. Red was delighted.

"This way." Red realized Erik was holding her hand. The sensation wasn't the firm grip of a human hand, but she could tell where it drew her nonetheless. It was more like atmospheric pressure on her hand and not at all unpleasant, especially considering whom it was holding her hand. *We're holding hands,* Red thought with a thrill, then remembered they were going sleuthing into a possibly dangerous situation. The thought brought her emotions down a peg.

They approached the old science building and climbed the steep steps. Red grasped the heavy handle of one of the massive oak doors and pulled. The door flung wide. She felt his hand grasp hers again as soon as they were through the door; it slowly swung shut behind them.

Only two students were in the hallway and they appeared to be discussing something related to a paper pinned to a bulletin board. They didn't notice Red. Erik led Red through a door to the left and up a heavy wooden staircase to the second floor. The hallway on this floor looked very much like the one they had just left, a wide hallway with rows of doors on each side and a dark tile floor, kind of like a hospital from the forties, Red thought.

At the far end of the hallway, a male student pushed a lab cart in the opposite direction, his back to them. He was wearing a white lab coat.

"That's him. Roy." Despite Erik's breezy voice, he somehow succeeded in conveying a sense of alarm. "Act normal."

Act normal? What was normal in a college building? Red didn't know. She was just a high school student. She quickly pulled her hood over her head. Was this normal college student behavior? She didn't know but neither did she have a choice, since Roy would surely recognize her. She wished she had a book or something in her hand. Feeling a sense of panic, she glanced around, then spotted a ladies room halfway down the hall. Red forced herself to casually saunter in that direction.

As she turned into the ladies room, she briefly caught a glimpse out of the corner of her eye of the guy in the lab coat turning into the last doorway on the left. He glanced in her direction. Her spine tingled, sending chill bumps down her arms. She was glad of the hood hiding her hair and features.

Once inside, Red breathlessly sat down against the row of sinks and combed both hands through her hair, trying hard to slow her breath and calm down.

"You okay?" came the breezy, yet gloriously male, voice from the space beside her.

"I think so." Her voice was a little unsteady.

A sound from the first stall made Red quickly duck into the empty stall at the end of the row, her face hot with embarrassment. The woman in the other stall must think her totally bonkers for talking to herself. Thinking quickly, she said very clearly, "Let me call you back in a few minutes." *Thank goodness for cell phones.*

She waited until her ears told her that the girl washed her hands, used the hand dryer, and finally left.

When she was sure they were alone, Red put her lips close to the crack where the stall door was hinged and whispered loudly out into the room. "Erik."

"Right here."

She jumped, realizing he was actually in the stall with her.

"Relax." He laughed.

"What if I'd come into the stall to actually use the bathroom?" she asked, feeling a bit annoyed and yet strangely excited by his proximity.

"What? In the middle of a spy mission? I think not," he retorted with amusement. "Besides, I could have simply averted my eyes."

"Yes, but how would I know whether you were looking or not?"

"How do you ever know whether or not I'm watching?"

She felt a tingle. Red could sense a playfulness from Erik and it thrilled her. But this high was followed almost immediately by regret, given Erik's situation. This was as far as their flirtation could go. But maybe if she was able to help him transform back ... *focus*, she told herself.

Hearing the bathroom door open again to admit a newcomer, Red decided it was time to move to another location. As soon as she was outside the bathroom, she felt

D.K. Reed

178

Erik take her hand and pull her to one of the doors midway between the bathroom and the end of the hall, on the opposite side of the hallway from the door through which Roy had disappeared earlier.

No one was in the hallway. Erik opened the door for Red and escorted her in with a small pressure on the small of her back. Red, not being used to being treated like a lady waltzing with a gentleman, blushed. The only time she spent with a guy her age was with Wali, and they spent most of their time kicking each other. Red was thoroughly enjoying this different kind of behavior from the opposite sex. Of course, maybe it didn't mean as much to him as it did to her. After all, how else could he show her where to go since she couldn't see him?

Once through the door, Erik led her to an inner room and silently closed the door behind them. Red studied the small space, which seemed to be a closet or a professor's store room, with floor-to-ceiling shelves on all four sides and copious pieces of lab equipment piled everywhere—balances, pH meters, and countless small metal and plastic meters Red didn't recognize. These were mostly at arm level, but in the shelves above were all manner of fascinating bric-a-brac: rolled maps jutting randomly out of a white plastic box and stuck intermittently throughout the shelves, feathery headdresses, primitive dolls, old notebooks. Red would love to leisurely explore this room.

Erik must've been searching for something on the bottom shelves because she heard a sound. Looking down, she saw the lower shelves were filled with stones and figurines made from stones, boxes of them. Box lids filled with small stones were being moved around.

"What are we looking for?"

"Magnets. Lodestones. Looks like Roy moved them. Hmmm. Let's check his desk."

Red felt Erik take her hand again and lead her out of the storeroom, then out into the hallway again. Red was relieved to see no one was in the hallway. Erik led her to the right this time, opposite from the direction Roy had gone. Past the ladies room and about halfway down the hallway, Red felt the hair stand on the back of her neck as she heard a door close behind her near where Roy had gone. She felt Erik's hand guide her to a water fountain conveniently positioned just a few feet to her right. Immediately, she got the message and leaned over the fountain, allowing her hood and hair to hide her face while she drank slowly.

She heard steps pass behind her as she continued to drink, trying to ignore the pink wad of gum stuck to the stainless steel drain. Thinking she might be drinking too long, she stood up and pretended to try to dislodge something from a side tooth with her fingernail and then drank again, just in case. Finally, Roy—she was sure it was him—disappeared into the stairwell.

"He's gone. Come on." Erik took her hand again and led her to a room just across from the stairwell. Red heard the knob being jiggled but the door didn't open.

"Locked, but come this way. I know a way in that's never locked."

They went back down the hallway and Erik opened another door. Red quietly slipped inside and once again found herself in a teaching laboratory like the one they had entered earlier. Again, she was led into a storeroom within the lab. This storeroom looked very much like the previous one, except it had another door on the opposite wall. Evidently, it was shared by two teaching labs. Erik opened the opposite door and they slipped in.

This room wasn't a lab so much as a shared office, for the graduate students, Red guessed. Five desks lined the walls of the narrow room, three on the opposite wall and two against the wall with the storeroom door.

"My old office," Erik explained.

"Oh." Red looked around the room. It was a narrow room with a huge industrial double sink at the far end. The sink was housed in a lab bench top that continued up the wall for about three feet. The bench top was all black and made the area look like serious lab space. Adding to this impression were scores of wooden pegs holding an array of lab beakers, flasks, and cylinders. Erik flipped a switch and rows of fluorescent lights snapped on, filling the room with high quality, very bright light. Yes, this was definitely a space intended for serious visual work.

Red noticed a picture of Erik pinned to the bulletin board over the desk at the end of the room. She strolled over, not sure where Erik was at the moment, curious but not wanting to appear too curious.

"This your desk?" she whispered.

"Yeah. I can't believe another student hasn't claimed

it," came the familiar windy voice. Red thought it was coming from the middle desk on the same side of the room halfway between the window and the door.

"Want me to help look for something?"

"No, I'll just be a minute."

Red wandered closer to Erik's old desk and browsed the contents. A shelf overhead housed a collection of science textbooks—everything from astronomy to nuclear physics. The desktop was fairly neat and didn't appear to be very dusty given that Erik had disappeared more than a year ago. In fact, it looked like someone had just been there. A pen lay angled as though someone had jotted notes and then left. A yellow notepad, half used, lay beside it, the top sheet clean with no writing. A stack of file folders lay to the right and a pencil canister to the left. Otherwise, it was very clean, like someone had sanitized it, taking away any notes or papers one might expect to find randomly strewn about on a desk.

Red glanced over the items pinned to Erik's bulletin board, her eyes sliding past a seminar schedule onto a mountaintop photo of Erik in hiking garb next to a very cute Xenia. Red felt a stab of jealousy. Maybe she *was* Erik's girlfriend before he went missing. Red should've known. A hot guy like Erik would have girls flocking around. What was she thinking, letting her heart get attached to such a gorgeous young man? And she was such a big tomboy.

Red tore her eyes away from the beautiful couple. Trying to look normal, she kept scanning the bulletin board. Several other photos were pinned to the board, but they were all of nature scenes and did not include any people.

Red heard the scraping sounds of a metal lock and a creak. She looked toward the sound and saw that Erik had pulled forward an entire shelf hinged to the wall. Behind it was an ancient metal safe door. A pair of tweezers was floating about the keyhole.

"Can I help with that?" she asked.

"Na, almost got it. Someone—Roy, no doubt—has been sticking things in the lock, trying to pick it. I need to dig out a couple of things jammed into the keyhole. He should've known this baby couldn't be picked." A moment later, he said. "Okay, key, please."

Red lay it on the counter, unsure of the location of his hand. She watched it float into midair, then turned away, drawn back to the photo of Erik and Xenia. Xenia's cheeks were flushed from an obvious climb, her legs and arms tanned, her glorious hair pulled back into a ponytail. Red noticed how neat she looked—how *together*. Red thought she saw impishness in her sideways grin. Despite her pangs of jealousy, Red thought she looked like someone she could like. She remembered the way Roy had treated her the night of the bird meeting and felt bad for Xenia.

She turned her gaze to Erik's image. Red saw his vitality—his sharp, dark, intelligent eyes, his golden skin, his bronze hair, showing a few golden highlights from time spent in the sun. His loose-fitting, gauzy, white shirt was unbuttoned almost down to his navel. Red almost gasped as she noticed the soft bronze chest hair covering his rock-hard pecs.

"*Yes!*" Red heard Erik's triumphant whisper and whipped around, as though he'd caught her ogling his photo.

But his attention was on the safe. With a loud creak, the safe door opened.

Red heard his intake of breath. Inside the safe, she saw three small, shiny black stones. Carefully, Erik took them from the safe and laid them on the counter.

Suddenly, she heard the sound of a key sliding into the knob of the door to the hallway. Then everything happened so fast she wasn't sure what was happening. She saw the safe door slam, the shelf shoved back in place, then felt something cold press against her as Erik's arm went around her back to grasp her by both arms, holding her tightly to himself.

"Just be quiet. And trust me. It'll be okay," he whispered quickly.

Red felt a strange tingling all over her body and then a kind of snapping feeling, as though someone had snapped a rubber band, but strangely, the feeling was all over her body and not at all painful. It was unlike anything she had ever felt before.

Chapter 14

Wow!

For an instant, Red lost sight, but then just as quickly regained it, though the world had transformed. It was as though someone had changed the channel. Colors were muted and the shapes all around them looked to be made of mist, rather than form – it was almost as though she had entered a cartoon, or a dream. Was she still conscious?

She caught movement by the door to the hallway, though the appearance was also hazy. A male ghostly figure stepped through the opening. She gasped, though the sound barely came out. The hideous figure jerked his face toward her and she froze, but amazingly, he didn't seem to see her.

What was this thing? He looked like a ghost—no, a zombie, she decided. His facial expression was blank, like someone sleepwalking, composed of a slightly glowing, gray haze. The hideous part was a glowing form within the hazy figure, parasitic, like a tapeworm or liver fluke. This form was smaller and strangely orangey, with beady black pupils and no irises. It was amorphous, loosely shaped like a human, but with arms and legs more like tentacles that reached throughout the gray form, frequently changing shape. It was difficult to look at. Since both forms were transparent, its face was behind the gray face and it appeared to be the driver of the body, like some grotesque crane driver at a construction site.

Adding to the disgust were a few smaller orange misty shapes of varying sizes, hanging off the gray form like remoras off a shark, some hovering close, looking for a place to attach. Like the larger, orange, tentacled thing, they also had beady black eyes with no irises. All were made of mist, their forms changing and pulsating with movement like amoebas. Red was horrified. She saw a brief, pained expression cross the otherwise blank, staring gray face. One of the gray hands tried to swat at the hovering parasites, but the gesture only sent them a few inches away and they came right back. It reminded Red of the cows on her grandparents' farm in the heat of the summer, the way they'd periodically swish their tails in a vain attempt to keep the flies at bay.

Another thing Red noticed that looked beyond odd was that when one of the hands swatted at the hovering orange things, the "real" arm didn't move with the gray form. The real or fleshy body was transparent, like a form painted on a window. In general, the gray form seemed to move with the body except when it swatted at the orange parasites—this was an independent action by the gray form and did not seem to involve the body. Was this a body and soul Red was seeing? But with evil spirits all around? Red felt a coldness creep all over her body. She felt both horrified and deeply depressed at seeing such a victimization of this body and the total loss of control for the poor gray soul. Had this being once been human?

Following closely behind the first monstrosity was another. The second figure was also a man, possessing a similar inner gray form and another inner, parasitic orange form. Its orange inner form was darker and murkier than the first man's and its black eyes brighter with what Red instinctively thought of as evil. Red watched as one of the smaller, remora-like orange forms flew to the second form, apparently trying for a hold. The orange form in the second man backhanded the smaller orange form, sending it flying away a few feet. It quickly returned to the first man and began again vying with the other smaller, orange remora-like forms for a hold.

Red came to herself and knew she had been staring at the monstrosities for several seconds. She felt Erik take her hand and slowly edge her away toward the side door. Still keeping her eyes on the hideous things, she sidestepped as quietly and slowly as possible, following Erik's pull. She couldn't believe these things couldn't see her. She sure as heck could see them.

As she turned her face away from the hideous creatures, she was shocked for another reason. She could see *Erik*. He didn't look like a ghost, but like a real person. Now it was the rest of the world that was hazy. The back of his head moved forward in front of her, his outstretched arm pulling her along behind him. He was practically naked, wearing only a pair of roughly made leather shorts, cave-man style. Red swallowed hard.

Before she knew what was happening, Erik had disappeared *into* the door. His arm still outstretched backwards, his hand still clasping hers, he pulled her along behind him. Without any other option, her hand, too, went into the door. The sensation was strange, like going through a cloud but also like the cloud was going through *her*. She could feel the door as she went through it, but it offered almost no resistance; it was cool and smooth, like gelatin. Utterly amazed, she could do nothing but let Erik pull her away from the hideous thing behind them.

The teaching lab they emerged into was dark, with only thin rays of muted light streaming in from the streetlights outside. They quickly crossed to the door leading back into the hallway and went through it without bothering to open it. In the hallway, Erik kept moving very fast, dragging Red along behind him without looking back at her. They glided right through the massive front doors and out onto the steps. Red looked down to see where to plant her foot and was shocked to see her foot was bare. In the same instant, she realized, horrified, that she was totally naked.

Jerking her hand from Erik's, she covered her nakedness as best she could.

"It's okay, Red, no one can see you." Erik still faced away.

"What about *you?*"

"Come further from the building before we say more," Erik said gently. "I won't look, okay?"

They walked about twenty yards across a grassy lawn to a central area surrounded by rose bushes. Erik kept his back to Red. She had no choice but to follow, her head slightly ducked, as though that would keep anyone from seeing her.

"I'll explain it all later when there's time. Just suffice it to say that I altered your molecules and it doesn't work on woven clothing because of the way the molecules need to cling to each other. I'll find something leather for you to wear very soon. But at this moment, the most immediate danger is that Roy will find the stones I took from the safe. That, too, I'll explain later, but for now, just understand that this is important to international security," Erik said, his voice low and urgent, still facing away from her. "I need to go back in and retrieve them now that I have you safely away. Just remember, no one can see you. Don't worry about your lack of clothing." With that, he turned and began to stride away rapidly.

"But I saw *you* in the window," Red called out, feeling panic well up at being left naked in the middle of a college campus.

Erik stopped abruptly and backed up until he was only a couple of feet away, turning his face to the side but still averting his eyes from her. "That only happens when the sun is very low in the sky. The light has to catch just right. And even then, it isn't like anyone would really see your body—they'd see you as a haze, like a ghost. Okay?"

"Okay, I guess. Thanks." Red was touched by his sensitivity in returning.

She watched him quickly cross the length of walkway between the rose garden and the building and disappear back through the massive front doors.

Red crouched behind the tallest rose bush and tried to digest what had just happened. Erik had said he "changed her molecules." Breathing deeply, Red worked at calming her jangled nerves. When she was younger, her mom had talked her into doing some yoga DVDs together and had encouraged Red to do deep breathing exercises when she felt hyperactivity coming on. Looking around to make sure no one was around—still unsure if she could trust this new invisibility—Red ventured to straighten up to perform a sun salute. She felt the action calm her and imagined oxygen bathing her inward tissues. She willed her heart rate to return to normal.

Hearing voices, Red ducked behind the bush again and saw two figures, hazy like the person in the lab, but thankfully without any orange parasitic forms inside their gray forms. The forms had facial expressions that appeared to be conscious and animated, like any face would be if the person was engaged in a pleasant stroll. Red could tell from their voices that they were both female. They seemed to be discussing diets, one telling the other she hadn't eaten processed grains for three weeks and felt much more energetic and less hungry.

Red forgot about their conversation, distracted by two beautiful beings floating above their heads. The beings seemed to be made of white light, much brighter than the silvery-grey glow inside each of the girls, with faces that looked unearthly beautiful, though she couldn't make out much detail. They were wearing some type of flowing white garments, with white glowing wings made of the same type of glowing mist streaming behind them. They glided through the air above the girls, weightless, aided by only the minutest movement from their graceful wings.

The beings appeared to be hovering over the coeds, keeping silent vigil, focusing only on the girls, not looking around at all. Red wanted to call out to them and ask them what they were, but at the same time, she didn't want to call attention to herself. They didn't seem to notice her, nor did the coeds. Red, acutely aware of her nakedness, was glad they didn't notice. She was becoming convinced, however, that Erik was right about her invisibility. Hadn't the hideous thing in the lab looked directly at her without any sign of comprehension?

As the two girls and their guardian angels, or whatever they were, disappeared down the walkway to the left, a thought occurred to her. Did *she* have a guardian angel? She quickly looked up over her own head and was awed by the sight of an equally beautiful form watching her from overhead. The instant their eyes met, however, she saw a look of shock on the face of the apparition. Apparently it perceived that she could see it, and it vanished in a streak of light. "Don't go," she whispered, sighing. She wished she had gotten a better look at it. She couldn't even tell if it had been male or female, or perhaps it was androgynous. She wanted so much to talk to it.

Red noted movement near her in the rosebushes. There appeared to be mists of brown and yellow hues in the bushes but without the faces of the grayish mists occupying the people. The movement wasn't directional, rather, pulsating and slumbering, as if it was the life-force of the bushes and they were dormant. Red felt strangely calmed by this realization. In the limited light from the streetlamps, her eyes explored the grass around her and saw a similar haze, though more greenish and slowly pulsating, like a giant's sleeping breath.

Then she saw three orange misty shapes the size of bats, apparently the same kind of things as the disgusting parasites on the gray form in the lab, fly toward her from across the yard, like insect pests. She felt her adrenaline surge, preparing to fight them off. She didn't know if her tae kwon do training would help against evil spirits, or whatever these things were. But her aggression turned out to be unwarranted; they hovered a few feet above her head for a second, as though sniffing the air to determine her vulnerability, then flew off in the direction of the two girls and their guardian angels. Red was greatly relieved and beginning to feel a desperate desire for normalcy, no matter how intriguing this adventure might be.

Red did more yoga breathing and began to relax again. She became mesmerized by the beauty of the world around her, as much as she could see in the almost darkness—the sun had set while they were inside and it was now evening. Looking up at the sky, she saw the stars looked pretty much the same as before, but every few minutes, a glowing white light, similar in appearance to the light of the guardian angels, would dash upward or downward with the speed of a shooting star. Red wondered if these were the angels, or whatever the beings were that hovered over the girls, traveling upward into the heavens or coming to Earth on some mission. Zip, zip. As she watched she saw the action repeated often, several times per second, a constant traffic.

Red was caught up in the awe of it and jumped when she suddenly heard Erik say, "Here, put this on." She had been gazing away from the direction of the front door and now swiftly looked behind her to see Erik offering her a leather trench coat, his eyes averted in a respectful gesture.

Red snatched the coat and quickly put her arms through the sleeves. It felt a little odd because it lacked a lining—Red guessed the lining must have been woven and so didn't survive the transformation. But she was very thankful the coat was long; it covered her like a dress. It was a little big and long in the sleeves, but she was able to clinch the belt and roll up the sleeves for a serviceable garment.

"Thanks," Red replied earnestly. "Hope you didn't have to steal it."

"Let's just say I didn't steal it from an innocent bystander. Roy'll be looking for it about now." Erik laughed. "Which will keep him occupied for a while, at least."

"What do we do now?" Red asked.

"Let's get you somewhere safe. I think I have a lot of explaining to do."

"Back to the bus?"

"Now that we're both transformed, I have a better way to travel. It's something I've wanted to share with another person—with you—for a while."

Erik stepped toward Red, an inviting smile on his lips, and offered his hand with a slight bow.

Red gently laid her hand in his. Their eyes met for an instant. His eyes were seething with questions. Then a sudden sideways grin transformed his handsome face, as though he'd just thought of something mischievous.

"Okay, on the count of three, jump, and I'll teach you something really cool that I discovered a while ago."

"Jump? What?"

"One, two, three." Erik jumped up and Red jumped with him, expecting to be drawn back down a split second later by gravity. To her immense surprise, they glided upward, as though they were underwater.

"Now, kick, just like you were swimming." Erik let go of her hand and began swimming upward. Red followed suit. Feeling like she should hold her breath, she was amazed at the feel of the air. It felt like the consistency of water. If she wanted to stay in one spot, she could; if she wanted to launch in any direction, she only had to propel her body like a swimmer. That must've been what those angels were doing before, she realized.

She looked up at Erik, who was twenty feet or so above her. He was making an almost flying motion, or some hybrid between flying and swimming, thrusting huge armfuls of air downward with his massive arms and kicking his feet in a sort of scissor kick.

Red tried the same motion and was amazed at her ability to push the air down so decisively. In fact, the air seemed thicker than water to her, though not to breathe. It reminded her of the flying dreams she'd had for years. In them she would kick and flap her arms and eventually lift off the ground. It was frustratingly hard in her dreams, but she'd often done it to escape something. Like now—that was precisely what they were doing.

"Come on, slowpoke." Red realized she could hear Erik's voice clearly. She hadn't noticed it until now, but since her transformation, it didn't sound like a ghostly, windy voice anymore.

"Are you sure this is safe?" Her voice felt shaky. She ventured a glance down. The ground was a long ways down now.

"Completely. Watch." Erik stopped swim-flying and began doing a breast stroke to smoothly come down to circle around her. He looked somewhat like a playful otter as he glided around until he was beside her. His only movement now was of a swimmer treading water, with the subtlest of motions from his outstretched arms and slowly scissoring legs.

"This is amazing." Red giggled as she began to relax. She took a moment to revel in the dreamlike quality of it all. She stopped trying to swim upward and instead just treaded air, and felt very safe. She could feel the molecules around her were somehow different in comparison to hers, so she was effectively weightless, yet she did have some gravity. And before, when she'd been in the rose bushes, she had felt just as attached to terra firma as ever.

"This way." Erik pushed off gracefully, swim-flying in a north-westerly direction. "We need to find a quiet place and make a plan. You must have a ton of questions."

"I'll say. Like, what the heck is going on?" *And was Xenia your girlfriend or not?*

"I know a good place to talk. Follow me."

Despite her anxiety, Red allowed herself to thoroughly enjoy the adventure. Her senses were on overdrive, taking in the sounds, smells, and sights as they flew above Georgetown, over the Clara Barton Parkway, and began following the Potomac River north. The air felt like cool silk on her arms and legs and her swim-flying became more graceful as she got the hang of it.

The night was clear overhead and she still could see occasional white lights shoot upward or downward. She had so many questions for Erik, but they'd have to wait. She couldn't help just living in this moment. It was such a grand adventure. She felt like a child on a Ferris wheel for the first time—no, better than that. Like a little bird first learning to fly. She had often wondered what that felt like as she sat atop a mountain during one of her family's many hikes. Red had related to animals in a special way all of her life. She often tried to think of what it would feel like to be a horse, or a cat, or bird. And now she knew—well, the bird, anyway.

Erik turned to the right, leading them up the C&O Canal paralleling the river. The moon, beginning to peek over the horizon, was almost full, giving them a glistening path easy to follow. As they followed the water, Red heard the honk of Canadian geese coming up behind them, obviously better at this flying thing than she. Red glanced backward and saw five or six coming up swiftly in a vee formation behind them. Just like the girls on campus, the geese appeared to have a glow, rather than a concrete presence, only this time the glow was bright silver. The geese honked at them, seeming somewhat annoyed, like a bicyclist ringing a bell for a bike path pedestrian to clear the way. Red felt an absurd urge to stick out her tongue at them. Before they came too close, however, they veered downward and glided to a graceful landing on the canal's crystal surface, causing silent concentric rings to ride up the canal.

As they continued fly-swimming over the canal, Red noticed she could faintly make out glowing shapes in the water, fish shapes and thousands of smaller, glowing shapes. In the forest, too, she occasionally caught a glimpse of a glowing shape scurrying in the underbrush or sitting in a tree, but she usually couldn't see them well enough to make out the type of animal she was seeing. Plants, too. Some of the larger trees had beautiful glows, slightly greenish, some more amber. Red got the impression that all life forms had a distinct glow.

They were approaching one of the old historic boathouses that had been built at each lock on the canal. This one appeared to be boarded up. Erik began descending toward a bridge, crossing the canal in front of the boathouse. Red followed him down. They both landed easily on the wooden footbridge. It had probably built by the National Park Service but was definitely with a style in keeping with the lock's history. A bench was conveniently positioned on the boathouse side of the canal, and Erik took Red's hand and drew her toward it. The canal created an opening in the heavily forested park on either side of the canal and towpath, allowing moonlight to filter through, now that an almost-full moon had risen. Red could see pretty well in the light. Her heart began to pound at his proximity and the fact that they were alone here together. There was no one else with whom she'd rather have been alone.

"Where to begin. Guess I'd best start from the beginning," she heard Erik say as he turned to face her.

CHAPTER 15

Intrigue

Erik took one of Red's hands in both of his and looked imploringly into her eyes. "I'm so very sorry to have gotten you involved in this mess. And I promise to get you out of it—and your Uncle Alistair."

"Where *is* Uncle Alistair?" Red asked. "I know you said he wasn't dead, but where is he?"

"Yes, your uncle is alive, at least he was when we lost contact." Eric turned his face away ruefully.

An awful thought struck her. "Does Roy have him locked up somewhere?"

"No, nothing like that. Well, not exactly. It's hard to explain." She saw him take a deep breath. He seemed to gain some kind of resolve and turned toward her again. "Sonia, I need to brief you on some absolutely secret information so you'll understand the situation. I'd rather you not know, because this knowledge is dangerous, but I have no choice. You're already involved." He closed his eyes with a pained expression and then resumed speaking. "I can't believe I was so stupid to get you involved like this. I didn't think Roy would come into the office, or I never would've brought you there. He normally spends most of his time in another—"

"Never mind that." Red was impatient for knowledge and didn't want to see him blame himself. "You know I'd have gotten involved anyway, with you or alone," she said. "Ever since I saw you—your face—in the window, I've been obsessed with solving this mystery."

"I suppose, but I still should've thought this through better. Anyway, what's done is done, so here it is." He took a long breath.

"The short story is that you and I have been transformed and are invisible, but are okay, and hopefully, with a little luck, we can be transformed back. The same goes for your uncle, except that he's been transformed in a different way. I don't know how to explain so much to you quickly except to start from the beginning," he said. "As you know, I'm a graduate student at Georgetown University. Professor Hamilton is on my graduate committee. Another of his grad students is Roy Oglethorp. He was a decent enough chap at first. I was working on a double master's degree in physics and global history." Erik gave a small chuckle. "I know the two don't exactly go together, but I'm obsessed with physics and how things work, as well as the history of human thought and imagination—how our species figures out how things work. And if the truth be told, I liked the sounds of the global history program at Georgetown because it's a dual degree with King's College—London and British history are other passions of mine."

Amazing. Red thought. "Wow, I'm obsessed with British history, too. Uncle Alistair was always telling me stories about Britain when I was little, and I love Jane Austen and the Bronte sisters. Heck, even Mr. Bean." Red, realizing the interruption, stopped talking and cleared her throat, a signal for him to continue.

He smiled. "Roy's getting his masters in theology." Red noted this was said with a slight curling of the lip and a humorless grin. "Well, Professor Hamilton had a grant to research—"

"You should call him Uncle Alistair. It sounds odd to hear him called Professor Hamilton."

"Okay then, Alistair. But I draw the line at calling him *uncle.*" Red thought Erik looked adorable as he said this, blushing slightly. "Alistair had some ancient stones he had borrowed from the Vatican, and he advertised for a graduate assistant from the physics department—me, of course. It was the most amazing opportunity to fall into my lap that I could've imagined. He wanted someone to research the molecular make up of these stones. We had one year to conduct the research, and as they were historical artifacts, studying the stones fit into both my courses of study.

"Coming from the Vatican, the stones are, as you might imagine, surrounded by legends and intrigue. They're called the Stones of Bothynus. *Bothynus* is Latin for 'meteor.'"

"That's really cool. So, you think they're named after a meteor?"

Red could see Erik loved talking about his work. "That's an excellent question. Yeah, my favorite theory is that they actually *came* from one or more meteorites. Each of the three stones is named, too. They're named *Lapillus Angelus,* the Angel Stone, *Lapillus Parvulus*—Latin for something like little 'one small stone', though we call it the Elf Stone. In some texts it's also called *Lapillus Vættr*—it's the Norse form of the name. I'm still not sure how that name got assigned." Eric looked deep in thought, and then shook his head, looking a little embarrassed for getting carried away by his passion for talking about the stones. "The third stone is *Lapillus Sideralis,* the Star Stone. Their monitory value is priceless, but their value to our understanding of the universe goes way beyond priceless." He said this with marked reverence.

Red listened intently to the story.

"The legends claimed that Solomon knew a secret about the stones and could use them to transform people into other things. For instance, he could transform people into angels with the Angel Stone, into elves with the Elf Stone, or make them totally vanish with the Star Stone. But no one else could make the stones work that way, so people thought the secret died with him."

Erik looked up, excitement on his face. "Then your Uncle Alistair, on visiting the Vatican while conducting research, spent some time with an old caretaker, who told him of the legends and showed him the stones. They'd been locked away in a drawer and forgotten."

"That sounds like Uncle Alistair. He never met a stranger and he could talk his way into Fort Knox," Red said fondly. "So I take it he somehow got hold of the stones?"

Erik nodded enthusiastically. "Yep. Alistair applied for an antiquities grant to study the stones and for permission from the Vatican to borrow them. *Voila*, it came through and we got to study them."

"And you discovered their secret?" Red asked incredulously, feeling this whole thing was much bigger than she would have dreamed possible.

"Yes. Well, at least some of their secrets. Not all. My part of the grant covered studying the molecular structure. Roy's part was about digging into ancient texts to see what he could turn up of their history and legends. As you saw, our desks were next to each other and so we spent a lot of time discussing the stones. I saw no reason not to share my work with him and I think he felt likewise."

Red shuddered, thinking of Erik so close to Roy.

"Then, a year ago last spring, Roy got a call from someone in Italy, responding to one of his inquiries. Like I said, that was his part of the project and he spent a lot of time on the phone and computer, searching for anything he could find out. Well, this caller claimed to have an ancient papyrus that mentioned the stones. Roy knew some Italian and used some of the grant money to buy a plane ticket to fly to Italy to try to buy or at least photograph the papyrus," he said. "Alistair was all for the trip and even arranged a special study program for Roy at the Vatican for the summer. I think he was hopeful Roy could acquire the papyrus for the university collection, as well as research the question at the place most likely to have information on the stones."

Red nodded attentively, trying to figure out what he was trying to tell her.

"Roy was gone for eight or nine weeks and returned—" Erik hesitated, and Red got the sense he was trying to put something very difficult into words "—very changed. It was obvious to me that something was drastically different, but he somehow managed to hide it from Professor Hamilton—Alistair. I tried to discuss it with Alistair but he was so busy with his work that he brushed it off, thinking it was stress or that maybe Roy had met someone on his trip. But to me, well, I didn't really believe in such things then, but as I'm sure you'll now attest, I felt he had become possessed by a demon."

Red took in a rapid breath, thinking of the orange parasite inside the gray form they had seen. "So one of those *things* was Roy?"

"Yes," Erik said sadly. "Here's the thing. While Roy was away, I cracked the code."

Red felt a thrill. "You figured out how to use the stones?"

Erik shook his head as if he didn't believe it himself. "It was right there in plain sight all along if anyone had bothered to study the stones in a lab setting, but I guess most of the time they were held at the Vatican, with so many more glamorous artifacts around to study," he said. "At first glance, the stones look fairly plain—each is encased in a smooth black onyx housing with a colorful stone inside it. The Angel Stone looks a bit like ruby, the Elf Stone like emerald, and the Star Stone, maybe something between sapphire and lapis lazuli."

Red thought a moment. "You said they look like ruby, emerald, and sapphire—so they aren't actually gemstones?"

"Good question," Erik said. "We thought they were at first. But a couple of easy lab tests showed they weren't. In fact, their molecular structure, as best I could tell, resembled materials found in meteorites. And that fit with the legendary claim that they fell from the sky." He paused, looking at her. "Have you taken high school chemistry yet?"

Red rolled her eyes, a little annoyed at the perceived condescension. "Yes. I got mostly A's my freshman year in honors chemistry." She tried not to sound defensive or smug. After all, she was talking to a grad student. She hoped he wasn't out of her league.

Erik blushed. "Of course you've taken chemistry, Red. I'm sorry, you're obviously an intelligent person. Please excuse my lack of social skills. I have always been such a nerd," he said. "I get so carried away when I talk about the stones. It feels so good to be talking to another human being right now, and especially…" he looked imploringly into her eyes.

Red beamed at his obvious discomfort, pleased that she could affect him so much. She smiled reassuringly, trying to retain at least some of her annoyance for coolness sake, and urged him to continue.

"Well, I figured out that the black parts were mostly carbon, bonded together by an unknown element, which I was hoping to identify. I was thinking that would pay my ticket to a Ph.D.," Erik continued. "These coverings seemed to keep the inner crystals, the colored part, from being active. Each of the coverings had two small openings about the diameter of a pencil.

"What actually cued me in was an etching on the bottom of the Angel Stone showing two oval shapes side by side, with

205

rays coming from one end, or going into one end, in this case. I realized that someone had sketched instructions on how to use them, but no one had been able to figure them out."

Red frowned, trying to picture the etching. "I think you've lost me. You had to put two of the stones together to get something to happen?"

Erik shook his head. "You see, that's what everyone must've thought—you put two of the stones side by side, and some form of energy would come out of one of the openings. But I began by questioning whether the energy might be going *into* the opening, rather than coming out. I tried every combination of positioning the stones, and studied their molecular structures, but nothing happened. And then it dawned on me. The kind of material that changes something about another's objects molecular structure is—guess." Erik was being playful. Red loved seeing the spark in his dark eyes, though with only moonlight the color was unrecognizable.

"Something radioactive?" Red ventured a guess.

"Very close. I was thinking along those lines, but then I decided to try everything I had around the lab first. I was in a fever to figure it out and didn't want to waste any time in getting a radiation permit. I tried heat and light. Nothing. Then, just as a bit of a lark, I thought I'd see what a magnet would do. And guess what?"

"It worked?"

"It worked." Erik's eyes gleamed with excitement, recalling the moment. "I was working with the Angel Stone mostly, figuring that if I succeeded in transforming anything, I'd rather end up with an angel than an elf. And the Star Stone was a bit scary to me—I didn't want to create any black holes or anything."

Red was thoroughly enjoying Erik's obvious pleasure in recalling his work.

"So I'd been positioning one of the openings of the Angel Stone against some other stones I'd picked up from the geology department, trying different types of material to see if anything happened. When I lined up a magnet against the other opening, something happened. There were some faint sparks and vibrations—as though energy was flowing from the normal stone into the Angel Stone. An instant later, *snap!* The stone had transformed. It was like a ghost of a stone. It had a faint brown haze glowing inside. In fact, for all practical purposes, it was invisible and without mass, but I could still make out the faint image with a microscope. I was so excited I spent all weekend running experiments on the anti-matter stone, as I thought of it at the time. I called your uncle and he came over and helped me run some experiments. It was great. We were so excited and I couldn't wait to tell Roy when he got back from Italy." Erik looked regretful.

"That Monday, Roy didn't drag himself into the lab until mid-morning and seemed, well, out of it. I assumed it was just jet lag since he'd returned from Italy only the day before. I told him the gist of what I'd learned, and took him into the lab to show him," Erik said. A shudder ran through him. "That was when I realized something was off. Something was wrong with him. His eyes had a blank look and it was really weird how big his pupils were, pretty much completely covering up the irises.

"He stared at the transformed stone for a few seconds, not moving, and began to pant, like he was going to be sick or something— or like he was getting angry. Then he turned to look me in the eye and his eyes glinted. It was the weirdest thing. His eyes glinted like a cat's eyes in a headlight beam. It was too weird for me. I wanted to talk this over with Alistair and see what he thought. But I wanted to get the stones safely put away first. We'd been storing them in an old safe hidden in the wall of the closet in our office—you know, the same one as today. We'd reasoned that since the building was one of the older ones and survived both the Civil War and the Depression that it'd hold up to anything. People weren't very trusting then and tended to be very serious about locking up their valuables. Alistair was smart to claim that lab and get that safe," Erik said. "I took the Angel Stone back to the safe. There was a weird instant when I thought Roy was going to snatch it from me, but he must've thought better of it since there were other people all around us. I locked it in the safe along with the other two and went straight to your uncle's house to discuss what we should do."

"So what does the stone actually do?" asked Red, anxious to hear more, especially since her fate seemed to be linked to this strange story.

"As far as I could tell, it effectively makes things invisible, but practically unaltered otherwise. For living things, like us, our bodies still work—our hearts pump and all that. Well, there are some differences, of course, like a little bit of energy goes a much longer way, so we don't really need to eat.

And, of course, you've noticed that we can swim in the air and push through doors."

Red nodded.

"But the way it works, and this is just a guess, is that the electron current produced by the magnet sets up a flow in the stone in the direction of the opening on the magnet end of the stone, pulling energy away from anything positioned next to the opposite opening. Alistair and I spent several hours outlining a research plan to study this new phenomenon. We called the project 'Snap To Grid' because the energy seemed to draw out for a few seconds and then sort of snap, as though all the electrons snapped into a lower orbital, or maybe it was the protons or neutrons snapping into a smaller size. We had just begun to reason through the possibilities."

"Is that what happened to us?" Red felt her voice tremble slightly as the realization of her situation hit her. *What if we can't transform back?*

Erik looked up imploringly, as if asking her forgiveness again. She smiled and he seemed to show some slight relief. "Yes, I now think the Angel Stone makes the protons and neutrons snap to a smaller size, but that the electrons stay the same. Do you know about quarks?" Erik looked expectantly, as if hoping for another mind to help him understand.

"They're like sub-sub-atomic particles, right? They make up protons and neutrons."

"That's right," Erik looked relieved. "There are different types of quarks. Protons and neutrons are made of up-quarks and down-quarks. There are other types of quarks in stars, but these are the main kinds here on Earth. The best I can tell, the Angle Stone works on either up-quarks or down-quarks, or, most likely both, but not electrons. That is the only way I can explain why we're still the same size—the molecules would have to be the same distance apart. The electron clouds would see to that. But the molecules themselves must be much smaller. That is why we're transparent. Bear with me, I know this is a lot of information, but I've had almost a year to think about all of this, I just couldn't do anything about it until an angel found the key." Erik's voice was heavy with emotion.

"Roxy."

"I'm sorry, what?"

"It was Roxy who found the key," Red confessed, though it felt good to hear him call her an angel.

Erik nodded and then continued, "Now that I have access to the stones again, I can try to reverse this. It should be as simple as turning a magnet around so that the current flows the other way. I hope it is. At least, that's what's happened so far with other materials," he said. "I'm very thankful Roy hasn't been able to access them. Guess he couldn't find the key either. He wouldn't be able to get into the safe without it, at least not without making lots of noise and causing a commotion in the building."

"Must have been frustrating to be stuck like this for a year and not able to get at the one thing that could fix your situation."

"Yes." Erik looked momentarily rueful and then brightened. "But we have the key now and hopefully we can go back to normal."

Red wasn't so sure she wanted to go back right away. This was the best adventure she'd ever had. And at this moment, it didn't really matter what their situation was as long as she was with him.

Red gazed into his eyes for an instant, feeling drawn irresistibly, then looked away, wondering if she only imagined he felt the same way. With an effort to re-focus, she continued her questioning. "What about the other two stones? And what about Uncle Alistair?"

"Yes, we're definitely coming to Alistair, but first I have to explain a little more about the stones. I did quite a bit of experimentation on them and never got the Star Stone to do anything. In fact, I'm not sure it's authentic. Someone may have switched it out at some point in history. At least, that's the idea that Alistair and I worked off at first. We focused on the other two for a few weeks. Still, it does seem to have similar characteristics with the other two, so I'm still hoping we'll figure it out eventually. Why the ancients thought it made things disappear, I don't know, unless they had seen it act on meteorites. But that's just speculation. Lots of work to do on it. Of course, we were only supposed to have the stones for one year, which is now over and has been wasted for the most part."

Erik sighed. "We had just started to experiment on meteorite fragments—we have a collection site near the Potomac, not far from Alistair's house. It may be that the Star Stone works on quarks that don't really exist on our planet. So to test that, it was either gather meteorite fragments or try to reserve time on one of the nuclear accelerators, and we weren't ready to let our cat out of the bag until we knew more. Besides, it takes a year or more to get approved for time on one of those and it's really hard to get. Maybe in the future ..." Red watched Erik look dreamily upward as though planning some grand scheme.

"Anyway, back to the stones. The other stone, the Elf Stone, *Lapillus Parvulus*—its name literally means 'little-one pebble.' The few experiments I'd run on it showed that it miniaturizes things. But then, those things were many times heavier than they should be. So it just concentrated them. I'd only tried it on a few types of rocks. The rocks weighed exactly the same before and after but were about one thousandth of their original size. Again, I've had lots of time to think it over and figure out the puzzle. I think it changes the electron clouds, making them smaller, but doesn't affect the quarks, making the molecules fall together into a much smaller space, but not changing the weight because the protons and neutrons make up most of the weight of a molecule and they remain unaltered."

Red nodded, trying to visualize what she was hearing.

"And then the second breakthrough came when Alistair and I started experimenting with the two stones together, both activated by magnets. We were pretty hopeful about that, but we'd only just begun to experiment. Once I get back to my original form, though ..." His voice trailed off. Red detected a sadness, and that alarmed her because she suspected he wasn't totally sure whether they *would* actually get back to their original forms.

As if he had read her thoughts, his brow creased imploringly. "Sonia, I'm so very sorry. I should never have allowed you to go to Georgetown. I should've thought of another way to save you from Roy. Maybe it was my selfishness that made me make the choice to change you, rather than finding some way to attack Roy. Or, maybe I could've distracted him long enough for you to escape. I'm sorry." His voice was thick with emotion. "I'll take you home now and somehow fix this mess, but I do not want to involve you any further. Do you understand?"

Red's inner warrior was miffed by this insult. She was no wilting flower; she was Red Sonja. "You didn't 'allow' me to go to Georgetown," she said emphatically, wanting to shake him. "I do as I please. You couldn't have stopped me, and this is the most amazing adventure I've ever had. Don't you see? This is my destiny. And Erik, as much as I like you, it's simply not in me to be a wilting flower. I *will* come with you and *we* will fix this mess."

CHAPTER 16

Answers

Erik was silent for a moment, clearly taken aback by the force of her words, then took a deep breath. "Sonia, what if we can't change back? Don't you understand?"

"We'll burn that bridge when we come to it." Red tried to lighten his dark mood with a joke. She could think of worse situations than being stuck alone in this state with Erik. And if Uncle Alistair was indeed alive, she couldn't sit idly by and wait—she had to help.

" 'Burn that bridge.' You may be more accurate than you think," Erik said in a dismal tone.

"Okay, let's focus. What about the two stones together? You said you made a breakthrough?" Red prodded.

Erik nodded and to Red's relief, continued. "Alistair was really excited about the implications of that. You see, using both stones in their activated form evidently made both quarks and electrons smaller, so that the concentrated weight was no longer an issue. If something shrunk to a thousandth of its original size, it'd weigh a thousandth of its original weight. It seemed to be just a miniature version of the original. Alistair thought it'd help solve world food shortages by making food easier to transport and store, and perhaps make it last much longer since the microbes that attack would also be on a different scale, but there is so much work to be done ..." His fists tensed, showing his frustration at not being able to do the work right now.

"When we get back to our original forms—and Sonia, I'll do everything in my power to make sure we do—" Red could hear a resurgence of emotion in Erik's voice. "—I'm going to figure all this out. Run more tests. Of course ..." he hesitated.

"What?" prodded Red.

"It's just that this thing seems to have destroyed so many lives. Roy, Alistair ... I don't really know if Roy is fixable or even for certain that Alistair is still alive."

Red realized that as much as she had thought Uncle Alistair to be dead a few hours ago, now she wasn't willing to even consider that possibility. "He's got to be."

Erik continued bleakly, "I sometimes feel guilty playing with this stuff, like it's over my head, like the whole thing is out of control, or controlling us. Maybe I'll figure out a way to destroy the stones, rather than doing more with them, just to keep them out of the wrong hands. I mean, the potential for misuse is enormous," he said. "Of course, the potential for good is also enormous. I just wonder if we can control something so powerful. I've been consumed with knowing all I can about these 'magic' stones ever since I first heard of them. I wanted my life to be spent solving the riddles and figuring out how to use them for good. Roy felt that way, too, at least, I thought he did. But look at him now."

"Magic is only bad if we use it selfishly and try to play god. You were obviously trying to use it for good." Red realized they were getting off subject and added, "What about Uncle Alistair?"

"Uncle Alistair." Erik gave a small chuckle. "That sounds so weird to hear him called 'uncle'. It's just that your Uncle Alistair seems the consummate professor, or even wizard, like Merlin. Ever a seeker of wisdom and one who doesn't believe in being boxed in with convention."

"That's Uncle Alistair, all right." Red smiled warmly.

"So, what happened on that fateful night? September 2, to be exact. Well, about a week after Roy came back from Italy, he said he wanted us to meet some dude named Lorenzo, who was supposedly flying in later in the week to discuss some ancient writings. He was some expert on ancient writings who worked at the Vatican museum, or maybe someplace nearby—it was never really clear exactly who he worked for. But he even convinced Alistair to have him as a guest lecturer in his classes that week. Alistair only had one class going that semester. As you probably know, he'd been semi-retired for a while so he could spend most of his time on our research. I don't know. It sounded fishy to me. I suggested to Alistair that the guy might be a phony, but Alistair wasn't worried about it. He thought I was overreacting. Said a lot of people around the Vatican act a bit differently because of the enormous weight of the atmosphere there. Alistair thought that was what was different about Roy—he'd developed a weightier countenance." Erik shrugged, then took a deep breath and continued.

"Roy knew about our findings that summer while he was away. We kept him posted. After all, he was part of the research team. He said he needed meteorite fragments for some demo Lorenzo wanted to try. I couldn't believe he'd let a stranger in on our research secrets. I hoped he hadn't shared much, though he supposedly had information that'd be helpful to us, so what could I say? Roy scheduled a rock run for that weekend. I was suspicious, but Alistair was on board with it. We did rock runs periodically when we needed stones for our research, though Roy was never great with helping out on that part of the job.

"Well, somehow it ended up that Roy and Alistair did the run a day early, on Friday, during one of my exams. Roy said Lorenzo wanted to do some trials over the weekend. I tried that morning to talk Alistair out of it because I didn't trust Roy. I mean, I just had a bad feeling about it all, but all I could do was agree to try to hook up with them after my exam. They were to meet at Alistair's house and take a canoe out to the meteor site, and I was to take a second canoe out there if they weren't back by the time I got there. Alistair wasn't sure he could remember exactly where to look. As I mentioned earlier, I'm the geologist of the bunch." Erik allowed his pent-up frustration to show. "Why Alistair didn't see how outlandishly fishy that was … I mean, Roy organizing a rock run." His lips pressed together.

Red felt her heartbeat pick up. This was it—she'd finally find out what really happened to Uncle Alistair.

Erik let out a sigh and collected himself. "Okay, here's the thing. The three stones are kept in the special safe, as I mentioned before. I don't exactly know why I did it but as I stopped by the lab to pick up my things from my desk, I took the Angel Stone from the safe and slipped it, along with a small magnet and the key, into my pocket. There were two keys to the safe. Alistair had one and I had one. We arranged that during the summer when Roy was away, when we found out how important the stones were. Roy was upset about that change because before this, one of the keys, my key, had been available to anyone in the lab. It was kept on a special nail inside the closet door. But Alistair suggested we might want to up the security. Anyway, I rushed over to Alistair's house—well, your house now." He smiled at Red.

"No, Uncle Alistair's house. He's just got to be alive," Red said determinedly. "I feel terrible that we moved into his house and he's still out there somewhere."

"Sonia, Alistair will be delighted that you have watched over his place. I'm sure he will," Erik said soothingly and then continued. Red bit her lip and refocused on Erik's story.

"So, as I was saying. I rushed over to Alistair's place and knocked. When there was no answer, I went on around back, thinking they must be on the river. I heard something inside that sounded off, like furniture scooting in the dining room. I took cover and looked in a window. I saw Alistair scuffling in the dining room with Roy and a stranger, this Lorenzo guy. Alistair pushed Roy away, but then Lorenzo grabbed him from behind in a chokehold and put a pistol to his head."

Red gasped and Erik quickly continued. "I knew I had to do something fast, and my tae kwon do wasn't enough against two guys and a gun. So I lined up the Angel Stone and magnet on the picnic table and stepped against it. I snapped-to-grid, just like you did." Red thought Erik looked sheepish again, clearly sorry for bringing her into all this. She gave him a commiserating smile. Erik looked somewhat comforted.

"I knew I was invisible to them, though I didn't trust it at first. They weren't looking my way so I tried the sliding glass door. To my surprise, my hand went through the handle, rather than grasping it. So I pressed on through the door. I tried to grab Lorenzo from behind but my arm went through his neck. I tried frantically to grab things to use on them but could only scoot items a little at that point. I wasn't able even to scare them." Erik laughed scornfully.

"Roy sounded different, like a snake. That bastard." Erik hissed through his teeth, then cleared his throat and took a deep breath. "He was saying to Alistair that he should leave the safe key with him before they went out on the river, just in case, and then he laughed manically. It didn't sound at all like the Roy I knew, and he certainly didn't look like himself. You know what he looks like from this state."

Red nodded with exaggerated agreement, shivering as she thought of the terrifying orange form inside Roy.

"The Lorenzo guy laughed, too. Then Roy reached his hand into Alistair's pocket and pulled out his key ring. He was still laughing and I wanted to get a piece of him so bad. Alistair grabbed the key ring and during the scuffle, the ring broke and keys scattered over the floor. Lorenzo tightened his hold on Alistair's neck and Roy punched him in the gut."

Red gasped. Beside her, she felt Erik shake with rage. "Lorenzo told him to pick up the key to the safe and hand it to them immediately or he'd kill him. Alistair said okay and they released him so he could pick up the key. He gave it to Roy, and gave him a look that should've made Roy ashamed, but it didn't. Then Roy and Lorenzo took Alistair to the canoe, no doubt planning on drowning him." Erik tensed, clutching his fists. Red could sense the extreme frustration coursing through Erik at not being able to help her uncle.

"The three of them got into a canoe with Alistair in the middle. Roy and Lorenzo did the paddling and they first paddled across the canal, then carried the canoe across the towpath and re-launched in the river, keeping the gun on Alistair. All I could do was follow them, trying to think of something to do to help.

"Then, something really surprising happened. I waded into the river. It was easy because the current had very little influence on me. I walked fast enough that I was able to make it into deep water pretty quickly. The water was over my head and I could see fish, lots of them. Not like I usually saw them, but as faint glowing essences. Some were really big. I didn't know the Potomac had so many big fish. I think they were gars. But, I was thinking of trying to overturn the canoe the whole time and was walking through the fish as well as the water," He paused, as though trying to decide whether to continue. "Okay, I know what I'm going to tell you won't make sense at first, but I'll try to explain. Brain waves seem to still work pretty much the same in this state as the normal state, and so, as I walked through the fish, my brain was at the same spot as the brain of one of the big fish and as the fish's head passed through mine, my thoughts went through the fish's brain, I think. I felt this overwhelming hunger for small fish. I paddled upward and discovered that I could still swim and didn't have to just walk on the bottom. I think my desire to help Alistair was somehow communicated to the fish, because when I broke the surface, I saw my fish hurl himself against the side of the canoe, startling the men inside. They all jumped, which made the canoe lean too far to one side and it overturned. The Italian thug lost his gun and Alistair was able to get away from them."

Red tried hard to digest this extraordinary story. Her heart felt like it was in her throat. "So Uncle Alistair got away?"

Erik nodded. "Yes, at least as far as I could tell. I went back underwater to find my fish friend. I did the brain thing with two bigger fish and thought of Roy and Lorenzo as enemies. It worked like a charm—the fish began attacking them. And those fish had teeth." Erik chuckled humorously at the memory, and Red could sense his ire.

"By the time they got out of the river, they had several nasty gashes and Alistair was long gone. That was the last time I saw him. I went back to the picnic table and the Angel Stone was gone. I didn't know what to do next. I was stuck in this state. I assumed that Alistair took it back to the safe. After all, he didn't know I'd transformed. And the safe was the only place we kept them."

"So those two got the stones?" Red suddenly started to think of all kinds of nasty implications.

"You forget that I used the Angel Stone on you." Erik smiled grimly.

"Oh, right."

"Alistair had given them a bum key," Erik announced in a way that Red thought showed pride for his mentor's cunning. "As you know, it's a very distinct key, but Alistair had a key to another safe in the department that no one was using and he gave Roy that key. Oh, they came back and retrieved all the other keys scattered on the dining room floor and searched every inch of the house. But they never found the right key."

"Why didn't they just pick the lock or blow off the door?" Red couldn't believe that in a year they hadn't been able to get into a measly safe.

"I know they tried—I followed them there many nights—but their options are limited. Alistair's lab is between the dean's office and an old observatory. With all the traffic to the dean's office during the day, and the observatory during the night, I suspect they didn't want to risk any noise from explosions or drills. But in the spring, the old observatory is going to close when they open the new one. I think Roy is waiting until that happens, and once there's no one around, they'll try to blast it open."

"So the thug is still here?" asked Red, feeling a bit sick.

"Yes, he was the other guy in the lab. He must've returned. I saw him around for a few weeks when they were searching the house, but haven't seen him since—until today. I'm pretty sure he's part of a cult, something called *Tyrannus-Novum*. The name means literally 'New Tyrants,'" Erik scoffed. "Anyway, he's part of some organization Roy got thick with when he was in Italy. I've done quite a bit of spying on Roy and have seen a couple of other strangers around him and he's disappeared for a couple of weeks twice. I think there's some back and forth."

"So, you think they took Uncle Alistair to Italy?" Red was almost afraid to ask.

"No, that's where there is some good news," Erik answered quickly. "I got a note from him. He's alive—at least he was a year ago—but stuck in an altered state." He paused. "He's an elf." Erik grinned at the way that sounded. "Well, actually, he's smaller than that, but he must have used the Elf Stone."

"Where is he?" Red felt torn between excitement and exasperation.

"Here's what I know. About a week after my transition, I figured out that I could ride the bus. All I had to do was get on board. No questions asked. Shockingly easy. So I went back to the lab to see what I could find—what Roy and his goons had done. They had riffled through my desk, of course, but little did they know that my lab notes were in Alistair's basement because we had been working there the night before the 'disappearance.' One of the first things I did when I learned to manipulate materials was to hide my notes in the basement so Roy and his goons wouldn't have any more information than I'd already told him about how to make the stones work. I believe that you found them." Erik smiled in an odd way. Red would've blushed if in a normal state, remembering how she had treasured his notebook.

"Getting back to the story … Alistair apparently waited until after my desk had been searched, assuming they'd have no reason to search it again, and left a note in one of the drawers of my desk. A tiny note, of course—I had to use a microscope to read it. He must have found a pencil in the lab and removed a small sliver of the carbon. Anyway, the note said that he's small and living in the lab. Remember how I said we had started to experiment with food storage? Well, Alistair was really excited about that and he and I had already miniaturized about two hundred and fifty pounds of apples, several cases of peanut butter, some wine … it might be the thing that saved him. He has had no shortage of food. I'm sure he may be craving some Maryland crab by now, or, knowing Alistair, a nice single-malt scotch." Erik smiled.

Red felt relief wash over her at the thought that Uncle Alistair might actually be okay.

Erik continued, "So your uncle is living in the lab, eating the experimental shrunken food, and drinking the experimental shrunken water and wine for the past year. I'm pretty sure he's still alive because I monitor the food when I can get over there and it's been disappearing. Though I hope it hasn't been mice eating it."

At the mention of mice she felt an instant of panic. Erik must have felt her tense, because he said quickly, "Sonia, I'm sure he's fine. Knowing Alistair, he's been collecting data on that state of being and is having a fascinating year."

"Can we go to him?" Red asked. "Have you seen him?"

"Yes, we can go to him, now that we have the key. And no, I haven't seen him. For some reason, these two altered states don't connect easily. It's kind of like being in another dimension, but I think that's an overused metaphor. He's

225

simply on a different scale than we are. But now that I have the key, we can transform back and figure this thing out as normal people for a change."

"You said there were two keys to the safe," Red said, remembering. "Where was the other one?"

"The other one was in my pocket when I transformed, so the transformed key would've been in my pocket when my pants dissolved. So it may be still laying in your yard. Or, the molecules of the metal may still be flying around in the air. It seems that only some things—mostly living matter—hold together well after the transformation. I hadn't gotten very far in the research yet and don't really know what happened to the key. It'd have been useless in its transformed state, anyway, since the safe isn't transformed."

"Why do you think Uncle Alistair made himself small?" Red asked, still trying to picture her uncle as a tiny elf.

"I suspect he made himself small to spy on Roy and his thug," Erik said. "I'm sure he thought I had the key and could just change him back later that day. I'd left the safe door unlocked since I had the Angel Stone and Alistair had the Elf Stone that morning. We weren't as careful with the Star Stone since we thought it likely to be a fake. Somehow, he managed to transform and get the stones locked back in the safe."

"How does he stay in the lab without anyone seeing him? He's not invisible," Red said, then flushed, worried that she sounded too school-girlish. *Of course he's not invisible.* What was it about this guy that made her care how she sounded? She wasn't used to being one of those girls that were meek. She squared her shoulders and was determined to speak up and be herself. "It must have been a rude awakening when he found out you were transformed, too, and lost the key."

"Well, actually, I don't know if he knows. I tried leaving a note for him in the same drawer, but there was no sign that he came back for it. I guess when I didn't find him in the lab the same day he transformed, he probably thought Roy and the thug killed me. Poor guy. I didn't dare leave the note there longer than a week. I was afraid Roy would find it. But I did write a very small note and placed it near the miniaturized food. I hope he saw it. I'm sure his mind has been working overtime, like mine, trying to figure out how to get out of this mess. It'll be wonderful to see him again and find out what he's learned."

"Well, what are we waiting for?" Red felt a rush of excitement.

"We need to plan this first, Red Sonja. I should've known you'd be itching for battle, with a name like Red Sonja." Erik smiled an electrifyingly beautiful smile. Red had never seen anything quite so compelling.

"Guilty as charged. I'd like to smash those demon parasite things against a wall." She knew her eyes were electric with excitement. They were two warriors about to enter the fray.

"Right now?" Erik said, his eyes twinkling. "Don't you have a curfew or something? Won't your parents have the police out looking for you?"

"No, my parents think I'm spending the night with Tatyana. It's still winter break for Annie and me. Mom and Dad have to go back to work tomorrow. They're probably already in bed." Red felt a little defensive at being questioned like a child. Was he emphasizing the difference in their ages?

Erik seemed to sense her irritation. "Sonia, I'm not trying to make you mad. I mean, I've seen your tae kwon do and how you've handled Roy these past few months. I know you're a strong woman and can take care of yourself. But it's my fault you're in this mess. I'm kicking myself for letting you come to the lab. I feel—well—protective of you." His expression seemed almost pleading.

Red felt confused. She felt hypnotized by his gaze. Slowly, she leaned toward him. She felt a little hurt by the emphasis on their age difference, but at the same time touched by his protectiveness. She wasn't used to having a protector. She'd always been the strong one in any group; she wasn't used to being with someone stronger, or equally strong. But then, she didn't need a protector. She was fierce and strong. Hadn't she proved that? "First of all, I'm almost seventeen. I'm less than a year from being considered an adult and my parents respect that. Second, my parents are adventurous and every member of my family has his or her own interests. We leave each other alone. Annie knows I had something up tonight and will cover for me. That's what we do. We watch out for each other. We don't try to control each other." Red had gotten a little more defensive than she'd intended but it felt good to set him straight about her family. It was one of the things that worked in her world.

Erik's eyes widened for an instant, as though he was surprised by her spunk. Then he nodded, seeming to accept her statement. Then, to her surprise, he looked at her with a provocative sideways glance, and said in a mock-sinister tone that sent a shiver through her, "So, I've got you all night …"

Oh my gosh. She swallowed hard. *What is he thinking? Whatever it is, I like it.*

Then, to her disappointment, he took a deep breath and broke away from her gaze. "Well, first things first: Alistair. We need to make a plan."

Red knew he was right and forced herself to refocus. Still, a part of her was hurt that he pulled away. She wondered if Xenia had anything to do with it. Her voice felt shaky as she responded, "Can't we just go and transform him back, now that we have the stones?"

"Yes and no. We have to get Roy out of the way first." Erik seemed to be purposefully looking away from her gaze. He rubbed his chin and looked skyward.

"Won't he be home asleep by now? It must be midnight."

"Sometimes he works all night at the lab. But we can certainly go look. I think, though, that we need to hatch up a Plan B just in case he's there. We have to make sure he's out for a while before we go in." He looked at her gravely. "Sonia, we have never changed a person back to normal yet, and there are no guarantees … I'm kicking myself now for my rashness in changing you."

"Erik, there were no guarantees when we transformed into this state, either. And haven't you been able to change other things back in your experiments?" Red wasn't sure whether she was trying to reassure himself or her.

"Yes, pretty much everything but woven material … and maybe metal." Red thought she heard a hint of humor in his voice at the mention of woven material and felt her skin tingle at the thought of how little they were wearing.

Trying to focus on the subject at hand, she said, "Okay, then stop worrying. This is a grand adventure and it's going to succeed. We're going to bring Uncle Alistair back, and us, too. That is, if you want to go back ..." She felt her playful remark was a success when she heard Erik gasp.

He looked into her eyes again briefly and swallowed before saying, "Really? You would ... Sonia. Hold that thought. Now we need to focus on Alistair and Roy. We first need to get Roy out of the lab, find Alistair, and transform him back. Then we need to figure out how to fix Roy. You know any good exorcists?" Erik raised an eyebrow sardonically.

"My mom might," Red said seriously. "She's friends with a priest."

Erik looked startled. "Sonia, seriously? That was intended to be a joke. You think this priest might be able to exercise a demon? Come to think of it, Alistair will probably have some advice on that, too, once we get him back." Erik rubbed his chin again and Red thought he looked adorable, trying so hard to concentrate. "So, to get Roy out of the lab, I'm thinking I should let the air out of his mom's tires. He at least pretends to be a responsible son and he'd go to help her."

"Too bad you can't use one of those big fish like you did before," Red said impulsively and grinned.

She saw one of Erik's eyebrows slowly rise. "Now, that's an idea. Well, we won't use fish, but maybe crows, or cats, or a dog. That's what we need. The owl certainly worked."

Something clicked for Red. "All that crow activity has been *you*? Oh, my gosh, I could strangle you. That crow scared the crap out of me." She unconsciously assumed a defensive tae kwon do stance at the thought of the crow's odd behavior.

She saw Erik assume an answering tae kwon do stance with a sparkle in his eye. "You're not the only one who's studied tae kwon do," he said playfully, standing up and beginning to circle his opponent.

"How do you know I studied tae kwon do?"

"I saw you and your wimpy friend sparring. Well, at first, I thought you were a lady in distress and I needed to rescue you. I didn't realize it was tae kwon do, though I suppose I should've known from your sparring calls," he said, and frowned. "You know, Sonia, I kinda wish you wouldn't do things like that. I mean, seeing a man physically attack a girl, especially a girl …"

Red remembered the fallen tree limb and felt a flash of outrage. "You injured one of my best friends with a tree limb!"

"Guilty as charged," he said, without regret.

"And you made a crow scare the living daylights out of me."

"Well, guilty, but that was meant as a courtship gesture. Come on, Sonia, we were in separate states of being. I had to use every tool at my disposal, didn't I?" Erik's amusement seemed to take on a worried tone.

Red was taken aback. *Did he say* courtship gesture*? All this time?* All the time she spent pining over him … could it be that he was he also pining over her? She didn't know what to think. She focused on circling him, ready to spar with the man she adored. She felt warm and euphoric and thought she could circle like this forever.

Erik stopped moving. His expression took on a seriousness, an intensity, an irresistibility. She stopped, too. Her heart pounded as he looked unwaveringly into her eyes. They stayed like that for a long time. It was impossible to tell. And then he looked down at her lips and slowly his face began to move toward hers. Red suddenly couldn't take it anymore and attacked him with a kiss that took them both by surprise. The kiss continued for a long time and they pulled away briefly only to rush together once more, claiming each other, desperately satisfying a starving urgency.

As they embraced, Red could feel the full length of his rock-hard body. How she had longed for this man. Her first kiss, though she knew this was more than a first kiss, more than a crush on a guy's picture. It was something she would never forget.

She heard Erik groan and felt him slowly pull away. "You're so beautiful. Sonia, I …" He took a slow breath and then grasped her hand and led her back to the bench. "Sonia, if we keep this up, we'll never rescue your uncle, and your parents will have me arrested. Of course, your idea of staying in this state just might have some merit …" He smiled playfully.

With an effort, Red forced herself to refocus. "No, you're right. We've got to get Uncle Alistair. So, do you think the crow thing could somehow be used to rescue him?"

Red settled back on the bench and listened with fascination as he explained how he'd developed the technique to physically superimpose his brain over another brain and exchange brain waves. "It's definitely not a perfectly controllable skill. I've tried it with many creatures and it's hit or miss. The first time I exchanged brain waves with Moon, I caught myself craving to eat a grub." They both laughed.

"Moon? Ah, that must be the crow with the moon-shaped scar on his beak," Red said, smiling at the realization. She *knew* something had been unusual about that crow.

"That's the one. He and I developed a connection over the past year. I think sometimes that if it weren't for him, the solitude would've overcome me." Erik's brow furrowed.

Red touched his hand. "Well, you aren't alone now."

Erik searched her eyes once more, beaming with warmth. "Oh, Sonia, how selfish I am. I should've left you alone."

"No, things happen for a reason. I am happy. Don't spoil it."

Red was delighted at last to get to ask all the questions she had wanted to ask for months. She felt like she was getting to know Erik as a real person, as a man, as opposed to a mere ghost. They talked long into the night.

She learned that Erik's dad, Viggo Wolfeningen, had disappeared in Iraq during the first winter of the war and was presumed dead. Red's heart wept for Erik; she'd only been a kid then, but had heard about the videotaped beheadings and hoped Erik's dad hadn't suffered such a fate.

Erik had been the man of the house after that. He had no brothers or sisters and his mom was alone without him. He had been fifteen at the time. After high school he'd gone to a college near his mom because he felt responsible for her. He considered himself lucky to get into Georgetown as an undergraduate and then to find a great graduate program at the same location.

His mom was a strong woman, Red learned. She'd worked part-time while Erik was a child, sometimes not working at all when the family was overseas. Still, his dad's disappearance had made Erik really worry about her and it had hurt him to know that his mom had had to endure the disappearance of both men in her life. He had wanted to write a note, but feared she would think she was being visited by a ghost. So he'd settled for watching over her. At least once a day he'd gone to her and done his brain-wave possession thing, implanting ideas into her mind that he was alive and well and would be coming home. That had seemed to help her sleep peacefully at night. He'd also suggested she develop a friendship with Ms. Catsworthy, which she did and which he thought had helped both women. But somehow they'd also began including Roy's mom in the group. Erik hadn't really liked having her included—not that she wasn't a victim of this as much as the others, but because her presence kept Roy in the picture. This put Erik on edge the whole year; he feared Roy's demons would make him do something evil to the three ladies. Just watching over the women had taken most of his time over the past year. Then, when Red's family moved in, and Roy started hanging around the neighborhood again, his watch-list grew. It had been more than a full-time job.

Red listened with compassion and gratitude and wondered what tomorrow would bring. Whatever it was, she thought, she knew her life would never be the same again after today.

Chapter 17

Tiny Wizard

Daybreak found Red soaring with Erik over the Potomac River, heading south to the difficult task ahead, but also enjoying the views and time together. As Red drank in the beauty of the neon peach streaks growing in the east, she felt like a new day was dawning for her as well. She was loved and treasured by the one she loved. How had this happened? Her whole life she had felt just a little inferior to others because of her ADHD. No guys, besides Wali, had ever shown any real interest in her. And, to be honest, she had never had any real interest in them.

Yet here she was, having fallen in love with a ghost. She was never the one who got the guy, the one who was rescued by the handsome prince. She had always been the rebel. She felt a mixture of joy and shock at this new experience. To be loved by someone so wonderful bolstered her own feeling of self love and made her believe what those who loved her had always maintained: that she was okay, that everyone had something to overcome and that was all right. Her issues had just always seemed a little more obvious than most other people's. She blushed as she remembered defying her first grade teacher by lying on the floor instead of sitting like the other kids during circle time. And in third grade, she remembered a sour kid calling her stupid because she was always the last person to turn in her work. Even those she considered her friends had occasionally snickered. She had felt so alone, so abandoned, so rejected, so unworthy of love back then.

But now, she knew she was worthy, and she was loved. Not because a man loved her—her inner feminist would never have allowed that—but because she could now see herself through the eyes of this wonderful being, and she liked what she saw.

As she flew, however, her euphoria waned and a shadow of a doubt crept in. *What if he's just grateful to have me here because he's lonely? Maybe he'd have loved anyone who turned up in that house.* She reminded herself that she was a strong woman and would be fine with or without a man. If he thought he loved her, so be it—she'd enjoy it, which her impulsiveness was urging her to do anyway. She'd enjoy the moment and focus on whatever she pleased. For a moment, she clung to this thought; it was like a shield from the outside world. No one could tell her how to focus her attention. That was hers and now she knew exactly what she wanted to focus on. So she focused on their kiss. She would've squealed if Erik hadn't been flying so close. Instead she looked across a few feet of air into his eyes. His warm smile made her heart race once again. Since they were soaring easily, he took her hand and stroked it with his thumb. She felt giddy with happiness.

Red glanced once again to the east. The colors were becoming more intense. The trees on either bank glowed with their greenish-pulsating energy. She heard bird songs and kept seeing small glowing forms of yellow energy. It intrigued her that the energy was always clear. Some of the human energies she had seen had been murky, especially Roy's. She shuddered, remembering the task before them, and wondered what the day would bring. She so hoped Uncle Alistair was still alive. She couldn't begin to imagine the awesome pleasure she'd feel if she could tell her family he wasn't dead after all. She thought of Ms. Catsworthy and felt an inward glow, knowing how happy she would be to find him still alive.

And the fact that she was actually flying was beyond ecstatic. She'd dreamt so often of flying, soaring over green fields and oceans. And now, was she really doing this? She felt adrenaline at the thrill of flying and just being above it all. She wanted desperately to tell someone of this most exciting adventure but knew she would never be able to really capture the thrill in mere words. *Oh, if only Annie were here.* She hoped there would be a way to show her what it was like.

Every few strokes Erik had to release her hand so they both could maneuver in their graceful air-swimming movement. Then he'd take it again. As they became more in-tune with each other, it became like a dance, a beautiful aerial ballet. Red looked at Erik and thought he recognized this, too. Without a word, Erik spun Red and then caught her. Red gasped and then laughed. Erik, obviously very practiced at this type of travel, gracefully planted a soft kiss on her lips and then spun her again. If anyone below could've seen them, Red thought, they'd have been in awe of the grace of this performance.

The light was growing to the point now that buildings began to appear as black forms against the pale sky. She could see two early morning joggers on the towpath below. She saw their essences, as well as their guardian angels hovering overhead. She remembered briefly that her own guardian angel had disappeared as soon as it realized she could see it. And, with all that had happened, it'd failed to register until now that Erik didn't have one hovering overhead, either. She looked toward him and was taken aback by his stunning smile. She felt a thrill run through her body and almost forgot her question. "Why don't we have guardian angels like those two joggers?" She gestured with a nod toward them; unlike her adroit partner, she didn't feel quite comfortable enough with flying to venture to point even for an instant.

Erik smiled and seemed to laugh to himself. "Oh, we have them all right. But they're the shyest creatures I've ever encountered. I tried for weeks to talk mine into coming back. Needless to say, I was lonely and could only catch a glimpse of her ... him on occasion. I called out, begged, cajoled, even shouted in anger once. Then I worried that I'd scared it away for good. But it never allowed me to communicate with it. Seems that once it sensed that I could see it, it was gone in a flash."

"That's exactly what mine did last night," said Red.

Nodding knowingly, he added, "I have some stories to tell of all the attempts I made to talk to mine. I'll tell you about

238

them when we have time. But rest assured, they're watching us. You can catch a glimpse from time to time." He hesitated and then gave her such a loving look she felt her heart would melt. "Sonia, I can't tell you how good it feels to talk about this with another person."

"I'm sure. There's so much going on around us." She looked to the east again and noticed they were passing an impressive tower.

Erik followed her gaze. "That's the National Cathedral."

"I thought it looked familiar. That's where I was confirmed. Only I've never seen it from overhead." She laughed, feeling giddy.

Erik smiled warmly, seeming to enjoy the fun. Then he pointed to a group of buildings a bit further to the south. "We're here. Georgetown. Let's land over near that bench to recap our plans."

A few minutes later, Red and Erik watched from a bench near the entrance to the old science building, no longer bothering to hide in the nearby bushes. Erik had explained that the only time they had to be really careful was when the sun was either rising or setting. He wasn't totally sure why—something about the wavelengths of the light—but he intended to add this research question to his graduate work when he got back to the university.

A few students were stirring. As it was Sunday, they all had bed-heads and were probably seeking breakfast. One guy in a puffy down coat, hands in pockets, was obviously hung over and seemed to watch the ground as he walked, intimating that the sun was too bright even at this early hour. His guardian angel dutifully hovered overhead. Red watched to see if she could see a hint of frantic worry in the apparition but only sensed serenity.

"Okay, you know what to do?" asked Erik.

"We go into the lab and if Roy isn't there, I'll watch the front door while you retrieve the stones," Red said. "If he's there, then we go to Plan B—letting the air out of his mom's tires."

"Right. Ready, comrade?"

"Ready, comrade."

How different Red felt this morning to be entering the building than last night when she escaped it. So much had changed. Erik was real and had kissed her. She almost squealed again with delight at the thought. And now they were going to be an awesome team and save Uncle Alistair. She felt excited and not even scared of Roy. Not with her Viking by her side.

It turned out that the coast was clear. Roy must have still been asleep. Red saw Erik motion her into the lab. It would only take him a few minutes to retrieve the key and get the stones, she thought. She took one last look through the glass of the main door and saw the courtyard in front of the building was clear. No Roy coming at least for a few minutes.

When she entered the lab, she was taken aback. She didn't see the Erik she had expected, but a beautiful glowing, crystal-clear, silver form. He was stunning. Clearly, he'd transformed. Now she was the ghost, she thought. She stopped short, not sure what to do.

"Sonia?" She recognized his voice, though the quality had changed, like he was speaking from a tunnel. "If you're in here, come and stand in front of me and tell me when you're there. I'll be able to hear you."

She realized he couldn't see her. She walked forward and stood in front of him. "I'm here."

"Okay, here goes."

She felt a tingling and then a snapping sensation and felt disoriented for an instant. Then she looked up into Erik's eyes as he bent to kiss her. Her senses were awakened and she lost herself momentarily.

"You are so beautiful," he said, squeezing her shoulders. She realized they were themselves again, whole and human. "I thought you were beautiful when I saw your essence, and then when you were transformed. But now, I can't believe here you are in the flesh, blushing and alive. And even more beautiful than I'd imagined."

Red felt in danger of her knees giving away. "And you, I can't believe you're really here. Flesh and blood and not a ghost." She felt her eyes fill with tears of joy.

"We have to get Alistair," he reminded her.

"What's a few more minutes?" She raised an eyebrow provocatively, trying for smoothness.

"I like the way you think," He bent and kissed her again. "Okay, here's the plan. Why don't you hide in the ladies' room until I can find a lab coat and get us both some decent clothes? I think I know where some janitorial work coveralls hang."

She thought of the last time she'd hidden in the ladies room, how other women kept coming in. "Do you have some paper and a marker? I think I'll make an 'Out of Order' sign."

Red watched as Erik rummaged around the lab. The marker from his desk was dry, having been abandoned for the past year. But he found one in Roy's desk drawer. He also pulled from Roy's drawer a twisted length of thin rope and a silver roll of duct tape. "What the heck is he up to?"

He handed her the paper, then took a lab coat from a hook behind one of the doors and slipped it on. Red realized she was disappointed that he had covered that glorious chest. With all that had happened, Red hadn't taken enough time to appreciate the view of Erik in a leather loincloth; sadly, now that his body was even more compelling in its real carnal aspect, pulsing with blood and vitality, he was covering it up.

"You ready?" he asked. She nodded. "I'll come back as soon as I can. And, remember, Sonia, we can no longer walk through doors. So don't bump that pretty nose." Erik smiled mischievously and tweaked her nose. Red smiled back, realizing how much she liked this guy. He had a sense of humor.

They peeked into the hallway. They were alone. Red slipped into the ladies room to hide, watching for a moment while Erik continued down the hallway, looking like a flasher, wearing only a lab coat.

She didn't have to wait long. He returned a few minutes later wearing a baggy orange coverall and handed her an identical one. "Put this on and then come back into the lab, okay? I left a mop beside the door as a prop." He was gone.

Red slipped out of the leather coat and into the coverall. She sighed as she looked in the mirror. *My first date and look how I'm dressed.* She did as much as she could to improve her appearance, washing her face and brushing her teeth with a finger, and then tried finger-combing her hair, now wild and tangled from the flight. She pinched her cheeks for some color and took a deep breath. *Ready or not, here I come.*

Back in the lab, Erik knelt down, opening two cabinet doors in one corner of the lab, and searched inside, careful not to move any of the items. Red held her breath, knowing her uncle was here somewhere. She heard Erik say quietly, "Just as I feared. I don't know where he's hiding right now. I can't call to him since I think our speech would be distorted to him and he might not recognize it was us and stay hidden, and I don't want to miniaturize and leave you alone here in case Roy comes back. So I'm going to set up an Alistair-trap. He could never resist a party."

Red watched him disappear into the inner closet and emerge with a box of party favors. "Your uncle always made sure each of his grad students got a little birthday celebration. He said it was too easy with the pressures of grad school to forget to be human." Erik laughed warmly. He pulled a Twinkie from a drawer, holding it by a corner of its cellophane wrapper. "I was hoping to save this, since they aren't being made anymore, but what better occasion to use my last Twinkie?" He placed the two cakes on a festive paper plate, pushed a birthday candle into each, and laid this aside with a box of matches. He then went back into the closet and returned carrying an empty box. He took a plastic birthday party tablecloth from the party favors box and wrapped the empty box with it.

"Is there anything I can do to help?" asked Red, puzzled at the frivolity of his actions when they were under such pressure to avoid Roy.

"I'm almost finished. But, yes, it'd be a huge help if you peeked out the door every few seconds to make sure he isn't coming."

"Okay." Red inwardly chastised herself for not having thought of that before and hastily went to the door to begin her vigil, alternately opening the door ever so slightly to peek out while continuing to watch Erik in his curious task.

Erik seemed to move quickly, wasting no time. He reached behind his desk and pulled out a piece of yellow poster board. Using the marker from Roy's desk, he wrote in large letters, "Happy belated birthday. Please blow out the candles and remain standing in that spot for your surprise. Welcome back. Erik." He lit the candles and looked at Red. "I'm hoping the candles will get his attention."

Red watched Erik tape the sign to the upside-down box. It now looked like a small but festive party table. He reopened the lower cabinet door. He was moving so carefully that Red was curious and left her post to peer into the cabinet. At first the space looked empty, but then her eyes could make out translucent shapes that looked like stacks of boxes. Most of the boxes had lids but some seemed to contain colorful shapes. Were these fruits and vegetables? If Uncle Alistair was in there and was equally translucent, he'd be impossible to spot unless he moved—even then it would be difficult.

"I'm surprised Roy has left this alone," she said.

Erik snorted. "He made fun of Alistair and me for doing this. He didn't have altruistic ideas like ours, at least, not after he returned from Italy. He probably forgot about this stash. Not worth anything without the stones."

Erik carefully pushed a few boxes aside ever so slowly and placed the wrapped box inside the space. He then placed the plate with Twinkies on the box. "Now, here's the tricky part. I need to light the candles and minimize the whole thing. Can you check the hallway again?"

"Got it." Red moved quickly back to the door and peeked out. "Coast still clear." She came back and sat on her heels beside Erik, who was now doing something with two of the stones.

"When I say 'go,' light the candle and then jump out of the way," Erik said. "Ready?"

"Ready," replied Red.

"Ok, go."

Red quickly lit the candles and jumped back. Erik pointed one stone toward the table and the other directly behind it. With a flash like that from a camera, the box was gone. Then Red realized that it wasn't gone, just tiny. "Are the candles still burning?" she asked, straining her eyes hard to detect any tiny glow.

"I think so." He bent down so his eyes were very close to the box. "Yep. Mission accomplished," he said triumphantly as he rose back onto his heels. "Keep a close watch on the door while I wait with the stones. As soon as he shows up, I'll reverse his transformation."

"Roger." This was scary but something within Red was battle-ready. She went to the door, her blood beginning to pump harder to a primal drumbeat, mentally running through maneuvers to subdue Roy in case he showed up. She'd buy time for Erik to help Uncle Alistair no matter what she had to do to keep him away.

Moments ticked by. Red alternately peeked into the hallway and back at Erik, who sat as still as a statue, the stones poised.

Finally, after what seemed an eternity, Red heard Erik gasp. She looked back and saw him make a small quick movement. At the same time, she caught sight of two men emerging around the corner down the hallway, heading toward them. "Here they come! Two of them."

Red heard a snapping sound and Uncle Alistair appeared, smiling as he savored a Twinkie. "Ah, the simple pleasures of life," he beamed.

"Quick, both of you, in the closet," Erik said.

She saw her uncle quickly obey, likely too disoriented to do anything but blindly obey someone he trusted, but she stood her ground. "No, I got this."

"Red, no!" she heard Erik shout-whisper. There was no time to reply. She flipped off the light switch as the key scratched in the doorknob. Red jumped back flat against side of the door and saw Erik mirror her on the other side. In the dim light she saw that Erik still had the stones in his hands.

The door opened. As Roy's arm reached for the light switch, Red heard two snapping sounds and Roy disappeared. The second man lunged at Erik.

Red wasted no time and launched herself toward the man. A few basic tae kwon do moves came instinctively to her as she threw him to the ground.

She saw the lights come on and heard Erik's voice say, "What the—"

It had all happened so fast that Red scarcely realized

which movements she had made. She found herself standing over Lorenzo, who was face down on the floor. His arms were behind him and she had a firm grasp on his wrists, pressing them upward toward his shoulder blades until he groaned, totally immobilized. "Get it off me," Lorenzo shouted in pain.

She heard Erik laugh as he speedily dropped beside her. He set the stones beside Lorenzo and said, "Okay, warrior princess, you'd better jump back or you're going to get minimized and have to fight this dude all night."

Red released her hold and threw her hands back in a surrender position. She heard two snapping sounds, and Lorenzo disappeared.

"Okay, now quick, we need to find Roy." Erik took a small beaker from the lab bench above and gently herded Lorenzo into the beaker as he tried to run away.

She saw Erik pick up a black rubber floor mat that covered the floor just inside the door where Roy had disappeared. "Quick, empty that trash can and bring it here," he said urgently.

Red emptied the few contents onto the floor and sat the can in front of Erik. He hesitated and looked around. "The paper towels for a cushion," he urged, gesturing toward a stack of brown paper towels beside the sink.

She quickly took the stack and scattered them around inside the can. Erik carefully bent the opposite ends of the mat upward so it formed a loose cone shape, and shook it into the can. He peered into the can, then moved it directly beneath an overhead light. "Got him," he said, satisfaction in his voice.

He took another beaker from the lab bench and lifted it down into the can to gently nudge Roy into the beaker. Then, picking up both beakers, he smiled. Red peered at the two tiny men sitting in their respective beakers. They both looked very much disoriented and scared.

"Okay if I come out now?" Red heard her uncle's familiar voice from the closet and ran to him.

"Uncle Alistair!" Red squealed as she threw her arms around him. He returned the hug like a human starved for companionship. They both cried and laughed at the same time.

Erik embraced Uncle Alistair, then stepped back and cleared his throat. "Um, I hate to break this up but I remind you that we're now guilty of kidnapping. I'm not sure if there is a law covering transforming people into elves, but I'm sure they'll come up with something. Professor Hamilton, I know you don't know all that's happened in the past year and we'll have to brief each other very soon. For now, suffice it to say that you were right about a lot of things, including the existence of angels and demons and that Roy and this other guy, an Italian named Lorenzo, are possessed with evil spirits. We saw them."

"No. You saw them?" Alistair was incredulous.

"I saw them, too, Uncle Alistair," Red chimed in.

"We need to get these demons exorcised, and hope these two will be so grateful they won't press any kidnapping charges," Erik interjected in a serious tone.

"I need a glass of water," Alistair said weakly. Red noticed he looked skinny and pale.

"Uncle Alistair, are you okay?" she said with concern.

"Oh, yes, yes, quite." He patted her hand. "It's just that, with all that food we miniaturized, we didn't miniaturize much water and since I didn't know how long I'd need to stay in that condition, I've been rationing water for myself. I have longed for months to drink my fill."

"You sit here and I'll fetch it," said Red. She filled a clean liter beaker from the tap in the lab. She handed it to Alistair and then did the same with another beaker, only this time, she went to the water cooler out in the hallway to fill it so it would be cold. As she returned, Alistair was polishing off the first beaker and was delighted to receive the ice-cold one.

"Ahhhh," he said with such satisfaction that Red beamed, not sure she could recall a time that she had so pleased anyone.

"Okay, are we ready to plan now?" Erik's eyes sparkled with obvious pleasure as he looked from one to the other. "Here's what I'm thinking," he continued. "We need to take these two somewhere and hold them until we can get a priest or a team to perform the exorcism. Red," he said, looking pointedly at her. "Do you think we can bring your parents into our confidence? That way we could use Professor Hamilton's basement to hold them. If not, then we can use my mom's, but I think there may be some screaming and the neighbors are more likely to hear it from my mom's basement. Your house is more secluded. You know that dug-out area in the basement? I think that's the best place for this—" he seemed to hesitate over the word "—exorcism."

He looked to Alistair. "And we need to find a very strong team of priests. Do you know anyone you can call who'd be willing to come right away?"

"Yes, I think so. I'll need to make a few calls," responded Alistair.

"And your parents?" he looked at Red.

"Yes, absolutely," Red nodded. "Well, my mom, anyway. My dad's a devout atheist and will probably be hard to convince about the demons."

"You just let me deal with my nephew," Alistair said with a sigh. "Always was such a stubborn lad." He rolled his eyes playfully and then smiled, first to Erik and then to Red. "My, it's good to be back."

CHAPTER 18

Call for the Priest!

The logistics for getting back to the mansion were tricky. Red and Erik weren't fully dressed and Alistair, though dressed, hadn't been able to use water liberally to wash his clothes and was in desperate need of a shower. Besides that, Alistair and Erik decided they needed to keep hidden until the matter of Roy and Lorenzo was resolved. So Red had to be the spokesperson for now.

She needed a phone and knew pay phones were pretty much a thing of the past. She also knew being barefoot in a janitorial cover-all might raise questions. But she was nothing if not creative. She peeked into the hallway. A few people were now stirring. She waited until she spotted the right candidate. She shyly approached a middle-aged, matronly-looking woman and asked to borrow her cell, saying her battery had died. The woman looked her over and said, with much concern, "Of course, sweetie. Are you in trouble?"

"No, no, no," Red said, laughing. "It's part of a birthday surprise."

"Oh, okay." The woman handed Red her cell, though now seemed a little suspicious about this alleged surprise. Red hadn't considered that someone might think the surprise might be her popping out of a cake or some other illicit activity. Frat parties were notorious for things like that, she had heard. The woman regarded her with patent disapproval.

"Have to call my dad." She smiled shyly and the woman seemed somewhat mollified, but not totally convinced.

Red quickly dialed his cell and turned her back to the woman for some privacy. Thankfully, he answered on the second ring.

"Dad, it's me," she said with a modicum of perkiness.

"Oh, hey, Red. Need me to pick you up? You still at Tatyana's?"

"Noooo." She hesitated. "Actually I'm at Georgetown and, yes, I do need you to pick me up."

"Georgetown? Red, what's going on? You in trouble?"

Red felt warmed by the concern in his voice, but didn't want him to feel alarmed. "No, no, Dad, not at all. In fact—" Red took a deep breath to begin. "Dad, I need for you to bring your wagon here right away. I also need for you to keep totally quiet about this, well, except for Mom and Annie. I mean, you can tell them that you're coming to pick me up, but there won't be room in the car so they can't come with you."

"What the dickens are you up to, Red?" She could hear bewilderment in his voice.

"Seriously, Dad, this will be the best surprise you've ever had. It'll be like Christmas and your birthday, heck, ten Christmases and birthdays." Red needed for him to grasp the seriousness and follow orders without asking too many questions. "I can't tell you, you'll just have to see it for yourself. Meet us at the loading dock behind Uncle Alistair's old building by the Dumpster. Do you know which building it is?"

"Of course I know which building, but what is this 'us'?" He was going along with this good-naturedly. Red loved her dad.

"Oh, and Dad, you may want to stop and pick up a couple of bottles of champagne on the way." She so loved this.

She hung up the phone and handed it back to the woman, who accepted her thanks graciously but glanced at her watch, obviously giving Red a gentle chastisement that the whole encounter had taken too much time.

Red thought she had never experienced anything as joyful as the reunion between her dad and his uncle. Her dad was speechless when Uncle Alistair emerged from the back door of the old science building. Uncle Alistair wordlessly grasped him in a hug and her dad clung to his uncle, choking something incoherent.

Red was mesmerized by the sight until she heard Erik prod urgently, "We should get them into the car before someone sees Professor Hamilton and starts asking questions."

"Good point."

Red and Erik guided both of them into the Volvo and Red took the keys from her dad, suggesting that the two sit together in the backseat to catch up. Her dad, who normally would have been aghast at Red's driving without having her learner's permit with her, didn't even question it, so Red knew he was still in shock. She knew she should also be in shock from all that had happened over the past twenty-four hours, but she felt oddly normal and in charge. Erik offered to drive but she simply said, "No, I'm good."

Red and Erik were too tired to talk on the drive home and listened to the flurry of questions, laughter, and exclamations of concern from the backseat. She saw that Uncle Alistair held a box carefully in his lap and suspected it contained Roy and Lorenzo. She heard him coach her dad that secrecy was absolutely essential for now and then listened as her dad called her mom and urged her to ask Ms. Catsworthy and Minah to come to their house as soon as possible for a very important bit of business. "Something like a surprise party," he said. Red giggled, wondering what her mom was thinking right now. She glanced toward Erik. Their eyes met and she almost forgot she was driving when she caught his vibrant smile. She swerved a little and snapped her focus back to the road.

At home, she watched her uncle and Erik keep their faces low and walk rapidly into the house to avoid any recognition from neighbors or people out walking. Luckily no one was around except her mom and Annie. Annie, after hugging her great-uncle, gave Red a big-eyed look. Then, glancing at Erik, a look of stunned recognition crossed her face. She turned to Red and grinned knowingly. Red blushed.

Immediately after the hugs, Uncle Alistair announced that he wanted to make a beeline for the shower. "Umm, where would I find a clean change of clothes?" he asked her mom, a little shyly. Red wanted to hug him again for his graciousness—he didn't seem even a little annoyed to arrive home after a year to find that people had moved in and rearranged all his things.

Her mom evidently realized that he assumed his clothes would've been packed away or given away and that her parents would be occupying the master suite. "Uncle Alistair, your room is pretty much as you left it. Yates and I didn't have the heart to move in there. It just didn't seem right. I guess we kept a little hope in the back of our minds that you'd return." A sincere tear trickled down the side of her face. An answering tear also trickled down her uncle's cheek.

Her mom continued, "We're so glad you're back. We will, of course, pack up and move back out now that you're back. I hope you find that we've kept everything in good order for your return." She smiled sincerely.

Uncle Alistair was obviously touched by the offer. He stepped forward and took both her hands in his, looking directly into her eyes. "Please, please don't talk of moving out. I couldn't be more delighted to find my family at home upon my return. And it would've been fine for you to take the master suite. In fact, I insist. There are two of you but only one of me. You should have the larger room."

Her mom leapt upon him in a grateful embrace, hugging him and cry-laughing. "Thank you so much. We'd be happy to stay with you here, if you're sure it's okay. But Yates and I are very comfortable in our room and I can't think of anything better than all of us living here together."

Red felt tears of joy swell in her eyes and looked around to see everyone present shared her sentiment. She watched as her dad stepped forward and squeezed her mom's hand and then smiled to his uncle. Uncle Alistair smiled back and the deal seemed to be set.

"Now, for that long-awaited shower, before I drive everyone from the house with my stench," Uncle Alistair announced cheerfully.

Red knew she'd never forget what she had seen today—the joy first from her dad, and then her mom and Annie, but the best was yet to come as Minah and Ms. Catsworthy arrived. The mother-son reunion was beyond joyful. But she was taken aback by the powerful emotions she sensed flowing between her great-uncle and sweet old Ms. Catsworthy. There was definitely more than casual friendship there, she thought. She felt her inner matchmaker's interest piqued.

And Erik. She basked in happiness as the family, along with Minah and Ms. Catsworthy, feasted and celebrated. She noticed that several times throughout the evening, Uncle Alistair disappeared—once to make phone calls, once to take the mysterious box into the basement, once with Ms. Catsworthy, and a couple of times with Erik, evidently to discuss plans.

Erik also pulled Red aside to invite her to sit with him in the backyard. "I'd love to take you for a stroll on the towpath, but need to lay low for a few days," he said.

"Oh, good point. We have some lawn chairs in the back yard. Want to sit there?"

"Perfect." He flashed the smile she loved so much. He had showered and changed into some clothes her dad loaned him and he looked so handsome. Red couldn't believe that he was her—her what? Boyfriend?

Her boyfriend. That sounded so good but also a little scary. Red's years of not being popular with the boys came back to haunt her. Her self-doubts attacked her almost every moment. Was he just grateful to her for rescuing him? Surely, a graduate student couldn't be interested in her, a puny high-school student. These doubts resounded in her head over and over. And what about Xenia?

As it was such a special occasion, her parents had allowed both Red and Annie to have a glass of champagne each. Better still, they weren't really policing them on their interpretation of *a glass*. As Red and Erik sat in the yard, Red wasn't sure if her light-headedness was from the champagne or from Erik and the moon. In this enchanting light of the full moon, Erik reached over and took her hand in his. Red allowed herself to enjoy the moment. There was so much she wanted to say, and to ask, but settled for making small talk. They laughed about their amazing flight the night before and made a lot of eye contact. Eventually, Red heard a throat being cleared behind her. Pulling her focus away from Erik with some effort, she turned to see Annie standing behind her.

"Erik's mom wants to go home and I said I'd tell him," she announced.

"Of course," he said, jumping up. "It must be getting late."

"It's two a.m.," Annie stated and then looked pointedly at Red's champagne glass with one eyebrow raised.

"Sonia, I'd better go home with my mom," Erik said. Still holding her hand, he pulled her to a standing position and faced her. He gently pushed one of her stray locks behind an ear and smiled another captivating smile. She smiled back and they mutually leaned into a kiss. Pulling back way too soon, he looked sideways at Annie, who was purposefully looking away. "More of that later," he whispered, "but tonight I'm remembering what tiredness feels like in this body. It's going to feel strange to sleep in my old bed again." Erik shook his head regretfully.

Red sighed, feeling the effects of the champagne. She didn't want him to go and wanted to say something to that effect. As she started to speak, however, she noticed her voice sounded odd and whiny and stopped in mid-sentence with "But ..."

Erik seemed to sense her mood and smiled. "Believe me. I don't want to go. But, don't you have school tomorrow? And I'm wondering if you may have indulged a bit too much in the champagne—how much of that stuff did you have? You need some sleep. And, second, your dad—no, more like your mom, would fetch her shotgun if I tried to stay." Red watched one side of Erik's mouth turn upward adorably.

She had to agree. And seeing Minah's eyes light up afresh as they rejoined the others made Red feel a little selfish for wanting to keep him to herself. The experience of being in an altered state with Erik had made a huge impression on her and she knew a part of her would always long to go back. That had been just theirs.

But seeing the easy laughter all around the library as her uncle sleepily recounted details of his transformation made her glad to be back and surrounded by family. She noted that her mom, dad, and Ms. Catsworthy hung on every word and he seemed quite in his element. Finally, she said goodnight and went to bed, feeling the adrenaline wane and the weight of tiredness pull her into a peaceful sleep, filled with inner visions of flying over the canal.

The next day was Monday, and Red's first-ever hint of a hangover. She awakened at ten, feeling thirsty and having a slight twinge of a headache, but otherwise okay. She decided to go to school late, even though at Annie's urging, her mom had already called the school and reported her sick. She didn't want to get behind in any of her classes and needed to bring up her score in English composition. Her mom agreed to drive her to school mid-morning since she was working at home, and Red was glad to catch a little slack. In fact, her mom seemed to feel guilty for allowing her to stay up so late, and did not seem to suspect Red's over-indulgence.

On the walk home that afternoon, Red was having some difficulty keeping the necessary secrets. She so longed to tell Tatyana her exciting news about Erik that she thought she'd burst. Tatyana quizzed her about coming to school late and Red gave a vague response about not sleeping well the night before.

"Um-huh." Tatyana surveyed her with suspicion. "You aren't telling me everything. Red, I'm beginning to worry about your obsession with this ghost guy. You need to get out more. Tell you what. You and I will take a bus to the mall Saturday morning. We'll guy-watch at the food court. That should get your mind off ghosts. What do you say?"

"Oh, don't know about Saturday. I'll have to let ya know later. But I do have something to tell you—I just can't quite yet."

"Hmmm." Tatyana eyed her quizzically as they paused in front of her house. "If I didn't have a project due tomorrow, you wouldn't get off this easy. But you're going to have to tell me everything, and soon."

"Agreed." Red loved having such a good friend, and she was glad Roy was now captured so he couldn't harm her.

The thought of Roy made her quicken her step after leaving Tatyana. What would she find at home? She shuddered.

She caught up with Annie just as the mansion came into view. Four strange cars were parked on the road in front of their house, in addition to the two that were theirs. She and Annie approached cautiously and quietly entered. A palpable stillness was evident inside and she heard low voices coming from the library. They both dropped their daypacks onto stools as they passed through the kitchen and entered reverently, sensing that was the appropriate attitude.

A fire blazed in the grate, adding warmth and timelessness to the room and to the gathering. She and Annie found their mom, Minah, and Ms. Catsworthy in a deep conversation with a female priest whom Red recognized as

Reverend Joan, her mom's friend. Her dad was sitting apart from the group, reclined and staring out a window in deep contemplation.

As Red and Annie entered the library, the women rose and welcomed them. Their mom gestured for them to take a seat, saying, "Girls, I called Joan and asked her to help us understand what's going on with Roy and the other man. I mean, I know it's supposed to be hush-hush, but I knew we could trust Joan and wanted to pick her brain about ... well, demons and exorcisms."

Red's dad looked up from his contemplation. "And as you might imagine, I'm not at all convinced that Uncle Alistair's right about this. I think it's more likely some kind of hypnosis or brain-washing, but I'm keeping my mouth shut." He shrugged and then resumed his stare out the window.

Red learned that Roy and Lorenzo were in the basement in separate rooms. An exorcism team of priests and a psychologist had been working with them for several hours and would continue to do so until the exorcism was resolved. No one was allowed to go into the basement without a specific invitation from the exorcism team. There was no mention of their small size, so Red assumed that Uncle Alistair and Erik had taken care of that little detail before calling the others. Red tuned in and out of Reverend Joan's explanations and found herself wondering if the transformation had affected the demons or if size meant anything to them.

Red also learned that Uncle Alistair had arranged the exorcism team, as he was connected with a large network of experts in all areas of religion through his work at the university. They had immediately dropped everything and come to help—one from D.C., one from New York, and one flying in tomorrow from the Vatican. These priests actually specialized in exorcisms, Joan said. Red was surprised to learn that exorcisms were becoming better understood and studied. Exorcism teams tended to have at least one psychologist and sometimes a psychiatrist or neurologist, since it was often a mental or psychological crisis that precipitated such a severe lapse in judgment as to invite a demon in. Reverend Joan was there for the family, her mom said; though she wouldn't be assisting in the exorcisms, she had gratefully accepted the invitation for a rare opportunity to learn.

Red felt awed by the seriousness of the situation and a glance toward Annie told her she felt the same. She learned that Roy's mother had been told about the demon possession and had visited him earlier. Red shuddered at the thought of what that must have been like. Uncle Alistair was assisting the team and would likely remain with them until the process was completed and the two men were taken to a mental hospital for testing and treatment. Her ears perked up even more when her mom explained that Erik was assisting Alistair in the process and was presently out running an errand.

Red watched each face with curiosity as Reverend Joan read something to the group and then had them repeat statements renouncing evil. Presently, Red heard someone enter the front door without knocking and the sound of footsteps approaching. Her heartbeat picked up and then simultaneously sank when she realized it was Erik, but that he wasn't alone. He and Xenia walked silently past the door to the library without even a glance toward her. He had his arm around Xenia's shoulders and she leaning into him for support, her arm around the small of his back. Like one connected organism, they strolled past. Red heard the basement door close.

Red couldn't move. Erik and Xenia, together? She wanted to run, to scream, but she sat frozen in her seat. After a few minutes, she realized sounds could be heard from below. Screams, angry shouts, commands, maniacal laughter, and occasional chants issued from the basement.

Red lost track of time. She sat quietly while others around her alternately chatted and then sat silently. This felt like a wake. Somehow, snacks materialized, along with tea and coffee. Red's mom occasionally went into the kitchen and returned bearing yet another offering of hospitality. Red felt her tummy growl, but at the same time she felt nauseous from the sight of Erik with Xenia. She wanted to go to her room and cry but also wanted to be brave and support the effort, and no one else had left the group, not even Annie or her dad. Everyone seemed to sense that with the heaviness present, each person was needed to help support each other as well as the two unfortunate men downstairs.

Eventually, to Red's great relief, her mom suggested that the two girls should go to bed. They had a full day of school tomorrow and needed their rest. She was glad to escape as she walked quietly upstairs, said good night to Annie, and entered her room. Once inside the door, Red closed the door and leaned against it for several moments, her eyes closed. Still in shock from seeing Erik and Xenia together, she remained paralyzed for a few moments and then craved fresh air, suddenly feeling suffocated.

She broke from the paralysis, walked to the window, and raised it as high as it would go. The air was cool outside but not windy, so it was pleasant. The moon was almost as full as it had been the night before, casting light onto the two chairs in the yard below where she and Erik had sat and held hands. That was the last straw. The dam broke. She sank down to the floor inside the window, sobbing from her broken heart. What had she been thinking? A college student in love with her? Her clumsy self? Her tomboyish, tall frame? She continued sobbing for what seemed like half an hour before coming up for a breath.

A scratchy sound made her suddenly jerk her head upward. Moon was standing on her windowsill. "Oh, Moon. It's you." Her sobs became a mixture of sobs and laughter. "You silly bird. I know how you feel. Unrequited love. It's not pleasant, is it?" She reached up and stroked his smooth head with one finger. He made a clucking sound deep in his throat. "Would you like a hug?"

Moon eyed her with one black eye, clucked once, ruffled his feathers, and then clucked again. Red gently put her hands on either side of his vibrant little body and gave him a gentle squeeze. Then, reaching her lips down, she planted a kiss on the side of his beak. He clucked and eyed her intently, first with one eye and then the other. Red wasn't sure this form of affection was fully understood or enjoyed by Moon, but he did seem to take it in his stride and she hoped he appreciated that she was trying.

She gently removed her hands from the sides of his body and stroked the top of his head and down his back with a finger, cooing to him gently. He shuddered and clucked.

A slight knock at the door startled both of them and Moon flew away. Red wiped her eyes on her sleeves and blew her nose. "Who is it?" She was almost afraid to ask.

"It's me. Who else did you think? Santa Claus?" came Annie's sassy voice. Red felt a mixture of disappointment that it wasn't Erik and relief because she didn't want him to see her distraught like this. Annie's voice came as a warm welcome balm.

She opened her door and saw Annie's concerned expression. "You okay, Red?"

"Yeah, I guess the whole thing kind of got to me."

"Oh, I thought you were crying about Erik having his arm around that girl." Leave it to Annie to see straight through her.

"Okay, okay. Whatever." She swung the door wide, an invitation for Annie to enter, and threw herself onto the bed with a sigh.

Annie collaborated, following her inside and diving onto the bed beside Red. The two joked and bonded and Red felt much better. With Annie's help she began to feel good about herself again, strong. She felt appreciated. Annie let her know in no uncertain terms that no man was worth that much pain. That she, Red, was a cool person to be with and she didn't need a man to make her whole.

It's amazing, Red thought, as she stared at the dark ceiling after Annie had retired to her own room, *how important friends and family are. I love Erik but I don't need him. I'm okay alone. Life is beautiful. I'm loved and I love and that's all that matters. If Xenia makes him happy, then Xenia he shall have. I'm glad for the time we spent together, and if that's all there is of it, then so be it. I will not cry to him or attack him the next time I see him. I will be steady and serene. I will be indifferent. Then he won't have to feel guilty.*

Finally, she began to drift off to sleep. As she drifted, she distinctly heard a tapping at her window, but was too far gone to look up.

The next few days were uneventful. Red felt an odd kind of letdown after all the recent excitement. Like a robot, she rose every morning and walked to school. She sat through class, did her assignments, and dodged questions from her friends, especially Tatyana, who watched Red like a spectator, waiting for something to happen or for Red to make some grand confession, which she somehow managed to avoid. Red didn't see Erik again, nor did she see Uncle Alistair. A different assortment of strange cars was parked outside the mansion each day when she returned from school. When she asked for an update, her mom and dad just shrugged their shoulders and said she knew as much about what was going on in the basement as they did.

Then, on Thursday, Red came home to find that all the cars were gone. In the library, Red and Annie found an exuberant Uncle Alistair seated by the fire, holding a brandy snifter with amber liquid. His legs were stretched out in front, ankles crossed in maximum relaxation. Red noted that her parents were seated on the couch in a rare moment of togetherness, her dad's arm across the back of the chair behind her mom, her shoulder leaning into his chest. They were all laughing as she and Annie entered. It was amazing, like a storm had broken and the sun come up. The atmosphere almost made her feel cheerful.

Uncle Alistair jumped to his feet and stretched his long slender arms wide in an invitation for a group hug. "Come, girls, and give your old uncle a proper hug now that the world is once again in proper order." He beamed. Red glanced toward Annie questioningly; both shrugged and then in unison ran into his arms. He lifted them both off the ground in his exuberance.

"Uncle, don't break something," Red heard her dad exclaim, mostly in jest, but with some edge of true concern.

"Nephew, I feel like the father of the prodigal son. What was lost is now found." Then, to the girls, he said, "My dear student, Roy, is now free from the evil that has besieged him for more than a year and is now under expert care, with a full recovery expected." He laughed as he spoke, a tear glistening in each eye.

"That's great, Uncle Alistair." Red beamed.

"Yeah," agreed Annie.

"Girls, I know you need a moment to refresh yourselves after a long day at school, but please hurry back down and I'll tell you the full story."

Fifteen minutes later, Red had seated herself on the hearth near Annie, who was stretched on the floor in front of Uncle Alistair's chair. She was thrilled to be part of the audience for his tale. He seemed to love having occasion to be dramatic and told the story with grandiosity and flourish. Her dad also listened, with intensity, she noted, though he must already be familiar with parts of it. Her mom listened, too, but kept popping in and out, preparing dinner. Wonderful smells wafted from the kitchen as Red sat listening intently, in awe of the tale her great-uncle had to communicate.

The basement had been transformed into a makeshift medical unit on Monday, Uncle Alistair told them, with hospital beds and monitors. The personalities of both Roy and Lorenzo had been difficult to reach. The psychiatrist had checked on the men at least once a day. The team of priests that specialized in exorcisms had worked in shifts, allowing the young men time to rest between sessions. Counseling sessions attempted to draw their individual personalities out and separate the real person from the demon. After much effort, the real personality of each man had been available for communication for brief periods, allowing the priests to ask them to denounce evil and ask the demons to depart. Once this was done, it was a matter for the priests to command the spirits to depart in a formal ceremony. Red saw her uncle shudder during this part of his story. She learned that the departure for each demon had occurred while she and Annie were in school and her parents at work, so only the team of exorcists and Alistair had been present when this finally occurred.

Red was surprised that she actually felt compassion for Roy when Uncle Alistair explained how he'd gotten in over his head in Italy. Lorenzo had offered him an ancient manuscript on the condition that he participate in a secret ceremony. Uncle Alistair didn't go into much detail, but evidently Roy confessed to succumbing to the deal partly out of jealousy over Erik's success with his research. Red prickled a little when Xenia was mentioned—Uncle Alistair said Roy's mother and Xenia had been called in to try to draw out the old Roy. "It was really Erik that prevailed, though," said Uncle Alistair. It seemed Erik had been quite the hero, offering to take the demons into himself to relieve Roy of the burden. The thought made Red shiver and was glad it hadn't come to that; Roy had been touched by Erik's gesture and had finally been able to humble himself enough to renounce the demons and ask for help. The priests had pulled a fast one by commanding the demons to depart from Roy, then having Erik renounce them so quickly they couldn't actually enter Erik. This part of the process had been the most disturbing because the demons had fought back, Uncle Alistair said. He didn't go into much detail, but said Roy's face had appeared very strange. Red thought his far-away look spoke volumes, like a man who had seen a bloody battle.

Red was incredulous to hear that Roy, then, after a lengthy rest, had helped to reach Lorenzo. At one point, the team had been close to giving up. Apparently, the demon that had possessed him was a very powerful, ancient demon and Lorenzo had been in that condition since his adolescence. His own self was almost totally obliterated. He'd require much therapy, and since his mental and psychological development seemed to have halted at the point of his possession, his recovery would likely take years, Uncle Alistair said.

"His possession stemmed from his involvement with a cult, mostly in defiance of his parents," he said. Red was amused to hear a hint of grandfatherly warning in Uncle Alistair's voice when he told Lorenzo's story. He said he supposed Lorenzo had thought it cool at the time to carouse with this dark and mysterious group. Red saw his face tighten as he said the cult was still in existence. "And they're still very interested in attaining the stones," he said. "Lorenzo will likely have difficulty avoiding them when he goes to Italy." He said he and the psychologist were looking into international agreements for the mentally ill in the hopes that Lorenzo could be institutionalized for a while in the States.

Red was relieved but somewhat dismayed to learn that the stones had already been sent back under heavy security to the Vatican. "The year is up for our loan, and as a precaution, it seemed like the best thing to do," Uncle Alistair said. Still, she was a little disappointed. She should have known that being transformed had been a once-in-a-lifetime adventure and something she wouldn't likely get to repeat, but a part of her would have liked to have stayed like that—with him. She felt tears begin to prickle at her eyes and worked hard to suppress them.

She only half-listened to the remainder of her uncle's account, feeling a bit sick as she wrestled with conflicting emotions. It was great to hear that a happy ending had been accomplished, at least in part, for the two young men, and she knew she should focus on that. But hearing Erik and Xenia's names mentioned together had made bile rise to her throat. She tried to recapture the serenity she had found before, and glanced over to Annie, but she was absorbed in their uncle's story.

She vaguely heard Annie ask about animals—something about demons being sent into a herd of pigs. This captured her attention. She noted, too, that all the others in the room had begun to stare alternately at Roxy, now sleeping on top of a row of books in the bookshelf, and Buddy, totally unconscious in front of the fire. She actually felt a little humor begin to tickle her throat. "Our team did not have to resort to those methods. No demons were sent into your pets," Uncle Alistair quickly assured them. All were obviously relieved, but Red suspected each animal would be watched a little more closely for a while.

Red's mom called her and Annie into the kitchen to help with the final meal preparations. Red was given the task of setting the dining room table and fetching extra chairs from the basement. "Why do we need extra chairs?" Red asked.

"We have guests," she answered as she drained a large steaming pot of broccoli and some other vegetables.

"Who?" Red was almost afraid to ask.

"Let's see ... Ms. Catsworthy, Minah and Erik, Roy and his mom, Xenia, and ... oh, yes, Reverend Joan. That's seven extras, plus the five of us, which makes twelve table settings," she said. Then her mom was quickly gone, her head ducked into the pantry, oblivious to the bomb she had just dropped on Red.

Red felt faint. Not only would she have to encounter Erik, but Xenia, too. And, to make matters worse, even Roy would be there. He might be different now, but shouldn't he be in a mental institution or something?

She quickly arranged the table settings and went to the basement for the extra chairs. The basement looked strange. Things had been moved around and large sections seemed to have been swept clean. She guessed the hospital beds and equipment had been removed earlier that day along with the patients. The extra chairs were still arranged in a couple of semi-circles from the exorcisms, rather than folded and stacked in the usual way. She carried up two folded chairs in each hand, her hands hooked through the slats. She did her tasks hurriedly and quickly slipped upstairs for some solitude before her mom could snag her and assign another task.

Once inside her room, she didn't allow herself to waste time having another cry. She had cried enough. She was getting a little less gushy now, and had a little more self-control. She had little time to steel herself, though; the guests would arrive any minute. She stepped into the shower, allowing the warm water to soothe her aching soul. She took her time. Let the guests arrive without her—she needed to take care of her inner child now.

Once she had towel-dried her hair and put on fresh jeans and comfy sweater, she applied a little makeup, though her inner rebel wouldn't allow her to overdo the beautification. Erik could take her as she was, or go off with Xenia. She'd not belittle herself enough to slather on makeup and perfume to compete with another woman. Besides, she thought, thinking of the beautiful Xenia, with her white-blue eyes and bronze skin, the woman looked like a goddess. She couldn't compete if she tried. In a rebellious answer to these musings, she removed the sweater and donned the silly T-shirt Annie had given her for Christmas, topped by an old faded flannel shirt left unbuttoned. *There. That'll show him I don't give a damn.*

She shoved her hands into the pockets of her jeans and went downstairs, determined not do battle. Well, unless provoked.

CHAPTER 19

A Stroll on the Towpath

Red mustered all the nonchalance she had inside of her as she entered the library. Her traitorous eyes, however, flew straight away to Erik, seated on the couch with Xenia and Roy. He looked up, beaming at her, a warm and brilliant smile. She nodded briefly, then quickly looked away, feigning indifference. Both Erik and Roy rose. Roy approached her. She froze for a moment, recalling their former encounters.

Roy put his palms up in a sign of surrender. He moved cautiously and timidly toward her. The others in the crowded room didn't seem to notice; the conversations continued to flow as Red stood frozen, unsure whether she needed to assume a defensive stance as Roy crossed the room.

"S-Sonia," Roy stammered. He looked imploringly into her eyes. "I am so sorry for the way I acted. It wasn't me. I do remember everything, though, and, well—I'm sorry." He shook his head, looking downward, as if he was ashamed now to look at her. Before Red could speak, he continued, "I owe you so much for helping rescue me from the condition I was in." He reached for her hand clasped it between his own.

Red was taken aback. This was a totally different Roy. Red thought he seemed sincere; she wasn't one hundred percent sure she could trust him, but was mostly willing to forgive and forget. "It's all good," she said.

He squeezed her hand before releasing it and smiled a brilliant warm smile. Wow, she thought. He was actually kinda cute. She'd have never guessed.

She was further surprised when he teasingly added, "And that was some tae kwon do move. Remind me not to mess with you again."

Erik appeared, giving her right shoulder a squeeze. This shocked Red, sending an electric current through her. Somehow, she wasn't expecting this forwardness. Sure, they had been close like that a few days ago, but that was before he had apparently remembered his flirtation with Xenia. She smiled briefly but insincerely at him and then looked quickly away.

Erik looked confused, but at that moment Uncle Alistair, now assuming his rightful role as the head of the family, announced that dinner was served and said everyone should make their way to the dining room.

Red didn't look at Erik again until she sat down at the table. She expected him to sit next to Xenia, but was comforted a little when he sat down beside her. She guessed that meant he was going to try and let her down easy. She noted that Xenia seated herself next to Erik on his other side, though, between him and Roy.

Red scarcely registered the food. Her emotions were too vexed and her thoughts too scattered to take in anything else. She was very quiet and pretended to listen to conversations across the table, nodding occasionally so it would look like she was listening. She ate a few bites of something—perhaps some bread. Erik asked a few questions about how her week had gone and she replied dutifully in monosyllables.

Then, after what seemed hours, the meal was over. People were rising and retiring back to the library. Roy was leaving early because he was still recovering from his ordeal and needed rest. Red moved with the crowd, but felt herself being pulled aside by a hand grasping her arm.

"I thought you might like to take a moonlit stroll with me along the towpath," Erik said softly into her ear.

Red stiffened. *Okay, this is it. Our "Dear Jane" talk. Now is the time for the other shoe to fall.* She could hear it now: *You're a nice girl and I like you very much, but …*

Red nodded, just wanting the whole thing to be over. She couldn't stand much more. She remembered her conversation with Annie about standing on her own and straightened her back. Erik handed her ski coat to her. Surprised, she took it. How did he know where to find it? Oh, yeah, he'd stalked her for a year. She scoffed silently. She put on her coat and followed him outdoors like an automaton.

Outside, the moon was still bright, though not as brilliant as it had been the weekend before. Erik took her hand as they descended the yard and then the path through the woods to the towpath. *Oh, he's really going all the way with this gallantry thing.*

Once on the towpath, Erik stopped, and, using her hand as leverage, he turned her to face him. "Okay, now that we're alone, I need to know what's going on in that gorgeous head of yours. I know this has all been sudden for you and I may have assumed too much, too fast. You need to tell me how you feel. I can't read your mind—well, at least not anymore." He smiled, apparently remembering. Red flushed as he continued. "I know you're young, several years younger than me, at least, and I promise you I'll back off if you need it. You still have a lot of life experiences before you. I'll bet you've never even been to a prom yet."

Red looked away. He had been looking straight into her eyes and the intensity was beginning to be too much. *Oh, why does he need to do all this? Just say it!* She wanted to scream. Hot tears rose to her eyes. She was thankful for the dim light. Maybe he wouldn't see the tears.

He used a finger to turn her chin back toward his face. "You need to tell me what you want. I'm willing to wait. I want you to have the freedom to grow up. You still have high school to finish and then college. I want you to experience everything good. I don't want to hold you back. But you have to talk to me."

Red strengthened her resolve. "Erik, this was fun. I mean, flying and all. But it's okay for you to have Xenia. I'm happy for you." The last part was said in an almost whisper and with forced conviction.

"Xenia? Sonia, what are you talking about?"

"Your girlfriend, Xenia. Rachel and Daniel told me

Xenia was practically your girlfriend." Tears were streaming now steadily down both of her cheeks.

"Oh, I get it now." Erik captured one of her hands, raised it to his lips, and kissed it. "Sonia, *you're* my girlfriend, if you'll have me. What do you think I've been trying to tell you? Xenia is *Roy's* girlfriend. Oh, sure, there were times when she used me to try and make him jealous because he was so pompous—that's just Roy. But Xenia and I have never even kissed."

"But you had your arm around her the other day," Red pointed out. "You looked like a couple."

"No, I was comforting her, like a brother. I was so distraught last week trying to help Roy that I didn't even realize you'd seen me bring Xenia in. But I guess it must've looked like that." He grimaced, apparently realizing what she'd been through in the last few days. "Oh, Sonia, please, can you forgive me? I've been such an ass. I should've called. I just had so much going on and wanted to leave you alone because I knew you had school. Oh, sweetie." He embraced her tenderly. She sobbed for a moment into his shoulder, not quite fully able to accept that he really did love her, but gradually allowed the joy to return.

Erik pulled back enough to face her, and asked with an irresistible quality to his voice, "Can you forgive me for my stupidity?"

"Yes," Red responded, throwing her arms around his neck.

She felt his face turn toward hers. He kissed her, first tenderly and then more demandingly.

Too soon for Red, Erik pulled back and said hoarsely, "Guess I should get you back inside. After all, it still is a school night for you and I don't know how well you've been sleeping, but if it's anything like me, not at all well."

Red sighed, but knew he was right.

Then to her delight, he added, "But before we go in, I want to ask you on our first official date. How's tomorrow night? Should I pick you up at six?"

"It's a date," responded Red, "I mean, it's the least we can do after having spent the night together already." She winked and he raised one eyebrow. They laughed and then walked back up the path together hand in hand.

Red was so happy with the feel of his warm hand intertwined with hers and the scent of him still in her nostrils that she almost failed to register the caw of a crow overhead. She heard Erik laugh softly and they both said together, "Moon."

CHAPTER 20

Annie's Party

Annie's fifteenth birthday, February twenty-first, was on a Thursday. She was going to have a birthday dinner with her family that night, and planned a sleepover party with her best friends for the following night.

During the day, her friends brought cupcakes and a giant Mylar Batman balloon to school. Red knew that according to the custom of their peers, Annie had to carry the balloon around school all day, tying it to the back of her chair in each class. Annie's friend Nyah had also slipped into her room after school on Friday and erected a life-size cardboard figure of the Hulk in a half-crouched position. Red puzzled at how much Annie and her friends were into the super-hero theme but enjoyed watching her beam with appreciation for all the attention she was getting. And Red was happy that Annie was getting attention from others, because she had definitely been preoccupied with Erik lately. Life was good.

The most fun of all the birthday activities turned out to be the family dinner. This was because of a scheme Uncle Alistair and Annie had concocted. They had spent a lot of time in the preceding evenings hidden away in the basement. Each time Red had seen Annie, she had beamed with a mischievous sparkle and if asked about it, simply pressed her lips together and raised her eyebrows.

Besides Erik, who was now a regular fixture at the mansion, the only extra person Annie had invited to dinner was Ms. Catsworthy. The longer they cohabitated with Uncle Alistair, the more Red began to realize that Ms. Catsworthy was much more than a neighbor—she held an unspoken position as a member of the family. But she had evidently not been in on Annie's secret, either.

This *pièce de résistance* for the evening came after dinner when the family retired to the sitting room. The cake was presented as usual, accompanied by the Happy Birthday song, and candles blown out. Her uncle asked those present to indulge him for half-an-hour, the first ten minutes of which they'd need to wait while he and his grand-niece set up. Then he disappeared into the basement and Annie went upstairs.

When they reappeared Annie was wearing a swimsuit and Uncle Alistair was carrying a glass bowl and a strange gizmo that looked like a remote control connected to a small telescope. The glass bowl, Red saw, was being used as an aquarium.

He set the bowl down in the middle of the room. It contained several smooth stones and bright green aquatic plants and was filled with crystal-clear water. Red strained her eyes to see if there were any fish but there weren't. Her uncle placed a Popsicle stick on the water's surface, then pushed it to the side, waiting just a moment for the water ripples to cease, until the Popsicle stick sat quietly floating on the water's surface against the glass wall of the bowl. He then arranged several yoga mats on the floor beside the bowl.

Red watched curiously as her uncle stood next to the aquarium and looked toward Annie, who had been stretching in one corner of the room. "Ready?" he asked. She nodded and giggled, then walked gracefully toward the bowl, like a gymnast. She stopped in front of the bowl and touched a finger to the water, apparently testing the temperature. She then backed up a few steps and assumed a gymnastics ready-stance, with one toe pointed forward. She looked at Uncle Alistair again and nodded. He raised the gizmo, peered toward the telescope, and pointed it toward Annie. "Three—two—one—GO!"

Annie took a few carefully choreographed long strides and leapt. The entire room gasped as she launched herself into a beautiful dive toward the tiny aquarium. Out of the corner of her eye, Red saw her dad lunge forward as though to try and catch her. Red heard a snapping sound and Annie disappeared.

Red barely heard the faint plink in the water of the bowl, then the sound of a chair scraping across the floor. Her father gasped and swore. Red looked up to see her mom slide to the floor in a faint. Ms. Catsworthy rushed to help her back to her feet, looking pale herself.

Red bolted toward the spot where Annie had disappeared. "Please, please, don't be frightened," she heard Uncle Alistair say, who had apparently not expected such a degree of shock from the audience. "Annie is just fine. Behold." He gestured toward the aquarium. Red was awestruck as she peered into the aquarium and watched a very tiny and transparent Annie climb onto the Popsicle stick as though it was a surfboard. She looked up and waved. "Whoa," Red couldn't help but shout. She shook her head in amazement and thought how she should've known to expect something incredible like that from Uncle Alistair.

Red was speechless as she watched her uncle kneel down, very carefully reach into the aquarium, and pick up the stick on which Annie sat. He quickly placed his other hand beneath it to protect Annie in case she fell, and smoothly set the stick on one of the mats. He looked around at the others and smiled. "Please, everyone, step back. Our Annie is fine, I assure you." Red, her shock starting to abate, noted with amusement his attempt at showmanship.

She saw him once again raise the gizmo, point it toward Annie, and press a button on the remote control. She heard another snapping sound and Annie instantly reappeared in her original size, seated on one of the mats in the same position as she had sat on the Popsicle stick.

Red heard her mom gasp and saw both parents rush forward and hug Annie. Her mom was crying.

"Mom, it's okay. I'm fine," Annie said.

"Don't you ever scare me like that again, young lady, or you'll be grounded until graduation! Do you understand?"

End notes

[1] Quote from: E.O.E. Somerville and Martin Ross. 1984 (1899, 1908 and 1915 stories first published). *The Irish R.M.* Penguin Books, Ltd. Harmondsworth, Middlesex, England.

[2] Quote from Heathcliff in: Emily Brontë. 1947. *Wuthering Heights*. Thomas Cautley Newby. London.

[3] Quote from: C.S. Lewis. 1952. *The Chronicles of Narnia: The Voyage of the Dawn Treader*. Geoffrey Bles. London.

[4] Quote from: Edgar Allan Poe. 1845. *The Raven*. Wiley and Putnam. New York.

[5] Quote from: C.S. Lewis. 1943. *Perelandra*. The Bodley Head. London.

"Yes, Mom. Sorry. I guess I didn't think about that," Annie said. "But wasn't it cool?"

"I guess," Her mom admitted grudgingly, glancing toward Uncle Alistair with a hint of reproach in her look.

"Dear Kaye," Uncle Alistair said. "This is entirely my fault and I'm so sorry to frighten you. That was certainly not my intent. It just seemed like such fun." Red felt a little sorry for her uncle, whose voice sounded regretful.

"Well ... okay. I guess I have to admit it was pretty awe-inspiring," her mom said, finally seeming to relax and enjoy the idea of what had just happened.

Red felt the whole room seem to breathe a collective sigh of relief.

Red turned to Erik, who now stood beside her. "I thought you guys sent the stones back to the Vatican." Red noticed that Erik, who had been very quiet through the whole episode, seemed to have a twinkle in his eye. She began to suspect he had known about the surprise in advance.

"Officially, we did. But Professor Hamilton had a few fragments and shards, not much more than dust, really, that he collected from the original container the stones were shipped in. That's what we've used all along for our research. As with any artifact, the standard protocol is to only remove samples from the specimen as a last resort, and then, only from an unobtrusive spot and as little as can possibly meet the research needs. But we didn't need to, because we found such a treasure-trove of dust in the container."

"Erik," Red said thoughtfully, rubbing her chin, "I have a favor to ask."

***

On Saturday morning, Red waited for Erik. Her request to Erik was to borrow Uncle Alistair's remote control gizmo to communicate once more with their friend, Moon, and somehow help him to move on from his infatuation with Red. Moon had continued to appear at Red's window almost daily with various colorful offerings and she felt sorry for him. Plus, she was secretly a little creeped out by his amorous advances.

When she'd quizzed Erik about her uncle's remote control gizmo, she'd learned it was equipped with options for activating fragments from either one or more of the stones. The control used at Annie's party wasn't the only one they'd created, either. Her uncle had a stash of dust and fragments from each stone and had made controls for the team to use in answering different research questions, mostly for experimenting on different types of food storage. There were several versions. The research team had labeled them STAG controls, an acronym for Snap To Alternate Grid, though that particular acronym was chosen in part because the Hamilton family crest contained a stag.

Erik had asked her not to mention to anyone that they were going to use one of the STAG controls. She already had an inkling of the importance of keeping quiet about the stone fragments. She knew those present at Annie's party had been family or trusted friends and had agreed to maintain secrecy—her uncle would've never used a STAG control for entertainment purposes if he hadn't totally trusted everyone present. Erik had even suggested that if word got out, organized crime and corrupt governments would come after them, worse even than Lorenzo's Italian cult. The comment had made her wonder about Lorenzo. She supposed only time would tell if that cult would still be a threat now that Lorenzo was freed from his possession.

As she dressed for the day, she had a chilling foreboding of what her uncle's decision to keep the stone fragments might someday bring upon them, but tried to put that from her mind.

Erik arrived at about eleven o'clock. "I have a surprise for this afternoon," he said. Red hoped it was a repeat of flying over the canal.

They wasted no time in slipping out the back for a hike on the towpath. It was a lovely almost-spring day and Red thought a walk would be a pleasant way to occupy her time while Erik took care of her plan for Moon. Red relished in the fresh air as they made their way down the footpath that connected the back yard to the towpath. "There's a spur that heads down to the river just ahead," she suggested.

"Good idea. I think I know the place and there should be enough cover there," Erik said. He slipped an arm across her shoulders now that the path was wide enough to walk abreast.

Red slipped an arm behind his waist and they walked the short distance in easy silence. Red thought he seemed as happy as she felt.

On reaching the spur, Red was glad to see no one else was there. For the transformation using the Angel Stone, she remembered clothing had been an issue – how could she forget? She watched as he stripped down to a new suede leather loincloth. She didn't realize she was gawking until he winked. She blushed. If she lived a thousand years, she'd never forget the way he looked in a leather loincloth. *Wow.* "Did you get that at the mall?" she teased.

"Hey, this was tailor-made."

"By whom?" She raised an eyebrow.

Erik laughed. "By yours truly. Hey, I'm nothing if not inventive."

She grinned. "So, should I wait for you here? I mean, I can't really zap you back to normal up the towpath. I can see us now, strolling down the towpath with you dressed as Tarzan." Red couldn't help but smile at the mental picture.

"I guess you've got a point there. Finding Moon might take a few hours, or even multiple attempts. I know where Moon usually roosts, but his foraging grounds vary." He thought for a moment. "How's this—we can meet back here in an hour. If it takes less time, I'll find you. You should be able to hear me. If it takes longer, we can decide then. Hopefully I can get some sense of how far away his flock is within the hour."

"Sounds like a plan."

She watched Erik pack his clothes into his daypack and pull a STAG control out of the outer pocket.

"Ready to do the honors?" he asked, handing her the control.

"Of course," Red said cheerfully.

Erik showed her which button to push first and which to push to transform him back. Feeling just a little nervous doing something so extreme, she mentally braced herself, then pointed the STAG control at him and pressed the button. Instantly he was gone. She gasped despite herself.

Now there was nothing to do but wait. She set off, walking north on the towpath to enjoy the hour. She heard several birdcalls, even her favorite, a wood thrush. She marveled at its crisp, clear notes. She heard lots of robin songs, also a favorite. She heard and saw several crows, but not Moon, at least not that she could tell. She was just a little sad thinking she'd be losing attention from him, even though she knew it was best for him. She felt there was just something really compelling about being able to communicate with another species and envied Erik a little in his opportunity to peek inside the mind of another species.

At just under an hour, she returned to the place where Erik had disappeared. She was a little startled to hear her name whispered into her ear. She giggled and looked up and down the path to make sure no one was around. Then, to make doubly sure no one saw what they were doing, she stepped behind some bushes. She asked Erik to stand in front of her and pressed the button. A snap and there he was. She couldn't believe how beautiful he was to her as he appeared wearing the suede loincloth and that killer smile.

She handed him his daypack but couldn't resist a kiss with this jungle-man before he became a modern man again. She stepped toward him with a challenging smile and was delighted when he hooked a hand around her lower back and pulled her to him. They kissed a long, deep kiss and eventually

Red grudgingly handed him his daypack. She really did want to get another opportunity to fly.

They feasted on strawberries and Nutella sandwiches. "Are you ready for your surprise?" Erik asked. "We're going to fly again."

Red was delighted to find her guess about the surprise had been correct. But she was really surprised to find he had brought a leather bikini for her to wear. She laughed richly when he presented it.

"Hey, do you know how difficult it was to find that? I actually did buy that at the mall. I thought it'd be better for freedom of movement than Roy's leather jacket," he said. "And, yes, it did enter my mind to suggest a clothing-optional flight." His eyes twinkled mischievously. Red had a hard time focusing with that visual image in her head.

The flight surpassed her expectations. The assurance of his regard along with the absence of the stress they had been under before allowed them to play in the air like otters. Red knew that no matter how long she lived, she would never be able to fully describe the experience to another living soul. But this just increased the bond she felt with Erik.

To add to her joy, Red saw Moon the very next day in her backyard with a mate. She knew Erik had implanted an idea of a beautiful female crow—he had admittedly not wanted to talk about how difficult it was to conjure up the fantasy. Red smiled at his wry humor on the subject. She was also grateful to him for going beyond her request and implanting ideas in the minds of Midnight and Roxy, as well as Snagglepuss and Fluffmuffin, Ms. Catsworthy's

Himalayans, that birds tasted bitter. This had been done to help ensure a long and happy life for Moon and his future offspring.

"Atta boy, Moon," she called from her open window. He was too busy to bother with a response, but continued clucking and posturing to the sleek female crow, which eyed him with a mixture of interest and studied indifference. Red beamed with delight and quickly speed-dialed Erik to share the joy of success.

She plopped down on her bed dreamily, feeling like all was right with her world. At the sound of his voice, her heart leapt. "Hi, sweetie," he said.

She loved their recent closeness and was thrilled he'd used a term of endearment and decided to reciprocate. "Hi, babe. Guess what I just saw?"

"Um, an angel?"

Red quickly realized her mistake—asking someone who'd seen so much more of metaphysical realities. How could she hope to shock him? "No, nothing like that. Better. I saw Moon's new girlfriend."

"Whoa, that's awesome," he said, clearly delighted.

"You did it," she said. "Thanks."

"Anytime. Anyone else you want me to alter?"

Red laughed. "No one who comes to mind at the moment. Hey, you didn't get into any trouble for using the STAG control did you?"

Erik's voice took on a more serious note. "No, but I'm not sure having them around is a good thing."

Red sat up. "What do you mean?"

"Oh, probably nothing. Just something that's been bugging me a little lately. Professor Hamilton and I were on the same page when it came to the seriousness of returning the stones to the Vatican securely. And we're on the same page when it comes to the seriousness of keeping the STAG controls top secret and definitely locked away from the rest of the world while we do our research. But he does take a lighter approach to letting family and friends in on our little secret. I mean, I wouldn't have done what he did at Annie's birthday party and I sometimes worry that he's a little absent-minded and even careless with the STAG controls."

"But you don't really think anyone in the family our any of our friends would betray you to the cult, do you? I mean, Roy was possessed beforehand. But now, everyone involved with the stones is clean. Right?"

"Yes, of course, Red. I'm probably being silly. I just keep thinking of that old saying, 'Loose lips sink ships.' Guess I'm just worrying too much. Don't you think another thing about it, okay?"

"Okay."

But as she ended the call, Red felt as if an icy finger had traced up her spine. As happy as she was with Erik, she couldn't help but feel a sense of foreboding about the Stones of Bothynus.

What if this whole ordeal wasn't over after all?